MURDER IN AN IRISH BOOKSHOP

"Can I see someone's torch?" Siobhán said. Oran was closest to her and handed it over. She maneuvered the light toward the back where the sound had originated, sweeping it left and right until she found the exact spot along the back wall. There, a woman was slumped to the floor against a bookcase. Eyes wide open, glassy, and un-blinking. Books had rained down around her.

Siobhan recognized the beautiful, mercurial author.

For everyone else, life would go on, but for aspiring author Deirdre Walsh, hers had just come to an abrupt and startling end...

Books by Carlene O'Connor

Irish Village Mysteries

MURDER IN AN IRISH VILLAGE

MURDER AT AN IRISH WEDDING

MURDER IN AN IRISH CHURCHYARD

MURDER IN AN IRISH PUB

MURDER IN AN IRISH COTTAGE

MURDER AT AN IRISH CHRISTMAS

MURDER IN AN IRISH BOOKSHOP

MURDER ON AN IRISH FARM

CHRISTMAS COCOA MURDER
(with Maddie Day and Alex Erickson)

A Home to Ireland Mystery

MURDER IN GALWAY

MURDER IN CONNEMARA

Published by Kensington Publishing Corp.

Murder in an Irish Bookshop

CARLENE O'CONNOR

Kensington Publishing Corp.
www.kensingtonbooks.com

KENSINGTON BOOKS are published by

Kensington Publishing Corp.
119 West 40th Street
New York, NY 10018

Copyright © 2021 by Mary Carter

All Kensington Titles, Imprints, and Distributed Lines are available at special quantity discounts for bulk purchases for sales promotions, premiums, fund-raising, and educational or institutional use. Special book excerpts or customized printings can also be created to fit specific needs. For details, write or phone the office of the Kensington special sales manager: Kensington Publishing Corp., 119 West 40th Street, New York, NY 10018, attn: Special Sales Department, Phone: 1-800-221-2647.

The K and Teapot logo is a trademark of Kensington Publishing Corp.

ISBN: 978-1-4967-3082-4

First Kensington Hardcover Edition: March 2021
First Kensington Mass Market Edition: February 2022

ISBN: 978-1-4967-3085-5 (ebook)

10 9 8 7 6 5 4 3 2 1

Printed in the United States of America

Given this book was written during a worldwide pandemic, I want to dedicate it to all of us who lost someone, healed someone, stayed home, wore masks, protested, pitched in, sacrificed, and loved. Also to the astronauts who gave us hope and a view of our precious earth without borders.

This book is also dedicated to Leah, whose husband contacted me during the pandemic. She shares the same birthday and I was happy to celebrate with her by naming a character after her. Cheers!

Acknowledgments

Thank you to my editor, John Scognamiglio, and my agent, Evan Marshall. I am so lucky that these men are so supportive, always willing to help with plot questions or advice. Thanks, Evan, for lending your "agent hat" to this book. Thank you, Caroline Lennon, for giving voice to all my characters. Thank you to all my friends, colleagues, and acquaintances willing to share recipes, tips, info, and support. Thank you to Bridget Quinn, Andrea Carter, Susan Collins, Kevin Collins, Lorraine, Tracy Clark, and Annmarie and James Sheedy. My family is always there for me, so I'd like to thank them as well: Carl and Jill Carter, Pat Carter, Melissa Carter-Newman, Amelia Newman, Elijah Newman, and Matthew Newman. Thank you to James and Vincent Collins, who cheered me up during quarantine with their beautiful singing and dancing. Never stop! Thank you to my neighbors who dropped cookies and treats at my door and helped celebrate my quarantine birthday: shout out to Kari Bloom, Marie Guillory, and Nathalie Gribinski!

Chapter 1

The Twins' Inn looked cheery in the orange glow of the morning light. Kilbane, County Cork, Ireland, had a back-in-time charm that often took visitors by surprise. Once befuddled that anyone, let alone Padraig and Oran McCarthy, would open a bookshop here, after spending some time in Kilbane and witnessing its charm, it made perfect sense now. Kilbane may not have held the same bustle as an Irish city, but there was no doubt it had character. Everyone was fast asleep—perhaps the argument that had broken out last night had taken its toll—and now residents were blissfully unaware of the trouble to come. It was a powerful feeling, knowing something they did not. The kind of power a writer well knows, playing God, crafting his or her stories. A tinge of red on the horizon foretold the approach of ominous weather. It was fitting; a storm was brewing in more ways than one. The pair of gray wolfhounds who had perched last night like statues by the office door, their regal bodies stiff, their ears alert to every sound, was nowhere to be seen. Asleep inside no doubt. But not for long. *Good boys.*

Everything, in the space of twenty-four hours, had changed. Human beings never had enough. They were bottomless pits of need. *Insatiable.* The argument played internally on an endless loop:

You can't do this.

I am already doing it.

I'll ruin you.

I'd like to see you try.

Don't push me. You. Are. No one. You. Are. Nothing.

Words said in anger. Give it time. Give it a chance. Patience. The most powerful virtue of them all. And time had gone by. There had been no more mention of this preposterous idea, this act of outright betrayal. One could almost breathe again. Go to bed without worry pressing down like an anvil. Wake up without the dread of a ringing phone. *Damage control.* One hoped it was all forgotten. Forgiveness was another matter. But then this. A note. Five little words written on a piece of paper taped to the door. Five little words. The proverbial cat was out of the bag, and he was already screeching. The cat might have nine lives, but humans did not.

One might argue that in the act of putting those five little words to paper, the writer was to blame for what was to come. The valley of death. *Walk, my lovely, walk.* There wasn't much time. Every detail must be considered. It would cause waves, of that there was no doubt, and adjustments would have to be made. No choice, no choice, no choice. Don't think. Do. Action was character. The method was there, in and out like a soft breath, no need to think twice. Poison. Who needed old lace when arsenic alone would do? Thank heavens the purchase had been made when this avoidable debacle first began. The regular Web now held the same opportunities as the Dark Web. What had been once unthinkable was now easy-peasy. Guided by gut instinct, and backed up by preparation. Preparation was always key. And everyone knows: *practice makes perfect*.

And now, the skies had come to play. Thunder and lightning, nature's stamp of approval. Ireland would see heavy thunderstorms over the next few days and warnings of power outages abounded. The ideal setting for a murder. Atmospheric. *You did this. Your death was brought on by your hands. I am but a messenger.* But first, the details. It was always in the details. The crime scene would tell a story, and a story needed to be shaped.

Chapter 2

Siobhán O'Sullivan wouldn't have believed spring was here (at last!) were it not for clear evidence on her morning run. Bluebells, daffodils, and snowdrops paraded their colors in planters along the footpath and in back gardens, sedge warblers and swallows sang from trees sprouting shiny green buds, and the light breeze was embedded with the scent of approaching rain. *Renewal.* It put an extra zip in her morning run through her village.

Mike Granger, who was sweeping the footpath in front of his fruit and veg market, waved as she ran by and she waved back. Otherwise there were only a few souls in sight. The early birds. Was it any wonder her morning run was often the best part of Siobhán's day? Most of the other shops in Kilbane were still dark: Sheila's Hair Salon, Annmarie's gift shop, and Gordon's Comics wouldn't open for another several hours. A faint light was on in

Liam's hardware shop; he would most likely be opening soon and closing late as folks rushed in to buy candles, batteries, and peat for their fires. Severe storms were expected in the next few days and rumors of power outages had everyone scrambling for supplies. O'Rourke's Pub would be dark until lunch but then they would be jammers. Even the ladies who power-walked in their tracksuits seemed to be sleeping in. When she passed the caravan park she noticed a few Travelers were up and one of their donkeys was happily grazing by the river. The lad seeing to the donkey gave her a nod and she nodded back. In the distance, a farmer plodded along the road pushing a wheelbarrow.

How she loved the near solitude of the mornings. Shop fronts, awash with pinks, blues, and yellows, were muted in the morning light, giving off a mystical glow. The sound of her runners on the pavement, the toll of Saint Mary's church bell, its spire rising proudly above her medieval walled town, and the presence of their gorgeous ruined abbey bolstered Siobhán's spirits and kept her moving forward.

She headed for King John's Castle and the town square, eager to reach her destination even though she knew it wouldn't open until ten this morning. The entire village was over the moon about the new bookshop opening today. Oran and Padraig McCarthy, a married couple who had just moved from Galway, had announced the opening of the bookshop last month, and since then Siobhán had run past every morning, anticipating the wonders to come.

She'd been plagued with guilt that she hadn't had time the past few years for pleasure reading, and she was determined to change that. A nice birthday prezzie for herself, maybe even a romance. And a Maeve Binchy of course, or maybe two. Her mam had been a big fan and reading them would almost be like having a visit with her. She'd have to hide any romances from Macdara Flannery, or there would be no end to the teasing. Then again, she could tease him about the plethora of paperback westerns clogging his bookshelf. (And she'd be lying if leafing through them hadn't conjured up images of Macdara in a cowboy hat, galloping in on a horse. But not a white one—she was perfectly capable of saving herself. She just liked the image of him in a cowboy hat, galloping through town, holsters on the ready.)

She would buy each of her younger siblings a book too, and encourage them to read every night before bed like she and James used to do. She passed King John's Castle and there it was to the right, the old building that had been vacant so long, the previously dusty windows now covered in velvet blue curtains, the sides painted a fresh green, the sign above in navy and gold:

TURN THE PAGE

COME FOR THE VIBES, STAY FOR THE SCRIBES.

The day was finally here. A bookshop in Kilbane. Why had it taken so long for someone to open one? They had the library, and of course one could drive to Cork or Limerick, but finally there would be one just down the street. She for one would do everything she could to support them. She wondered if the impending rainstorm would be good or bad for business. In her experience at the bistro, rain could either keep people out or drive them in. She had a feeling that they would turn out in droves for the bookshop, even with thunder and lightning in the forecast. Unfortunately, not everyone behaved during storms; they were a little like full moons that way. But keeping townsfolk from the bookshop was too big of an ask. Not that they were nosy, per se (aside from the regular curtain-twitchers), but everyone had been waiting anxiously to meet the owners, Oran and Padraig McCarthy. Besides, it might be fun to cozy up in a bookshop during a storm. Customers could then flock to Naomi's Bistro with their purchases and sit by a roaring peat fire. They could stay open late; Siobhán would take the shift herself. Potato and leek soup and brown bread would go well with the rain. Apple tarts for dessert. Yes, soups and desserts would be well stocked. And if townsfolk were in the bistro, happy out for a feed, she could at least keep an eye on them. She made a mental note to stop by Liam's hardware shop herself for candles and torch batteries, and then she would pop into the market for loads of crisps and chocolates.

Hopefully Oran and Padraig wouldn't find life in Kilbanc too mundane after the hustle and bustle of Galway City. To her dismay, they'd kept to themselves thus far, not venturing into Naomi's Bistro for a cuppa, not even to say hello, not even once. Eoin had even dropped off a welcome basket of scones and nary a reply. Opening a new business was time consuming, that was probably all there was to it. She'd make sure to personally invite them to the bistro. Turn the Page. She loved it. Just like she'd soon be turning the page to her twenty-ninth birthday, three days from now. It was hard to believe her twenties were nearly gone. Starting a new chapter. She was now eager to return home, shower and dress for work, so that she could hit the garda station early and time her break to coincide with the bookstore's opening hour.

She was back at the bistro, showered, dressed in her garda uniform, and halfway through her first heavenly cappuccino, when she heard pounding on the door to the bistro. Startled, she opened it to find Bridie, a neighbor and employee, bedraggled and breathing hard on the doorstep. Had she just come from a spin class? "Hi, luv. Did you lose your key?" Siobhán asked, before she caught the look on Bridie's face. *Troubled* was putting it mildly. It was only then that Siobhán noticed a basket in Bridie's hands with a pie on top. Lemon meringue from the looks of it. A card on top of the basket said: *WEL-COME*.

"It's for the bookshop owners." Bridie did not step inside. Her brunette curls were sticking to the side of her pretty face, her breath still labored. "She's dead. She's lying near the bookshop, and she's dead." The words came out in a rush. "You know she never leaves the inn. What in heaven's name is she doing lying on the footpath near the bookshop?"

"Who are you on about, pet?" Bridie was in shock, the signs evident on her face and in the way her words tumbled out incoherently.

"I've been minding her. I tucked her into bed last night, and she was fine. And by *fine* I mean she argued with her book club, or maybe it was the twins—you could hear her yelling from the back garden, like. And she returned in a horrid mood. Everything I did was wrong, and of course she was going to school me. And I know it's no time to complain, but you know how she is. I brought her chicken soup. Do you think there was something wrong with the soup? Maybe it was something someone brought to the book club? She was fine last night, I tell you she was her miserable old self!" Bridie gasped and slapped her hand over her mouth.

"Take a breath." Siobhán reached out, set the basket with the pie down, and then took Bridie's hands. She breathed in by way of example. Bridie finally copped on and took a deep breath. Tears pooled in her eyes. "I was going to call the guards when I saw you run by. I need to call Father Kearney. Do you think it was her heart? Or old age? It couldn't have been the chicken soup. Why was she wandering out in this weather when she hasn't gone beyond the inn in over a year?" Bridie grabbed Siobhán's shoulders. "I made the soup. I ate the soup and I'm fine. Do you think she was depressed because she sold the inn? Jesus, Mary, and Joseph. What was she doing out and about at this hour of the morning?"

By now Siobhán had pieced it together, and she too could not believe it. Margaret O'Shea, the former owner of the Kilbane Inn. "Margaret?" Siobhán asked. "Are you on about Margaret O'Shea, luv?"

Bridie nodded, tears pouring down her cheeks. "She's dead. She is lying on the footpath near the bookshop and she's dead."

Chapter 3

Siobhán's disbelief remained until she was on the footpath standing over poor deceased Margaret O'Shea. She was lying perhaps twenty feet away from the shop, feet facing it, as if she had been heading straight for it. Her walker lay on its side next to her but didn't appear damaged. She was dressed in a thick gray jumper and wool skirt. Her face, always stern in life, looked peaceful, and her eyes were blessedly closed. Her arms were by her sides, hands palms out. Her handbag had landed a foot away, and a pair of glasses poked out from underneath her shoulder.

Standing at the top of the town square, Siobhán could see King John's Castle to her immediate left, and the Kilbane Garda Station across the street. Margaret O'Shea had undoubtedly not been the first poor soul to die in the town square (given its turbulent history she was most likely one of many), but she was the only one in these modern times, and even though she'd been a stern woman at times, Siobhán had always had a fondness for her, not to mention a great deal of respect. Until a year ago she had run the Kilbane Inn all by herself. To be running a business at seventy-something years of age on her own was something to be proud of. A profound sadness enveloped Siobhán as she stared down at her. "How did I not pass her on my run?" Siobhán wondered out loud. They must have just missed each other, which meant that Margaret had not been deceased for very long.

Bridie stood behind her, and having lost her battle with her tears, she was now openly weeping. "What was she even doing here?" Bridie wailed. "It must have taken her ages to walk."

"Maybe one of the twins dropped her off." The Kilbane Inn, now named the Twins' Inn, was run by identical twins Emma and Eileen Curley. Margaret still lived in her room on the premises, and as Bridie had stated earlier, she had not left the grounds in the past year. Had the excitement of the bookshop opening caused Margaret to venture out? Siobhán leaned closer to the walker. "There's no mud," she observed out loud. The journey from the inn would have required passing through sections where there was no footpath, only farmers' fields. If she had walked here, there should have been muck on her walker. Perhaps she'd taken the roads, a choice that would have lengthened an already long walk for a woman in her condition.

"It doesn't make any sense at all," Bridie said. "It's just wrong seeing her lying here."

Siobhán agreed. It did feel wrong. Had Margaret O'Shea known this would happen, she would have been mortified. Even looking at her felt wrong. "Perhaps she's here for the same reason you were," Siobhán said, scouring the ground for a pie, or tin of biscuits. "Leaving a welcome gift for the McCarthys."

"She was a big reader," Bridie said. "But the ladies in the book club always brought her books."

"What's the story?" At the sound of the deep voice behind them, they turned in unison. Macdara Flannery was approaching with two additional guards. She should remember to call him Detective Sergeant Flannery in front of everyone else. Even though he would be chuffed to bits if she called him her fiancé.

"It's Margaret O'Shea," Siobhán said. "Bless her soul. Bridie found her."

"How did you know she was here?" Macdara asked. "Poor dear." He bowed his head in front of the body, and once he was done he pulled a notebook out of his pocket as he turned to Bridie.

"I was going to leave a welcome pie at the door to the bookshop," Bridie said. "I nearly tripped over her in the dark."

Macdara glanced down the side street visible from their spot on the corner. There, a giant hand-painted sign loomed over the building depicting a gentleman with a raised pint: BUTLER'S UNDERTAKER, LOUNGE, AND PUB. Sometimes a cheeky board sat out front that read: *Patrons Wanted Dead or Alive*. Today the footpaths would remain clear as everyone prepped for the storm.

Siobhán knew where Macdara's thoughts were at this moment. He didn't want to leave Margaret lying here. He wanted to call Butler's and have her taken to the funeral home. If a death was unexpected and/or suspicious, the state pathologist would need to be called in. In those cases the body could not be moved from the scene. His eyes met Siobhán's. "What are you thinking?"

"She was fine last night," Bridie said. "More than fine. She was a spitfire at the book club. I brought her chicken soup."

"She's in her late seventies, luv," Siobhán said. "Her health has been declining this past year." She glanced at the handbag. "She wasn't robbed. There are no signs at all of foul play." And given the pristine state of her walker she had most likely been dropped off by someone at the inn. But why this early? The bookshop wasn't even open. Perhaps she wanted to avoid the crowds. Was someone coming to pick her up?

"You don't think it was the soup, do ye?" Bridie asked.

"I don't see any evidence of that," Siobhán said. "This wasn't your fault."

Bridie gasped and nodded. "I'll call Father Kearney," she said.

"I'll call Butler's," Macdara said. "Let's get her out of sight before businesses start to open." He was right. No doubt Margaret was looking down telling them to hurry up and do their jobs. He looked down at Margaret. "I'm sorry, luv. Rest in peace." His eyes fell to the bookshop. "I'm going to need you to call the McCarthys," he said to Siobhán. "Ask them to postpone the bookshop opening for at least a day while we do our due diligence on this one."

Fantastic. She had a feeling that even Bridie's lemon meringue pie wouldn't sweeten that news.

The next morning, it wasn't until Siobhán showered and changed from her run, and planted herself in front of her cappuccino maker in the dining room, that she remembered. A new garda was starting today. Aretta Dabiri. She would be Ireland's first female garda of African descent. Her father had immigrated to Ireland from Nigeria. It was cause for celebration. After the sad day they'd had yesterday, welcoming a new garda and resident was just the cheer the village needed. That and the upcoming opening of the bookstore—Turn the Page.

The McCarthys hadn't even answered her phone call yesterday; they had to send the gardaí to the door to ask them to postpone the opening while they canvassed the area, and had the twins check on Margaret's room back at the inn just to make sure there was nothing amiss. The only strange bit so far was that no one at the inn had admitted to giving Margaret a ride into town. Siobhán had been sure it was one of the twins. Of course, Margaret had friends in the village, so it was probably just a matter of time before they learned who picked her up and dropped her off. But until that point, it was going to gnaw on Siobhán. After one of the twins entered Margaret's room, she assured the guards there was nothing amiss, apart from the smell of bleach. This, she claimed, was not out of character. Margaret was a tidy woman who fiercely believed that cleanliness was next to godliness. And Margaret insisted on doing her own cleaning because she highly valued her privacy.

Granted, Windex was her preferred cleaning solution, but there were no signs that anyone had broken into her room. The previous evening the entire ladies' book club had met in Margaret's room, along with visiting Irish authors who were in Kilbane to celebrate the bookshop's grand opening. It made sense to the twins that after such a gathering, Margaret chose to use a stronger cleaning solution. She was a bit of a germophobe. Despite being a tidy woman, she had still refused the twins' offer to upgrade her room. It smelled musty, the twins relayed, no matter how much Windex or bleach she used. Most of them had partaken of Bridie's chicken soup and none of the others had fallen ill. It appeared that Margaret O'Shea had died of natural causes.

Margaret had no close relatives, and no one saw any need to call in the state pathologist. It would have been better if she had died peacefully in her bed, but what's done was done. Father Kearney scheduled an evening mass, and the twins were seeing to the funeral arrangements. Given Margaret had still been living on the property, they felt obliged. It was no surprise the events had momentarily shifted thoughts of the new garda to the side. But now, the day was here, and Siobhán's excitement returned. She could not wait to meet Aretta Dabiri.

The smell of rashers, sausages, and black and white pudding drifted into the dining room. Her brother Eoin was up and starting brekkie. Brown bread was cooling on the racks; Siobhán had been up hours before her run preparing the pans and sliding them into the cooker. It probably meant she'd be crashing in the afternoon, but maybe all the new events of the day would keep her hopping.

"You're up early," she said when Eoin ambled out. He was looking sharp in a black apron, his hair combed neatly back. There were days she had a hard time processing the change, how the Yankees cap always turned backward had disappeared from his head, and his skin had cleared up. Eoin O'Sullivan was now handsome. She could see a lot of her da in him. And his culinary skills and artistic skills had progressed, making him a catch. It

was no wonder the bistro had seen an uptick in young female customers. So far, her younger brother had been
pretending not to notice, but the mystery of why the baseball cap was gone and he was always neatly turned out
was solved. Siobhán wondered if there was one lass in
particular he was trying to impress, or was he just bask-
ing in the attention of many? He was the face of Naomi's
Bistro and she couldn't be prouder.

"James woke me up when he snuck out this morning,"
Eoin said.

"Snuck out?" Siobhán asked. "Where was he off to?"
Their oldest brother, James, had just returned home after
months in Waterford with his fiancée, Elise. She did not
return with him. He'd been in one of his moods lately, as
dark as the weather. Siobhán wondered if he was having
second thoughts about the wedding.

"I asked the back of his head," Eoin said. "But it didn't
answer."

Siobhán sighed. If it wasn't one thing, it was always
another. Just then a piercing tone rang out, something
akin to the sound of an animal being tortured. Ciarán, the
youngest of the O'Sullivan Six, had taken up the violin.
And they were all suffering for it.

"I thought you told him only to play in the field near
the abbey," Eoin said, slapping his hands over his ears.

"He can't do that with this weather," Siobhán said,
flinching as another screech rang out. This was all her
fault. She had bought Ciarán the violin and set him up
with lessons the minute he uttered that he wanted to play.

Eoin's gaze fell to the window and, beyond it, the dark
skies. "How do we know he's not causing the weather?"
he clipped.

Siobhán gave him a playful push, then winced as Ciarán's out of tune screeching continued.

"Shut it!" a voice yelled out from their rooms above the bistro. *Gráinne.* Her sister was not a morning person. Come to think of it, she wasn't an afternoon person either, and the verdict was out on the evening.

"I have to practice," Ciarán yelled back.

"You're scaring Trigger!" Ann, the youngest O'Sullivan girl, screamed. Trigger was their Jack Russell terrier. To be fair, he was afraid of everything. He once huddled under Siobhán's bed for an hour after a leaf had blown his way in the back garden.

"Give him ten more minutes," Siobhán yelled at the ceiling. Not that they could hear her. Not that they would listen if they could. Ciarán, instead, stomped downstairs clutching his violin. "Good work, luv."

Ciarán narrowed his eyes. He was a teenager now, on a growth spurt. His voice was starting to crack. He didn't let Siobhán ruffle his head anymore. "I'm hungry," he said. "It takes a lot of energy to practice."

Siobhán and Eoin made an effort to keep their faces as still as possible. "Brekkie is on," Eoin said. Ciarán placed his violin on a nearby table and disappeared into the kitchen. "And Chris Gordon is on his way," Eoin added as he gestured to her cappuccino machine. She set her mug down and picked up one for him. It was a small thing, making his cappuccino, but she loved mothering her siblings in whatever way she could whenever she could. And just because she was fantasizing about smashing the violin into a million pieces, or shoving it into the fire, didn't mean she was going to do it. Hiding it would be more humane.

The cappuccino machine hummed and purred and frothed. Now *that* was music. Hopefully, Ciarán would one day prove them wrong and learn to play the violin. Until that day, they were all going to need ear plugs. "Chris Gordon," she said. "This early?"

"You have no idea," Eoin said with a shake of his head.

Chris Gordon, the only American man living in Kilbane, owned a comic book shop in town. Or graphic novels, as she'd been taught to call them. He had movie star good looks, but you wouldn't know it by his personality. Lately, he'd taken an aversion to wearing shoes. The past few times Siobhán had been in his shop, his large feet glowed from the neon socks he'd sprouted. If she passed him outdoors, he was always in sandals, still with the socks. "What's the story?" Given this was a small village, they knew their locals. The neon socks and sandals were just the beginning of his quirks. Chris Gordon was not one of their early diners. Sometimes he didn't even open his graphic novel shop until noon. Maybe reading about vampires was turning him into one.

"He's out of his mind about the bookshop opening," Eoin said, giving her a nod as she handed him his perfectly frothed cappuccino. "Freaking out," he said, making air quotes and putting on an American accent.

Siobhán laughed. "Why?" This wasn't entirely a shock—the Yank was prone to dramatics.

Eoin shrugged. "He views the new bookshop as competition."

"I highly doubt they're going to sell comic books. *Sorry.* Graphic novels." Eoin had mad artistic skills and had begun writing graphic novels a year prior. They were a big seller at Gordon's Comics. The heroine of his comics was loosely based on her. Or at least the long auburn hair he'd given the character made everyone think so. She did have a new appreciation for graphic novels, but she didn't think Chris Gordon had any reason to see the bookshop as competition. Like she said: storms brought out the badness in many.

"He's beside himself. Threatening to sue."

"Sue?" Suing a bookshop for having the audacity to open? She took her mug and headed upstairs. "Wish him luck with dat," she called out.

Ciarán, violin now abandoned, bounded past her on his way back up the stairs, sloshing cappuccino on her and the stairs. "Slow down," she said as he careened past. "And get a towel to wipe up the stairs."

"I'm looking for Trigger." She still wasn't used to how low his voice was now. It instilled her with an unreasonable panic. "I'm going to apologize by giving him this rasher." He waved a rasher.

"Storms are coming, luv. He's under one of the beds." Their Jack Russell, Trigger, did not do storms. "And you've nothing to apologize for. Practice makes perfect." She sighed. When did she become the type of person who said things like that?

"Morning," Ann said, coming down the stairs. She caught Siobhán's eye, then mimed playing the violin and slapped her hands over her face with a mock look of horror.

Siobhán laughed and patted her blond head. "Watch your step, I spilled cappuccino."

"I have a game tomorrow, I can't break me neck," Ann said, practically sliding on the bannister to avoid the spill. Ann was the star player of her Camogie team.

"Your game is going to be canceled, pet. Storms are coming in."

"Can I stay home from school then?"

"No. Don't forget your brellie."

"No fair. Gráinne gets to sleep in."

If Gráinne had just gone to university like Siobhán had urged, she would be up in the mornings with the rest of them. Instead, her job as a personal stylist at Sheila's Hair Salon started at ten. "Comparing yourself to other people is only going to bring you misery," Siobhán called down the stairs.

Ann groaned. "My family are the ones bringing me misery this morning." Siobhán laughed. What a relief to hear someone else say it.

Chapter 4

Once at the garda station, Siobhán spent the morning on paperwork. She'd heard Garda Dabiri was immersed in her own endless stack of forms to fill out, and Siobhán would officially meet her in the afternoon. Her plan unfolded brilliantly, and she was able to coincide her first break with the bookshop's opening. A long line stretched from the door. She couldn't believe it. The crowd was even larger than she had been anticipating. Who knew that Kilbane was this starved for books? In this technological age it was heartwarming, and she soaked up the electric charge in the air. But for all the positives, Siobhán felt a nibble of worry.

All of these people weren't going to fit into the bookshop, and she was leery that Oran and Padraig McCarthy might try to cram them in past capacity. She wanted to be a customer first, not slap the new owners with a citation for overcrowding. But the concern was soon mitigated when the ten a.m. hour struck. The door flew open and there stood a man in spectacles, a black turtleneck, and a white wooly jumper, grinning ear to ear as he took in the line. Siobhán recognized Oran McCarthy from the photos on his Web site. He was likable in a scholarly way. She pegged him to be in his early forties. With his black pants and turtleneck, white wooly jumper, and black glasses beneath a mop of curly salt-and-pepper hair, he somewhat resembled a human sheep.

Siobhán was mentally trying to count how many people were in front of her when folks began turning away from the door, sour looks stamped on their faces. That was curious. Oran McCarthy seemed to be conversing with each person who stepped up to him. Then the person would do an about-face and slink away. Was the opening postponed again? Why not just make one announcement? And then someone in line finally entered the bookshop. It continued on in this manner, some being turned away, others entering, and Siobhán was considering cutting the line to get the lowdown, when finally, she was the one standing in front of Oran McCarthy. She waited for a friendly hello and was ready to introduce herself when he spoke first.

"What say you?" He stared her down, and if her shiny gold badge intimidated him, he didn't let it show. Up close his thick glasses enlarged his intense brown eyes.

"Pardon?"

He looked over her shoulder. "Next."

"Wait." *What on earth?* "How ya?" she said.

"Goodbye."

She frowned. "I say I want to go into the shop."

His eyes fixated on her garda cap. "Is this official gardaí business?"

She really wanted to say yes. "No."

He didn't hesitate. "Then what say you?"

What say she? Had she mistakenly arrived at some reenactment of a royal ball? Siobhán squinted at him, wondering if he'd been tipping the bottle. He seemed perfectly sober. Wait. Was this Shakespeare? "To be or not to be," she said.

He shook his head. "Not to be."

"I say, I want to go into the bookshop and have a look around."

"Next," he called out in a loud voice, looking to the person in line behind her. Siobhán was soon nudged out of the way. Flummoxed, she stood off to the side, determined to watch what would unfold. Oran held up a finger to the next eager customer, then turned to her, his intense eyes boring into hers. "Goodbye," he said firmly.

What nerve! Her hands clenched into fists at her sides. Shame heated up her cheeks as she headed back to the bistro for a feed. If she wasn't going to get into the shop, she might as well nibble away her stress. Either that or whittle away her stress. She could whittle a dagger and imagine stabbing him with it. She'd eat first and whittle second. From the way she was feeling, nothing less than an entire pan of apple tarts would do. With ice cream and fresh whipped cream, of course. The anger she felt coursing through her was primal. A feisty redhead . . . how she loathed being a cliché. *What say you?* How dare he? Who talked like that? What was she supposed to say? *I'll huff and I'll puff, and I'll blow your house down?* Had certain people been given a secret password to utter? And if so, why wasn't she one of them?

* * *

One shop's rejects were another's fortune. Naomi's Bistro was crammed with those given the boot from the bookshop. Gráinne had even stepped up to help Eoin and Bridie ferry plates between the kitchen and dining rooms. Bridie was still putting on the cheer, but Siobhán knew her well enough to know it was all an act. She assured her they would have a lovely memorial for poor Margaret and that she had died a natural death. Had they not been jammers due to the weather, Siobhán would have insisted on Bridie taking a few days off. The sky outside was darkening, as if the mood of the heavens had just taken a turn, and one could feel a sense of collective anticipation hovering in the air. Siobhán was just about to head back to the garda station when Macdara Flannery burst in with a petite woman by his side.

Despite looking light enough to pick up, the woman radiated strength; perhaps it was her perfect posture, or the crispness of a brand new garda uniform. She had beautiful dark skin and watchful brown eyes underneath her regulation blue cap with shiny gold shield. This must be Garda Dabiri. As Siobhán headed toward them, her attention was arrested by the canvas bag in Macdara's hands. It was green and navy blue, the gold logo splashing the title: TURN THE PAGE.

Siobhán gasped. "They let *you* in?"

Macdara cocked his head and gave her one of his looks. It was totally unfair that his sky-blue eyes and lopsided smile were his weapons of choice. "You sound shocked."

"What say you?" she mimicked, dying to hear the appropriate response.

He grinned. *"Shut your eyes and see."*

Whatever malarkey this was, she was going to give out to him later. Her eyes flicked to the woman beside him. "You must be Garda Dabiri." She smiled, hoping the woman would know her frustration was all aimed at the handsome Detective Sergeant next to her.

Garda Dabiri smiled and waggled a finger. "You can call me Aretta. Unless we're on a case." Aretta had a lovely Dublin accent. Siobhán hoped her experience growing up in Ireland had been a good one, but they had loads of time to share personal stories.

On a case. She had ambition. Just like Siobhán had already heard. Aretta Dabiri was the buzz of Templemore Garda College. She had moved to Ireland with her parents and siblings when she was a wee girl. Originally from Nigeria, they had settled in Dublin. Aretta's father came here to study at Trinity College, and had eventually become an Irish citizen. Siobhán was looking forward to working with Aretta and getting to know her.

"Lovely to meet you, I'm Siobhán." She leaned in. "Or Garda O'Sullivan if we're on a case."

"I know all about you," Aretta said, flashing a bright smile. "You're the talk of Templemore."

"I was just thinking the same about you."

Macdara patted his stomach. "Can we continue this bonding process while we sit?" he said. "I'm so hungry I could eat a small horse."

"Shut your eyes and see," Siobhán said. She held up a finger. "One moment . . . There's brown bread in the oven."

"You're not running away to Google it, are ya?" Macdara's grin was way too big for his face. She whirled around and zoomed into the kitchen, where she indeed whipped out her smartphone and Googled *Shut your eyes and see*.

James Joyce. Dubliners. Interesting. She had never finished a Joyce novel, something she'd never dare say out loud. Every time she'd given it a go she ended up falling asleep. No fault of the author of course; instead she was pretty sure she had some kind of undiagnosed reading-sleep syndrome.

She returned to the dining room. Macdara and Aretta were in the two-seater by the window, Dara's favorite spot. Even the locals knew to keep it open for him.

"You quoted James Joyce?" she said, hands on hips. *Not a chance.*

He held up the bag and dangled it. "Proof is in the pouch."

She slid her eyes over to Aretta. The corners of her mouth were struggling to suppress a grin. "I suspect you're a big reader," Siobhán said.

Aretta gave a little shrug. "I wouldn't want to be telling on my boss on my first day," she said.

They certainly had a fresh one. She'd get over that soon. "It's good to have a reader on the force."

"Are you a big reader yourself?"

"A big reader?" The question sounded innocent, so why did it make Siobhán want to curl up in the corner? She had always meant to be a big reader. Besides devouring Maeve Binchy, her mam hadn't been a big reader, but her da certainly was, and had always encouraged it in his children. He loved history, biographies, and literature. Between her father's love of reading and listening to her customers chat about their latest reads, she was proud of the great Irish writers past and present. James Joyce, Edna O'Brien, Roddy Doyle, Seamus Heaney, Oscar Wilde. Those were only pebbles in an ocean of them. Colum McCann, Tana French, Paul Murray. All authors she meant to read. A customer had once accidentally left a Marian Keyes novel behind and hadn't Siobhán stayed up all night reading? Yes. She'd laughed and cried and was a wreck the next day. That had been about a year ago. Had she done enough to encourage her siblings to read? No. Aside from books at Christmas, of course she hadn't. A reading holiday, that was what she needed.

Gráinne wasn't a big reader. But Eoin definitely was. And didn't James love his history books, just like their da? Siobhán had maintained a regular library schedule with the young ones. But frankly, she had no idea how much Ann or Ciarán read for pleasure. Mostly school assignments, she guessed. Here she was, failing them again. Would she have been a big reader if she'd gone to Trinity College instead of Templemore? Maybe she would do nothing but eat apple tarts all day while pondering it.

"She didn't get into the bookshop if that answers your question," Macdara said, after her long silence, practically purring he was so happy.

"Just because I haven't yet set aside time to get through Joyce doesn't mean I'm not a big reader," Siobhán said.

"Wonderful," Aretta said. "What are you reading now?"

She could feel her cheeks heat up. "I'm between books right now, which is why I'm going to the bookshop as soon as me shift is finished." *Shut your eyes and see.* Oran McCarthy was going to be the one given an eye opener if he didn't let her into the shop this time.

"They're closing early today," Macdara said.

"What?" Siobhán hadn't realized she was shouting until she saw Aretta flinch.

Macdara nodded as he nudged the brown sauce closer to him and eyed the kitchen as if telepathically calling out for his sausages. "Seems they have big-time authors to greet."

"Big-time authors? In Kilbane?"

"They've been in town for two days. Something I didn't find out myself until we had to push back the opening of the bookshop."

Right. Those must be the visiting authors the twins had mentioned. Siobhán had forgotten all about it. They certainly weren't getting off on the right foot with these owners. Was that why they were playing games about who got to enter their shop? "What a way to greet them," Siobhán said, referring to the visiting authors and thinking of poor Margaret lying dead on the footpath. "Do these visiting authors know about Margaret O'Shea?"

Macdara nodded. "I heard Margaret was in one of her black moods, and they all witnessed it. It sounds as if the poor woman wasn't feeling well all along."

Margaret had been a character, and her moods were often stark. "Rest in peace," Siobhán said, crossing herself.

Irish authors in Kilbane. She hadn't had much time to think about it, but it was exciting. What a perfect way to encourage her brood to read more, herself included. Siobhán would go mental if she didn't get a look inside that bookshop, especially since Dara had already been inside. "The line to the shop was awfully long," she said. "Do you think I should pop by right now to make sure they're not over capacity?" She held her breath. "Officially, like?" *Desperate times and all that.*

Macdara waved his hand like she shouldn't bother and brightened as Bridie approached with their breakfasts. Macdara had the full Irish breakfast, but Aretta only had a small bowl of porridge. Perhaps she was too nervous to eat on her first day. "I think they're fine given most people were booted from the line," Macdara said to his heaping plate. "As you well know."

He was enjoying this way too much. "If Irish authors are coming to the bookshop I'd better check the capacity."

"You'd better, boss," Macdara said with a nod and a wink.

Aretta lifted an eyebrow. "Boss?"

"Of my heart." Macdara placed his hand over his chest. Siobhán rolled her eyes. He was really laying it on thick this morning. Whereas they used to hide their relationship, now that they were getting married, Macdara had turned into a pile of mush. He'd better sort himself out. He'd been pressuring her to set a date for the wedding. Just the thought of it made her feel tied up in knots, and not the wedding kind. She had given it a lot of thought and had decided that a wedding at thirty sounded about right. She hoped he wasn't going to be disappointed with the wait.

"I'll leave you to your food and check back at the station after I've popped into the shop." *Shut your eyes and see,* she repeated to herself.

"You can't use the same quote," Macdara said as she was halfway to the door.

"What?" She hated when he seemed to read her mind.

"He won't let in repeats. All the easily Google-able ones are out."

What on earth was the matter with that man? She had half a mind to give him a good shake and the other half to slap him. "Not a bother," she sang.

Chapter 5

Her father's bookshelf was in the corner of Siobhán's bedroom, and *Dubliners* was on the first shelf. She would just bring the book, and if Oran McCarthy wasn't happy with the quote she picked out, she'd knock him on the head with it. Besides, she was going on official garda business.

On the way, hustling ahead of her on the footpath, Siobhán spotted Leigh Coakley, or rather she spotted Leigh's unmistakable golden curls bouncing as she hustled toward the bookshop. Coakley, the owner of Blooms, a local flower shop, was also an aspiring writer. She must have felt a presence behind her, for she whirled around, her hazel eyes alert. She relaxed when she saw it was Siobhán.

"You put the heart in me crossways," Leigh said, holding a book and a bouquet of roses in every color imaginable across her chest. She looked around, then leaned in and whispered, "Ever since poor Margaret O'Shea I've been a bit on edge. You know yourself."

"I know. Tis awful."

"Isn't it though?" Leigh shook her head. "She was in some mood the night of our book club."

"I heard." Siobhán eyed the roses in Leigh's hand. "Going to the bookshop?" *Are those roses a bribe?*

Leigh nodded, her expression radiating excitement. "I hear not everyone gets in."

Siobhán was thrilled to be able to impart some wisdom onto the locals. "You have to quote James Joyce."

"Or Seamus Heaney," Leigh said, mentioning the famous Irish poet/playwright and nodding. *"History says/don't hope on this side of the grave."*

"Pardon?"

"It's a Seamus Heaney quote."

"Of course," Siobhán said brightly. "I brought *Dubliners.*" Siobhán lifted the book.

"It can't be ubiquitous."

"I'm aware."

"Speaking of my ladies' book club . . . would you like to join?" She held up the book in her hand. *Musings on a Hill,* by Nessa Lamb. "I've just started it but I'm already hooked."

Siobhán had never heard of the author or the book. She knew the answer should be yes, that she'd love to join a book club. And it did sound lovely. But also, time consuming. "I wish I could. We're training a new garda, so my calendar is chocker-block."

"Aretta Dabiri?"

News did travel fast. "Yes," Siobhán said. "Garda Dabiri."

"I heard she's a voracious reader, so I intend on inviting her to the book club as well."

"Wonderful." Siobhán hesitated on the next question. It could be considered poor taste, and did it even matter? But curiosity had gotten the best of her. "Do you know what Margaret was so upset about that evening?"

"I heard one of the authors ruffled her feathers. Lorcan Murphy I believe it was."

"What happened?"

"Apparently, he had a bit too much to drink and stumbled into her room instead of his."

That sounded alarming. A strange man bursting into one's room would give anyone a fright. "Wasn't her door locked?"

"She had just gone in herself and was turning to lock the door when it opened."

"And?"

"And that was it. He didn't get a foot inside, mind you. After gathering inside Margaret's room for the book discussion, we were finishing up in the back garden—those of us who wanted a drink. Margaret, as you know, was a tee-totaler, and so out of respect we decided to imbibe in the garden. You could hear her hollering at the poor man all the way from the back garden. The names she called him. We didn't even realize Margaret knew all those words." Leigh shuddered at the memory. "Even the pair of wolfhounds turned tail."

Siobhán laughed. Then her thoughts returned to Margaret and she sobered up. "The poor dear."

Leigh waved it off. "Lorcan Murphy meant no harm. His room is next to hers. It was an understandable error." She sighed. "Still. He gave her quite a fright."

"But you saw her after that? And she was alright?"

Leigh cocked her head. "I didn't see her during that or after. Lorcan Murphy came out to the back garden and told us what happened. Believe me, the poor man was mortified."

"I see."

"You don't think it has anything to do with her death, do you?"

"No, no. I'm only curious," Siobhán assured her.

"If you change your mind, you're welcome any time."

"Change my mind?"

"About the book club."

"Thanks a million, I'll keep it in mind." What was she afraid of? Falling asleep every time she tried to read the chosen book? Yes, because that is exactly what would happen. Then she'd show up to the book group and end up looking like an eejit. Unable to comment on the theme or scope, or poetic descriptions. Drool on the pages. No thank you. She sighed as they reached the bookshop. Once again there was a long line. "I'm on official business, I'll see you later," Siobhán said as she headed to the front door.

When she drew close, Oran McCarthy pointed like the Grim Reaper. "The line is back there."

"I'm afraid we need to discuss capacity."

He sighed. Then turned his sign to CLOSED. "I hope this isn't a trick to get in."

"I have a copy of *Dubliners* right here."

He pursed his lips. "Word is spreading. I'll have to change it up."

There was a groan from the line as he ushered her in and shut the door behind him. "I've only fifteen in at the moment, and our capacity is a hundred and twenty."

Siobhán eagerly stepped in, enveloped by the lovely scent of paper and pulp. The shop was gorgeous. Wide pine floors, antique cream paint on the walls, and matching pine bookshelves filled with colorful spines lined every wall. She couldn't wait to start touching them. She was still thinking of perusing the romance section but didn't see any signs above the shelves delineating the genres. She spotted a giant poster by the register, propped up on an art easel:

IRISH AUTHOR NIGHT
VISITING AUTHORS:
NESSA LAMB
DEIRDRE WALSH
LORCAN MURPHY
VISITING LITERARY AGENT
DARREN KILROY

She didn't recognize any of the names. Of course, Nessa Lamb was the author of *Musings on a Hill*, but she only knew that from running into Leigh Coakley. Her fingers would be sore from Googling. "Tomorrow night," Siobhán said as if she hadn't already heard. "How wonderful." Her eyes drifted to a shelf near the counter where another poster stood that read: STAFF RECOMMENDATIONS. They were not alphabetical or even ordered according to year, and the handwriting was small and seemed hectic, as if the writer was in a race to get down the overflowing list of names: James Joyce, Roddy Doyle, Bram Stoker, Maeve Binchy, Geraldine Quigley, Anne Griffin, Niamh Boyce, Jonathan Swift, Samuel Beckett, W.B. Yeats, C.S. Lewis, John Banville, Seamus Heaney, Patrick Kavanagh, Colum McCann, Tana French, Paul Murray, Colm Toibin, Emma Donoghue. Andrea Carter. Adrian McKinty. She was getting dizzy.

"Just a wee start," Oran said. "Padraig is still working on the list." Siobhán nodded. At this rate, if she wanted to read even half of the names on that list, she would need to quit her job.

Oran shifted, then shoved his thick glasses up with his index finger. "I was hoping I could have a few guards on duty for the author readings."

"Why is that?"

Oran pointed to the poster. "Why, it's Nessa Lamb, of course." He peered down at her from his glasses, waiting for a certain reaction to the name Nessa Lamb.

"Of course." She had never heard of her before today. "She has mad fans, does she?"

Oran blinked repeatedly. "I would certainly hope so. In Galway and Dublin she would, so."

Was he trying to say they weren't cultured enough in Kilbane? Then why had he bothered setting up shop here? "Even so, how rowdy do book fans get?"

"Nessa Lamb fans should be calm enough, alright. But what about Darren Kilroy?" He waited for a response.

"I see," she said when she couldn't come up with anything else.

His eyes narrowed in disapproval. "You know who he is?"

She'd had enough of his snobbery. She pointed to his sign. "Is this another test? To see if I'm literate? He's a literary agent as we can both see there." Her blood pressure was ticking up.

Oran cleared his throat. "I meant no offense, Garda. None at all. He's Michael O'Mara's literary agent."

"Right, so." Michael O'Mara she'd heard of. You'd have to live under a rock not to. He was the author of the popular fantasy series starring a dragon. What was the name of the series? She was too young to start forgetting things, wasn't she? *The Dragon Files*. That was it. From what she knew, the dragon could no longer breathe fire and was on a quest to restore his power. There were at least twenty installments, maybe more, and the poor thing was still breathing vapors. "Michael O'Mara's agent, that is impressive."

"Tis," Oran said, sounding friendly for the first time. "And he has agreed to sign one of our emerging Irish authors by the end of the week. It will really put us on the map."

"Sign one of them?"

Oran sighed. "Represent them. Become their agent."

"I see."

"It's a huge deal."

Siobhán nodded. "Do you have Michael O'Mara's books in stock?" Maybe herself and her siblings could all start reading them together in the evenings.

"The Dragon Files?" Oran scrunched his nose. "No. We only sell literary fiction and history."

"You're joking me."

He thrust his chin up as if she'd just challenged him. "I certainly am not."

"No fantasy?" He didn't blink. "Romance?" He pursed his lips in disapproval and shook his head. "Science fiction?" Another shake. "Thrillers? Graphic novels? Murder mysteries?" Her pitch and volume went up as he rejected each genre with a look of pure disdain.

"Do you not understand what I mean when I say literary fiction?" He nearly spit out the words. He certainly had a big mouth for a Sheep Man.

Another male voice piped up from somewhere behind Oran. "I disagree with him and am diligently working to change his mind if that makes you feel any better." He pointed to the Staff Recommendations. "As Oran mentioned, I am still working on this list and I intend to keep it very inclusive."

Oran seemed to shudder. "They'll just have to purchase *some of those* elsewhere."

The other man sighed and gave Siobhán a look. She took a moment to study him. He was planted behind the register, hiding behind a huge stack of books waiting to be shelved. He had similar glasses to Oran, but was a good ten years younger, dressed in denims and a T-shirt with a black blazer. Hip. And very handsome. If Oran was the Sheep Man, this must be his herder.

"That's my better-younger-half, Padraig," Oran said. "His leniency in books notwithstanding."

"Nice to meet you. I'm Siobhán O'Sullivan. You need only call me Garda O'Sullivan if I'm on a case." Padraig took in her uniform, saluted with a grin, then returned to his book. Friendlier than his husband but not chatty. *Noted.* "I also own Naomi's Bistro with my siblings. We do hope to see you both there soon." She waited for some kind of reaction or acknowledgment. *Tanks for the basket of scones!* No such luck. Were they low-carbers? Vegans? Should she mention they could cater to all dietary needs?

"Here's a flyer for the event tomorrow," Oran said, handing it to her. "I need the guards to make sure no one enters with any kind of tree nuts on their person."

He pointed to a *WARNING* notice on the flyer, splashed in red: No nuts of any kind!

"I'm afraid you don't know this village," Siobhán said. "There'll be a room full of them."

Oran frowned, but Padraig burst into laughter.

"This is very serious," Oran said. "We've been warned that Deirdre Walsh is deathly allergic to tree nuts."

"I'm only messing with ya. I know it's a very serious allergy. You should double-check everyone at the door. And make sure you don't go over capacity."

She glanced at the schedule for Irish Authors Week. The authors would be doing a signing on her birthday. Now that was special. She could buy each of their books and have them signed to her. Or maybe to the O'Sullivan Six. This might encourage her brood to read. And as far as her birthday . . . she'd planned on warning everyone, including or maybe especially Macdara, not to make a big fuss over it, but no one had mentioned it. Just as well. Unless they were planning something. They'd better not be. "What about children's books? Do you have children's books?"

"Children can read literature," Oran said. "Or an adult can read it to them."

"Are you joking me?"

"Let me stop you right there. I will never be joking you."

Cheeky.

"It's true," Padraig said. "He's entirely humorless." Oran threw Padraig a look, Padraig shrugged. "Unless it's Bloomsday and then he's cheerful all day and into the evening. You'll see yourself on the sixteenth of June." Bloomsday was an official celebration of James Joyce, named after the protagonist Leopold Bloom, in *Ulysses*. The Kilbane Theatre often had readings to celebrate Bloomsday; they'd be thrilled to have support this year.

Oran and Padraig smiled at each other. At least Oran seemed affectionate toward his husband. But what kind of business owner starts off his grand opening by kicking people out of his shop and poking fun at them?

"Do you have any books by Marian Keyes?" she squeaked.

"We definitely need to get in Marian Keyes," Padraig said. He put his hand on his heart. "I loved *Rachel's Holiday*. And do you follow her on Twitter? She's hysterical." From the way Oran's face was contorting, he did not agree.

"No," Oran said. "We do not carry any books by Marian Keyes."

"One day," Padraig said. "One day soon."

"Maeve Binchy?" If Oran said no to this the day might seriously end in fisty-cuffs.

"Of course we have Maeve Binchy," Oran said. "Do you take us for savages?" Padraig rolled his eyes behind Oran's back and gave her another shrug. "I'd better get back to the line," Oran said. "Feel free to browse while you're here."

"Tanks."

Padraig's gaze remained on her as Oran headed for the door. "I promise I'll work on him."

Siobhán smiled and nodded, and then thought there was way too much smiling and nodding for the sour mood that had enveloped her. Padraig was going to have his work cut out for him. Now what was she going to do? She'd rather have her brood here, and she was still disappointed there were no romances, or adventure books, or children's books. Was she a simple person? Didn't everyone have a right to like what they liked?

"Finally," Leigh Coakley said as she burst into the shop, petals falling from the roses in her hand. "Where's Padraig?"

Siobhán and Padraig turned. Leigh's coat was now off, revealing a yellow suit with a red rose pinned on the lapel. She was bright and jarring. She handed the colorful bouquet of roses to a confused Padraig.

"I'm Leigh Coakley," she said. "I run the flower shop in town. Blooms."

"Blooms!" he said with a laugh. "We were just speaking of Bloomsday."

"No relation, but we do make arrangements for every occasion." She gestured to the roses cradled awkwardly in his hand. "Please accept those as a welcoming gift." He blinked as if her suit was blinding him, inhaled the scent of the flowers, and smiled. He set them on the counter.

"Thank you." His nose began to twitch and he gave the flowers the side-eye. Was he allergic?

"You're welcome." She stared at the flowers. "Do you not have a vase?"

"We haven't unpacked everything yet," Padraig said.

"I should have brought you one. I just assumed you had one of your own."

"Don't worry, I'll fetch something soon."

Leigh bit her lip, looking as if she'd just handed him a goldfish and it was flopping around on the counter gasping for a bowl of water. "I simply must have copies of all the visiting authors' books." She pointed to the sign. "Deirdre Walsh, Nessa Lamb, and Lorcan Murphy."

"Wonderful," Padraig said. He pointed to a table in the middle of the store. "You'll find them all right there."

"Including Michael O'Mara?"

"I'm afraid not." Padraig lowered his voice as if he was afraid Oran would overhear.

"But his agent will be here," Leigh Coakley said, sounding outraged. "Some people are speculating he might make a surprise visit himself!"

"They would be wrong," Padraig said. "But Darren Kilroy will be here. And by the end of the week, one of our lucky visiting authors will have him as his or her agent."

"But you must have copies of *The Dragon Files* somewhere in the store?" Leigh threw a glance to Siobhán. "Rumor has it Gritana might get his fire back in the new release."

"God willing," Siobhán said, then crossed herself.

"I am afraid we are not carrying O'Mara's books at the moment," Padraig said carefully.

Leigh Coakley gasped. "My ladies are not going to be happy to hear dat." She flicked her eyes over to Siobhán, then back to Padraig. "I have a very active ladies' book group."

"Wonderful."

"They were expecting *The Dragon Files*."

"I hope you and they will attend regardless."

"Irregardless."

"Regardless."

"I don't tink so."

"You don't think you'll attend?"

"I think it's *irregardless*."

"Whatever you tink is best."

Irregardless, or regardless, Siobhán O'Sullivan needed her headache tablets. She picked out *North*, by Seamus Heaney, *Light a Penny Candle* and *Tara Road*, by Maeve

Binchy, and a book by each of the visiting authors. She paid for them, and as she dropped them into her new Turn the Page bag, a trill of excitement ran through her. A simple canvas bag held entire worlds within it. Characters and images that would materialize with the opening of a page. Emotions that would well in her from another human being at another time and place taking pen to paper. She couldn't remember when a purchase had pleased her more, not counting chocolates. What a good omen for her birthday.

An image of Margaret O'Shea lying dead on the footpath rose to mind, squashing her happiness. *What was she doing there on the footpath, hours before the bookshop was slated to open?* How did she get there? Why had she ventured out that morning when she'd done nothing of the sort the past year? It had to be to visit the bookshop. And given she was a big reader and had hosted the book club the night before, maybe there was a connection. If Margaret O'Shea had been that excited to visit the bookshop, she should be standing here right now with her own worlds tucked into a canvas bag. Terribly, terribly sad. Perhaps it wouldn't hurt to poke around, ask a few questions. She could speak with the authors soon at the bookshop. That settled that. Three visiting authors and a big-time literary agent. And only one of them would get signed. How exciting. For one of them. Unfortunately, two of them were going to be in for a world of hurt.

Chapter 6

The next evening, Siobhán and Aretta arrived at Turn the Page, to once again find a full crowd standing on the footpath. It looked as if everyone who had attended the morning mass for Margaret O'Shea was here, only the somber black outfits were replaced by cheerful spring colors. Soon, a sleek limo pulled up in front of the bookshop. "You don't see that often around here," Siobhán observed. Except for funerals. She left that bit out. For a second she wondered if the limo was for her. A surprise. For her birthday. *Tomorrow*, she reminded herself. Then again, wouldn't the perfect way to surprise her be to plan something for today when she was least suspecting it?

They were definitely up to something. Not one of her siblings, or her fiancé, had even mentioned it. No dinner invites, no leading questions about what she might like to do for her special day, no sneaky hints of a surprise to come, no teasing that she was growing old. They were either up to something, or they were horrible, horrible people. Her focus returned to the limo.

The driver, a short but energetic man in a dark suit, jumped out of the vehicle and held the door open as if royalty was about to emerge. The authors were here. Excitement shone in Aretta's eyes as a glamorous woman stepped out. Dressed in a shimmering skirt, suede coat, and sunglasses that swallowed her pretty face, Deirdre Walsh was still recognizable to Siobhán. She had looked each of them up last night. The black-haired beauty was the one with the tree nut allergy. She'd self-published a dense literary novel, and someone (Siobhán had a feeling it was Deirdre herself) had dubbed her the Female James Joyce. Holding a book against her soft suede coat, she scanned the crowd, as if trying to figure out if they were friends or foes.

Oran stepped out of the crowd. "Deirdre Walsh," he exclaimed. "Welcome, welcome, welcome."

Three welcomes. My, my, my. Aretta was trying to peer around Deirdre and into the black mouth of the limo.

"Who are you waiting for?" Siobhán asked her.

"Nessa Lamb. I hope I can get an autograph." Aretta reached into her pocket and pulled out a worn paperback. *Musings on a Hill.* "It is filled with great insight."

The comment struck a chord of fear in Siobhán. This was why she hadn't joined the book club. What if she read it and didn't find any insights? What if they turned to ask her what she thought and all she could say was that she enjoyed reading it with a lovely bag of crisps and chocolate that melted on her tongue? Siobhán had mused plenty on hills, but never once thought of writing about it. Were some people just born scribes?

Next, a middle-aged man with purple-rimmed glasses and a lavender suit emerged from the limo. Spring had certainly started to infuse people's wardrobes. Had a memo been circulating that everyone should dress like colorful Easter eggs and Siobhán had missed it? This was Darren Kilroy, the agent. He stopped and held out his hand, helping a petite brunette out. Unlike the others, she was dressed in muted shades of gray. It made the dozen red roses she was carrying stand out.

"That's her," Aretta said.

Nessa Lamb looked as mild and sweet as her surname. She blinked at the crowd, then looked away as if it physically hurt to maintain eye contact. The last to emerge was a tall younger man, his curly black hair a sharp contrast to his pale face. He wore a brown blazer, plaid shirt, and denims. Apparently, he missed the Easter-egg-wardrobe memo as well. He smiled at the crowd and waved. Lorcan Murphy. The one who had mistakenly opened the door to Margaret O'Shea's room. Siobhán hoped she'd get a chance to ask him about it, although she had to be careful not to send ripples of alarm through any of them. She wasn't here to accuse anyone of anything untoward, she just hated loose ends.

Siobhán had researched all of the authors last night and despite being an "indie author," meaning he self-published all of his works, Lorcan Murphy had the most commercial success out of the three. He wrote both murder mysteries and westerns. Dara had several of his westerns and Siobhán could tell he was eager to meet him. Siobhán was wondering why Oran had included him, as his books didn't fit Oran's literary criteria. That's when she noticed Padraig's right hand. He clutched one of Lorcan's books, *Under a Rust-Colored Sun.* On it, a cowboy

sat atop a horse, head down, hat covering his face, looking as if he couldn't go another minute, the sun (indeed
the color of rust) beating down on him. Siobhán knew
you weren't supposed to judge a book by its cover, but
just looking at the knackered cowboy made her want to
take a nap. But Padraig McCarthy was certainly a fan.
Good for Padraig. Maybe Oran would soon realize he
needed to open the bookshop up to books from all genres.

The authors were ushered into the bookshop first, followed by Siobhán and Aretta. Padraig stood at the door,
asking each person if he or she were in possession of any
tree nuts. Moments later she heard a shout. "Peanuts!"
Padraig said, pointing to Darren Kilroy. "He has a bag of
peanuts!"

Darren immediately put his arms up as if he was being
arrested. "Sorry, sorry," he said. "The bag has never been
opened. They've been in that pocket since I flew to Lon-
don for a book fair. It completely slipped me mind." He
clapped Padraig on the back, a bit too hard from the way
Padraig lurched forward. "Fair play to ye."

"Not a bother," Padraig said, righting himself and
straightening his tie. Although his face said it was indeed
a bother. "The bag has not been opened. Tragedy averted."
He glanced at Oran as if he was seeking confirmation.

"A bit of irony," Oran said. "No harm done." Siobhán
didn't see the irony, but she wasn't prepared to get
schooled by Oran McCarthy.

"I'll take them outside immediately and find a rubbish
bin," Darren Kilroy said, throwing an apologetic glance
to Deirdre Walsh, who didn't seem at all alarmed, and
hurrying toward the exit.

As soon as the literary agent returned and the authors
were seated, the patrons were let in, and soon the book-

shop was standing room only. Oran welcomed the audience and introduced their guests of honor. Nessa Lamb had published three books and she had won numerous awards for her latest book, *Musings on a Hill*. Siobhán caught Deirdre Walsh rolling her eyes halfway through Oran calling out Nessa's long list of accolades, but Lorcan Murphy bobbed his head, his face reacting positively to each one.

Deirdre Walsh had one title out, *Melodies*, a weighty tome she clutched in her hand. Oran cleared his throat and read from a sheet of paper. "*Melodies* is an in-depth study of madness brought on by a matriarch's struggle for fairness and redemption." Deirdre mouthed the words along with him and then grimaced when Oran had nothing to add.

"Lorcan Murphy is the popular author of the mystery series *Dead Elf on a Shelf*—" Oran's introduction was interrupted by a burst of applause from Leigh Coakley and her ladies' book group. They all had red roses pinned to their outfits.

"Will you be keeping them in stock?" Leigh asked loudly. "We're big fans."

"We will of course," Padraig said before Oran could answer otherwise.

"Hopefully that applies to all of us," Deirdre said.

"Of course it does," Lorcan piped up with a grin. "And thank you to my fans." He gave a seated bow.

"Fans?" Deirdre said. She patted Lorcan's knee. "There's a first time for everything."

He tilted his head in her direction, and gave a shrug.

Nessa leaned forward. "Lorcan Murphy has more fans than you and I put together."

"It's not a competition," Lorcan said, waving his hand

and grinning like a Cheshire cat. "But look who's talking. You made the Forty under Forty list. Impressive."

"Thank you," Nessa said, eyes scanning the crowd for possible fans lying in wait. "What a thrill. I didn't expect it at all. It was such an honor."

Deirdre coughed into her hand and it sounded as if she'd spit out a word: "Baloney."

"A pleasure just to be noticed," Lorcan added, with a quick frown in Deirdre's direction.

Deirdre once again muttered something under her breath, but nobody seemed to catch it. Oran cleared his throat. "I'd like to direct my first question to Nessa Lamb."

"Typical," Deirdre said. Nessa Lamb threw her a searing look.

"You say you were not prepared for such an overwhelming reaction to *Musings on a Hill*?"

Nessa Lamb placed her hand on her heart like she was at a rugby game about to belt out the Irish national anthem. "It's been the greatest honor of my life. And I wasn't going to mention it, but Lorcan already let the cat out of the bag, so I might as well! Being called one of the hottest forty novelists under forty?" Her gaze flicked once again to Deirdre, who looked to be in her mid to late forties. "I never would have thought it." She laughed. "I finally have followers on social media. More followers than I know what to do with!"

A sound rang out, something between a snort and a laugh. All heads turned to Deirdre Walsh. Even she looked startled at her outburst. "Pardon," she said.

"I set out to write *Musings on a Hill* for myself." Nessa Lamb directed her comments back to the audience. "I am so humbled to receive all this attention. From fans and *agents*." This time her gaze fell squarely on Darren Kilroy before flicking away with a smile.

Let the competition begin.

"Oh, come on. I bet you wrote this little humble-brag speech while musing on that hill," Deirdre said. She looked to Lorcan and then Darren as if hoping to share a laugh, but both of them had suddenly spotted their favorite tome on the shelves and were staring at it with rapt fascination.

"I was never one for speeches," Nessa said, shaking her head. "But I am so touched that my words tumbled all the way down that hill and into this wonderful village." She turned to the crowd. "I can't think of a better place to announce *another* piece of good news. On the way here I learned that I've won the Irish Scribe of the Year award." The crowd erupted in applause. Siobhán watched Deirdre Walsh. Her face went scarlet in an instant. Had she applied for the same award? Nessa was still talking. "The cash prize will allow me to quit my job and live my dream of being a full-time writer."

The applause thundered. Deirdre fumbled for her bottle of water, and gulped it down as Darren Kilroy patted her on the back. She pushed Darren away, splashing water on the both of them. "Congratulations," Deirdre said through bared teeth. "I was up for that award myself as you well know."

Nessa Lamb looked stricken. Her hand was back on her heart. "I swear to ye," she said, addressing the crowd, "I didn't know. I didn't realize it was open to anyone who claimed to write a book." She said it so softly, Siobhán wasn't sure she realized it was an insult.

"Claimed to write a book?" Deirdre rose out of her

chair. Siobhán pictured ashes, and a phoenix rising. "What is that supposed to mean?"

"Nothing," Nessa Lamb said, her voice rising a little. "I just assumed there were certain criteria to be eligible for that award, and I must admit I've never even heard of you."

"Believe me," Deirdre Walsh said, "you've heard of me."

"No," Nessa said, shaking her head. "Not until today."

"Then you have no idea what I'm capable of, or the quality of my writing," Deirdre said.

"That is true," Nessa agreed. "I suppose readers can be slow to catch on as well."

Lorcan raised his hand. "Yes, Mr. Murphy," Padraig said, practically glowing with adoration.

"We indie authors should really stick together," he said, turning to Nessa and Deirdre. "This is getting a bit rude if you don't mind."

"One of you might not be an indie author after signing with Darren Kilroy," Oran McCarthy said. From the panicked look on his face, it was obvious he was in damage-control mode. "I'm sure he'll get you a big publishing deal, just like Michael O'Mara."

Darren Kilroy, who had just taken a sip of his tea, began to choke. It took him a few moments to recover. "There's only one Michael O'Mara," he said. "But I'll do me best."

"Michael O'Mara is a dime a dozen," Deirdre said. "If a woman wrote his books, none of us would probably have ever heard of *her*."

A gasp rang out from Leigh Coakley, who shot out of her chair. "Take that back."

"I will not," Deirdre said. She held up her weighty

tome. "I write about real people. Real struggle. It's fire-breathing dragons and hollow nothings mused about on hills you're all after? Is it? We're all supposed to sell out to the man, is that it?"

"Whoa," Nessa said. "My musings are not hollow. They're very deep."

"Those dragons represent the human struggle," Leigh said. "Underneath all that fire, and flying, Gritana is just like us."

"And they're very entertaining," another member of the book club said. "The way he tries to keep up with his pesky scales reminds me of my mani/pedi routine." The women in the book club laughed.

Deirdre shook her head. She zoned in on Oran McCarthy. "Then why don't you carry Michael O'Mara's books?"

Oran's face reddened. "That is under consideration," he said. "We've only just opened."

Deirdre chortled. "The old boys' club is alive and well."

"Several of my short stories have been published in renowned magazines," Nessa said out of nowhere. "And not one reviewer has ever called me hollow."

"Does anyone even read magazines anymore?" Deirdre asked. Her eyes scanned the crowd as if expecting an answer. "Except in the bathroom?"

At this point, Siobhán would take working with criminals over squabbling writers.

Lorcan shook his head. "Ladies, ladies, ladies. Where is your sense of decency and decorum?"

This time Nessa let out a snort. "Where was yours when you stumbled into some poor old lady's room in the middle of the night?"

"Hey!" Lorcan Murphy's face went scarlet. "That was an honest mistake." He crossed his arms and bounced his left knee. Nessa Lamb had struck a nerve. "I didn't sleep a wink after she screamed those names at me, and then to learn she passed away?" He shook his head. "That was a terrible thing to say. I would expect it from Deirdre, but you?"

"Me?" Deirdre said. "You would expect it from me? How dare you."

"I apologize. That came out wrong," Nessa said. "That poor woman." She crossed herself. Soon the entire ladies' book club was crossing themselves, and then the gesture spread to nearly everyone else in the room.

"It was dark," Lorcan said, still stung. "Her room was right next to mine."

"I'm sure the bottle of wine you consumed in the back garden had nothing to do with it," Deirdre said.

Nervous laughter rang from the crowd. Oran stiffened and he shot a look to Padraig, who didn't seem to notice. Instead, he was glued to the drama. Darren Kilroy rose. "I do not like this behavior. I understand you are all under a great deal of stress. All your books are worthy or you wouldn't have been invited. But I beg you. Either conduct yourselves with some decorum and decency, if I may quote Lorcan Murphy, or I shall be signing none of you."

"You may," Lorcan said. "Quote me."

Nessa and Deirdre took their seats. Deirdre slumped. "I'm more interested in readers than awards anyhow." She turned to Lorcan. "As are you I assume?" She had plastered a smile on her pretty face, but the tension was still heavy in the air.

Lorcan shrugged, uncrossed his legs, and crossed them the other direction. "I don't pay much attention to either, to be honest."

Deirdre laughed. "You're both full of blarney."

"Are you looking to sign award-winning authors?" Leigh Coakley asked Darren Kilroy.

"Sure, lookit," he said, when he realized they were waiting for an answer. "Who doesn't like to sign a winner? Doesn't hurt sales either, to announce you've won a prestigious award." He cleared his throat again. "But I do think we've gone off the rails a bit."

Nessa nodded her head in agreement. Her hand went back to her heart. "Thanks a million."

"Haven't you won the Blazing Saddle Award?" Padraig asked Lorcan. It was as if he wanted to keep the drama going.

Lorcan nodded. "I did indeed. And was nominated for the Six Shooter, but so far it's only grazed me." He chuckled at his own pun.

"Were you prepared for the success of *Dead Elf on a Shelf?*" Leigh asked.

Lorcan shook his head. "I did it as a lark on Christmas when me kids asked why the fecking elf hadn't moved off his shelf." The crowd laughed and Lorcan brightened up. "They thought it was because they were naughty." Heads began to nod in the crowd. "The next day I put a knife through the elf and poured some red sauce over him, and told the kids he was stabbed in his sleep because he was the naughty one." The laughter ratcheted up and Lorcan was loving it. "They started asking me who killed him, and before you know it I was killing every Elf on a Shelf over and over again." He began making a jabbing motion by way of demonstrating. One could imagine if he looked like that when Margaret O'Shea opened her door, it would have put the heart in her crossways.

The thought gave Siobhán pause. When he talked of killing, his eyes took on a glow. Was he telling the truth? Had he entered Margaret's room by accident? Or was her death anything but natural?

Chapter 7

Lorcan Murphy had finally stopped his stabbing gestures, and no one but Siobhán must have found it alarming, for the focus was still on *Dead Elf on a Shelf.* "Is it a children's book?" Oran said, turning to Padraig and wrinkling his nose.

"No, it's for the parents," someone in the crowd shouted out as Padraig nodded. Oran did not look impressed. Siobhán hadn't read it but now she wanted to. Fictional elves. Those were the kind of murder probes she wished she was tasked with solving.

"It doesn't seem very festive," Oran said, still confused. "Killing elves at Christmas."

"He doesn't just kill them at Christmas," Leigh volunteered. "Elves drop nearly every day of the year now."

"I don't understand this at all," Oran said.

"You must not have children," Lorcan said. "The parents get it."

"I see," Oran said. He cleared his throat. "Do you not feel any need to live up to our great Irish writers?" He gestured to a shelf. Above it on a banner featuring a rendering of Oscar Wilde was his message in capital letters: GREAT IRISH WRITERS.

"I'd say none of us can live up to the greats," Nessa said. "I'm honored just to be good."

"You two certainly are writers," Deirdre said. "Because you're spinning yarns right now." She shook her head as if disgusted. "Humble bragging is not a good perfume. Outright bragging is downright deadly."

Nessa glared at her. "It's better than outright desperation."

Lorcan laughed. Once again, Deirdre shot out of her chair as if it was spring loaded.

"Just you wait," she said. "I have a new project—an explosive tell-all—that's going to launch me into the spotlight. You'll be moping on that hill then and eating my literary dust." Her eyes bored into Nessa Lamb. "Convenient you mention your accolades but not your scathing one-star review."

Watching Nessa Lamb's face turn red was like watching a thermometer tick up. "I wouldn't be surprised if *you* left me that one-star review," Nessa shot back.

"If I had been reviewing it, I would have given you a falling star," Deirdre said.

A gasp sounded from Leigh Coakley. "You should eat your words," she said, shaking her finger at Deirdre. Behind her, the ladies' book club nodded in horrified unison.

"Mark my words," Deirdre said. "My new memoir is going to take readers by storm and blow people's minds."

"Memoir?" Darren Kilroy said, interrupting the shouting match. "Are you sure you want to write a memoir?" He sounded aghast.

"It's already done," Deirdre said. "Explosive!"

"I for one am not looking for memoirs, my dear," Darren said. "I can assure you of that." He shuddered.

"You'll change your mind when you read mine." Deirdre grinned. "And if you don't, someone else will snap it up. Mark my words."

"'Take readers by storm,'" Nessa added on. "'Blow people's minds.' 'Mark my words.' So cliché."

"I personally like to keep my mind intact," Lorcan quipped.

Aretta leaned into Siobhán. "If their books are as dramatic as they are, I might have to give them all a go."

"That's the spirit," Siobhán said. "Around here, we take our excitement wherever we can get it."

The morning of Siobhán O'Sullivan's twenty-ninth birthday was lashing rain. Margaret's burial would have to be postponed, which meant they'd postpone the funeral as well, and Siobhán couldn't help but feel relieved. It was her birthday after all. Cats, and dogs, and Guinness poured out of the sky. She smiled at the thought. Her mam used to say it was raining cats and dogs, and her da would add: "As long as there's a bit of Guinness mixed in, we'll be alright, so."

She wished they were here to watch her blow out the candles and tease her about her age. How could her twenties be nearly gone? At least she knew what she'd done with them. Raised her siblings, finished training at Templemore Garda College, became a garda at the Kilbane Garda Station, and got engaged to none other than Detective Sergeant Macdara Flannery. Those were all reasons to celebrate.

But she was starting to wonder if there would even be any candles. The morning came with not so much as a *happy birthday* from anyone. She expected Dara to show up at the door, with his lopsided grin and messy hair, and make her brekkie. If not him, then certainly her brother Eoin would greet her with an Irish breakfast, and maybe a homemade card with one of his brilliant illustrations.

And Eoin did make breakfast, for all of them, and for once the O'Sullivan Six sat in the dining room to eat. What a heap sat in front of them, plates full with eggs, rashers, sausages, black and white pudding, beans, and toast. But if Siobhán was hoping for a meaningful family connection, she was sorely disappointed. James, just home from Waterford, alluded to an upcoming appointment he was being very mysterious about, Eoin was preoccupied with the menu for the day, Ciarán had his head buried in his mobile phone, Ann was out of sorts about her Camogie match being canceled due to the storm, and Gráinne was flipping through a fashion magazine, every now and then gasping and tearing out a sheet. And as nice as it was to sit down with all her siblings, there had been no mention of Siobhán's birthday. "Is no one else excited about the bookshop?" she asked. She was greeted with half shrugs, a nod, and outright ignorance.

"Bookshop?" Gráinne said.

"Have you been living under a rock?" Siobhán asked.

Maybe working at Sheila's Hair Salon was detrimental to her health. All those chemicals erasing her brain cells.

"Dat's not nice," Gráinne said. "I'm only messing. Course we're all happy about the bookshop."

"Today might be a good day for all of us to go to the bookshop," Siobhán said. "Don't you think?" *Today. My birthday. The last one of my twenties.*

More shrugs. Not a word about her birthday.

That was their first mistake. The O'Sullivans were a celebrating type of brood, and Ciarán would remember any day that involved cake. They were up to something. But here they were, clearing the breakfast plates, and not one of them had uttered a word about it. It would have been impressive were it not so annoying.

"See ya," Ann said as she and Ciarán headed out the door.

"Have a good day," Siobhán called, briefly touching Ann's blond bob and squeezing Ciarán's shoulder on the way out. She followed them outside and watched them head down the footpath. Ominous black clouds swirled above. Ironic—if the power went out there would be candles after all, just not the kind she imagined. Maybe it was for the best. Did she really need to celebrate a birthday ever again?

She wasn't due to the garda station until later this morning so she whipped up six batches of brown bread, slid them in the oven, took her shower, and put on her garda uniform. She loved the navy blue with the gold shield. Guardians of the Peace. It was a nice job title to have, and even though she'd often played out what her life might have been like had her parents lived, she was proud to be a member of An Garda Síochána.

She removed the brown bread from the cooker and set it on the cooling racks. That should get the bistro through the breakfast rush if indeed the storm drove people in. When she got to the station, Macdara greeted her in his usual way. "Morning, boss," he said with a wink.

"Morning," she said slowly, waiting to see if he would add anything else. Like *happy birthday!*

"Pretty light day for you today."

"Is it now?" she asked. He nodded. "Is it a light day for you as well?"

He shook his head. "I'll be training Garda Dabiri up on basic protocols."

"Do you want me to do that?"

"I've got it. In fact, you can have the day off."

"The day off?" Was this the birthday surprise? A day off? "Are you joking me?" It would have been nice to know ahead of time. She could have had a lie-in.

"I would have let you know earlier, but a request for this evening just came in and I'd like to put you on it."

He must have read her mind. He had an irritating habit of doing just that. Was it going to get worse after they got married? Would she ever need to open her gob again? "What request?"

"I'd like you to man the bookshop for a few hours this evening. Seven to ten p.m."

"Man the bookshop?"

He nodded. "The authors will be signing copies of their books."

Was it a ruse? She had already planned on attending, but as a citizen. She mulled it over. "Why do you feel a guard is necessary?"

He sighed. "We've had a few threats come in."

Siobhán was on full alert. Macdara wouldn't joke about threats. "What's the story?"

"I think it's probably young ones, acting the maggot. A few veiled threats were called in."

Siobhán didn't want to imagine. "Any clue as to who made the calls?"

"Not yet," Macdara said."I hear Chris Gordon isn't thrilled about the bookshop opening."

News did travel fast. "Chris Gordon might be insecure but he's hardly one to issue threats."

"Even so, maybe it wouldn't hurt to pay him a visit as well. You can count that toward your hours."

The entire afternoon off did sound exactly like what the birthday girl wanted. "Anything else?" she asked.

"That's it." They were all excellent actors. But at least one of them should have said *happy birthday*—it would have been a lot less suspicious than this mass-amnesia act. "Not a bother," she said, heading for the door.

"Are you stocked up on candles?" he called out.

She stopped, held his gaze to see if he would mention her birthday or crack a smile. He did not. "Candles?"

"The storm. Good chance of a power outage."

"Right." Candles, matches, torches, batteries. Loads of chocolates. Crisps. A bottle of Baileys wouldn't hurt either. "I'll pop into the hardware shop. Do you need extra supplies?"

"All good, tanks."

"Right, so." She grinned the minute she turned her back. Whatever they were up to, it had to be something big.

* * *

There was a CLOSED sign on Gordon's Comics. Siobhán peered in the window to see if she could spot him, but it was too dark. She would have to ask Eoin to give him a bell. There was no way he was behind calling in threats to Oran and Padraig, was there?

Halfway home, the skies opened up and the rain poured out of the heavens. She jogged the rest of the way to the bistro. There was indeed a full crowd, driven in by the weather. She could hear chatter, plates clinking, and the sizzle of rashers on the grill. The talk, of course, was about the weather:

"Tis miserable, isn't it?"

"Ah, sure, lookit, it's pouring down on us."

"Tis only going to get worse as the day goes on."

"Do you think they'll cancel the author signings?"

"I'm sure they'll have candles, but I tell ye, if it keeps up like dis, lads, I won't be going out in it."

She headed upstairs to change out of her wet uniform. How long had it been since she had an afternoon to herself? *Ages.* Sadly, she had no idea what to do with it. She changed into jammies and her robe, then texted Eoin to bring her a cappuccino if he got a chance (it was her birthday after all, even if they wanted to pretend it wasn't), and once that was sorted, she took *Dubliners* off the shelf, curled up in bed, and turned to the first page:

THE SISTERS

There was no hope for him this time: it was the third stroke.

Before she knew it, Siobhán was lost in another world, a young man, a dead friend, and nasty old man Cotter. The writing pulled her in—no wonder everyone made such a fuss over Joyce—and although she was soon enthralled, she also felt stymied. Her work often consisted of death, and that brought up the image of poor Margaret lying on the footpath, and today, she was feeling every bit of twenty-nine. Perhaps she should save Joyce for another occasion. She sighed, put the book on her bedside table, and contemplated life. She needed a romance. Maybe an adventure tale. Something set on a sandy beach with the sun warming her bones. If only Oran McCarthy wasn't so rigid. How nice would it be to pop into the shop early and find something fun to escape into? Hopefully Padraig would be able to talk some sense into him. She closed her eyes, and before she drifted to sleep, realized now that she was getting old, she was going to need a lot more naps.

Although the bookshop was just down the street past King John's Castle, Siobhán had to fight the pelting rain and wind on her way there. She broke into a slow jog, mindful not to slip and do a face-plant on her birthday. Thunder rumbled, and lightning streaked across the Irish sky. She had her trusty torch tucked into her pocket. And how fortuitous. She arrived to find Turn the Page in the dark. Wasn't the author event slated to begin? She turned her head to the other side of the street, to find a blanket of darkness washed across her village. The power was indeed out, and the wind howled its outrage. She tried not to think about all the food stored in their multiple refrigerators back at the bistro. Hopefully, if nothing else, the lads would dig into it, and give food away to the locals. You can't win against Mother Nature, what would be would be. Such a turbulent way to spend her birthday.

Unless the power wasn't really out and the entire village was in on her surprise party.

Eejit. Just face it. Everyone forgot about your birthday. Even though she wouldn't put it past them, her brood wasn't capable of arranging power outages. She hoped it didn't last long; folks had a tendency to panic in the dark. Siobhán was feeling a bit uneasy herself. She took her torch out of her pocket, and slid the switch to ON. It emitted a high-pitch whine but did not shine. She shook it. Nothing. It was too dark to see if the batteries were in correctly; she was going to have to do without it. "Naughty torch," she said out loud. If Oran and Padraig were inside perhaps they were fetching their candles and torches. They seemed like the type of lads who would be prepared. After all, you can't read books in the dark. Unless they were e-books, but only as long as the charge lasted. Then again, everyone had been aflutter about the visiting authors, and distraction was the enemy of preparation.

The thunder rumbled as she reached for the doorknob. *It was a dark and stormy night* . . . Nothing else came to her. Definitely, not a storyteller. She'd have to leave the scribbling to the masters. The door to the bookshop squeaked open as rain pummeled the windows.

"Hello?" Siobhán called into the darkness. "It's Garda O'Sullivan." She took a step. The floorboards creaked. "Is anyone here?"

A loud bang could be heard, then someone cursed. *Gráinne.* Soon little flames appeared in the distance, one by one.

"Surprise," a chorus of voices yelled out.

"Jaysus," Siobhán said, placing her hand on her heart. "Did you make the power go out too?"

A laugh rolled from the corner of the room. Macdara. "Of course not," he said. "Took us by surprise as well." She heard a click and a torch shone from where she'd already pinpointed he was standing. He put it under his chin. The shadows were ghastly.

"Don't do that," Siobhán said. He laughed again but moved the torch away. There were more clicks and suddenly enough torches were lit for Siobhán to see people clumped together in front of a birthday cake in the center of the bookshop. She approached. "You shouldn't have."

"We were all set to turn off the lights when Mother Nature did it for us," Ciarán said. He sounded giddy with excitement. The authors were in attendance as well. Probably waiting to get this over with so they could sign copies of their books.

"Padraig is looking for more candles," Oran said. He stood to her left near Nessa Lamb.

"Not that there aren't enough on your cake," Ann teased. "Blow them out."

"Come look," Gráinne said. In stereo, the torches moved to the cake, giving it a spotlight.

BIRTHDAYS ARE MURDER
SOS
29

"SOS?" Siobhán said.

"You try spelling out Siobhán O'Sullivan in icing," Eoin said.

"No bother," Siobhán said with a laugh. "I love it."

"Perfect initials for a garda," Aretta said.

"It won't be Siobhán O'Sullivan for long," Macdara said.

"Right, so," Siobhán said, already weary of the attention. Not her initials for long? *Why did Macdara say that?* "Are you saying I'm dying?" she asked.

"What? No. No. Of course not. I'm saying you'll be Siobhán Flannery as soon as we set the date."

"Oh." Oh. *Oh. No, no, no.* She didn't like that one bit. She didn't have to take his name. Did she? Was that still a thing? Why did he have to sound so pleased about it? Siobhán O'Sullivan had a much nicer ring to it. He could hear that, right? Wouldn't he want to be Macdara O'Sullivan? That had a nice ring too. A thud sounded from the back of the shop.

"Padraig?" Oran said. "Is that you?"

"I'm here," Padraig said. All heads turned to the front of the shop where a torchlight bounced. Padraig was in the front, dripping with rainwater. But the thud had come from the back.

"Happy birthday to you," Gráinne started singing. Several others joined in. "Happy birthday to you—"

"Stop." Siobhán had to yell. The singing ceased.

"What's wrong?" Macdara asked. Shadowy faces, mouths still open from singing, stared at her, perplexed.

"Can I see someone's torch?" Siobhán said. Oran was closest to her and handed it over. She maneuvered the light toward the back where the sound had originated, sweeping it left and right until she found the exact spot along the back wall. There, a woman was slumped to the floor against a bookcase. Eyes wide open, glassy, and unblinking. Books had rained down around her. Pages were stuffed in her mouth. No living creature could remain so still. Siobhán recognized the beautiful, mercurial author. Her ebony hair melted into the darkness, leaving a pale, pretty face staring straight ahead. A shiver ran through

Siobhán as she recalled what she said about her memoir. *Explosive* . . . A scream rang out. Then several, as the others slowly caught on to the horrifying sight. Siobhán's heart thundered in her chest. For everyone else life would go on, but for aspiring author Deirdre Walsh, hers had just come to an abrupt and startling end.

Chapter 8

"Deirdre?" Nessa Lamb's words came out garbled. She gasped again, and then several others began to talk at once.

"Nobody move," Siobhán said.

"And stay calm," Macdara said. "Slowly make your way to the front of the shop."

"Are we supposed to not move or slowly move and make our way to the front?" Oran asked, panic growing in his voice. Siobhán snapped off the torch in her hand, but the others continued to beam their lights at the figure slumped against the bookshelf.

"Don't look," Siobhán said to her brood, putting an arm around Ann and Ciarán, steering them to the door. "Detective Sergeant Flannery is correct. Move slowly to the front, go out the door."

"It'll be pouring down on us," Leigh Coakley said.

"Nobody said you have to remain outside," Siobhán said. "But you can't stay here." She turned to James. "Help everyone to the exit."

"Of course," her older brother said with a quick squeeze to her shoulder. "Sorry about your birthday."

"We'll worry about that another day."

"Follow my voice," James said. "I'm leading a procession to the bistro."

"Orderly now, no need to run," Siobhán added.

Some people were slow to move. Macdara began tapping folks on the shoulder one by one. "We'll need everyone to vacate the premises."

"Oh my God, oh my God." Oran was stuck on autopilot, repeating the words over and over. Padraig brushed past Siobhán, on his way to the counter, his coat dripping wet.

She stopped him. "You were outside?"

"What?" Her question seemed to startle him. His eyes darted to the register. Was he worried about money?

"You're soaked," she pointed out.

"Yes," he said. "I had to run to our flat to get more candles." He reached into his pocket and pulled out a cluster of fat candles. It took a second for his eyes to land on the horror slumped against the bookshelf. "The European history section," he whispered. "Did she find the secret room?"

"Secret room?" Siobhán asked.

There was a beat and then Padraig McCarthy fainted dead away. Siobhán rushed to his side. "Padraig? Padraig?" She scanned the people heading for the door. "Oran?" She had to yell his name several times.

"Why are you shouting at me?" he called out in what

was undoubtedly a shout of his own. "I am following orders. I am moving slowly to the front."

"It's Padraig," Siobhán said. "He's fainted."

"Padraig!" Oran said. He rushed forward, his light bouncing at his side. "Not again."

"He's done this before?"

"Only when he's acutely stressed." Oran threw a glance toward the bookshelf where Deirdre lay slumped, and shuddered.

"What can we do?"

"I have smelling salts near the register." He took a step toward it.

"Halt," Macdara said. "I'll get them." The entire store was a crime scene. They were contaminating it every second they remained. Oran gave directions to Macdara, who finally procured the smelling salts. Oran knelt beside his husband and administered them. Moments later, Padraig lifted his head. "What happened?"

"You're alright," Oran said. "Let's get you outside."

"Should we call an ambulance?" Siobhán asked.

"I just need water," Padraig said.

"We'll get you to the bistro," Macdara said, giving Oran a hand in lifting Padraig to his feet. Siobhán followed them out.

"Oran," she said. "What did Padraig mean? Secret room?"

Oran was in no position to argue. "The bookshelf she's leaning against." He licked his lips. "It's a door. A secret passage."

"Where does it lead?"

"Nothing special. A back office. We did it as a lark."

The building had been vacant for a long time. It

abutted an alley. "Does this secret office have a door to the alley?"

"It does. But we've never used it."

That didn't mean someone else hadn't. "Do you have a key?"

"No. In fact we shoved a large bookcase in front of it. Padraig didn't like the thought that someone might try to break in. And we hadn't had time to change the locks."

Siobhán wouldn't be able to access the office and see what he was referring to until the state pathologist arrived to determine the cause of death and move the body. "We'll discuss this again," she said as Oran and Padraig headed with the others to the bistro.

"What can I do?" Aretta asked.

"Call Jeanie Brady, the state pathologist, then the forensics team, and the crime scene photographer. The station clerk will provide you the numbers."

"On it," Aretta said. She hurried off toward the station. The rain continued to rage. Siobhán huddled underneath the awning. If they could get the scene photographed, Jeanie Brady might give the guards permission to move the body to Butler's Undertaker, Lounge, and Pub. It wouldn't be possible to thoroughly document the scene with the power out, but electrical crews had also been notified as well as the volunteer fire department, and everyone was on the case. It was a good thing she couldn't sleep through storms anyway, for she knew in her bones that this was going to be a very long night.

"Is it for sure a murder probe?" Aretta asked. She stood in the doorway of Siobhán's tiny office at the garda station. They had a small amount of power from generators, but the lights were dim and Siobhán was having a hard time locating her extra notebooks and biros in the crowded mouths of her desk drawers.

Speaking of mouths . . . "She didn't stuff pages in her own gob," Siobhán said.

"It's possible though, isn't it?" Aretta asked. "She was a writer."

Siobhán pondered this. She'd heard writers could get a little whacky, but she could not imagine a scenario where one would literally eat their own works. Then again, they didn't yet know who wrote the pages residing in Deirdre's mouth. "The state pathologist will determine the cause of death. But I think we need to investigate for the *probable,* which is that this will be a murder inquiry."

"The killer couldn't have known the lights would go out," Aretta said. "Unless he or she caused the power outage."

"I think the killer saw an opportunity and seized on it," Macdara said. Siobhán let out a yelp as he materialized in the doorway.

"You're going to be the death of me," she said, placing her hand over her thundering heart.

"Sorry, boss."

Aretta frowned. Even in the waning light, Siobhán could see it. For whatever reason, she did not like the detective sergeant calling Siobhán *boss*. Perhaps it was intimidating to a new garda. Perhaps this was why romantic relationships were discouraged at work. Especially in an uneven power dynamic. And Aretta Dabiri did not know the pair well enough to realize they were capable of separating their love lives from their work lives. "You were saying?" Siobhán asked him.

"The killer did not make the power go out," Macdara

repeated. "But the idea of murder could have been in the planning."

"Won't the electrical crews determine what caused the power outage?" Aretta asked.

"Quite right," Macdara said. "But given the thunder and lightning, not to mention the fact that the entire village lost power, I'd say we know the cause, alright."

"I need to know everything that happened before I arrived at the bookshop," Siobhán said. "But let's not do it here. I for one could use a cappuccino."

"At this hour?" Aretta asked. It was nearing nine in the evening.

"You should go home and get some sleep," Siobhán said to her. "I'm afraid we'll be up all night."

Aretta set her gaze on Macdara. "Can I join you?" she asked. "It's good training."

"If you wish," he said. "But it wouldn't count toward your hours as we're not requiring it."

"Very well," Aretta said. "I wish to attend as a learning experience."

"Let's set up shop at the bistro, then," Macdara said. "Aretta, make sure you have a notebook and a biro."

She patted her jacket pocket. "Mission accomplished." They donned their raincoats, grabbed brellies, and headed off to the bistro. As they passed Gordon's Comics, Siobhán noticed a torch bouncing around inside. She paused in front of the shop.

"I never got to speak with Chris," Siobhán said. "But it looks as if he's there now."

Macdara followed her gaze to the shop and gave a nod. "Perhaps we should make sure he's alright."

"Why?" Aretta asked as Macdara stepped up and

knocked on the door. The torch inside immediately stopped bouncing.

"It's just a courtesy thing," Siobhán said. Aretta didn't need to be bogged down in all the local drama, there would be plenty of time for that. Inside the comic shop, the torch went out. Macdara knocked again. There was no reply. Macdara turned to Siobhán.

"He's acting squirrely."

She sighed. "We'll return in the morning. We can't force our way in."

Macdara slipped his business card underneath the door. "Let him stew on this."

"Just a courtesy thing?" Aretta said lightly as they picked up their trek to the bistro. The rain was still lashing out of the sky, and they increased their pace, keeping a hand on their hats lest the wind blow the blue caps with the shiny gold shields away.

"Rumor has it he isn't happy about the bookshop opening," Siobhán shouted in the wind. "But believe me, Chris Gordon is harmless. We just want to follow up is all."

"He's an American," Macdara said. "He's threatening to sue Turn the Page."

"On what grounds?" Aretta asked.

"It's just a rumor we intend to follow up on," Siobhán said, a little more forcefully this time. "And even if he said it, there are no grounds and I'm sure he knows it. Chris has a flair for the dramatic."

By the time they reached Naomi's, they were soaked. The bell dinged as they entered, and Siobhán could smell the peat as the fire crackled away in the main dining room. The bistro was now closed, but Siobhán could tell from the plates and saucers left on tables that many had come in from the bookshop. Her brood was all-in, trying to get a handle on the mess. And even though Siobhán tried to talk them out of it, Macdara and Aretta helped Siobhán clear the tables before they huddled around the fire. "This won't do," Siobhán said. "If I get to change into dry clothes, you two should as well. Macdara, James should have something you can wear, and Aretta . . ." Aretta was tiny. She would drown in Siobhán's clothes. "My sister Ann will be able to help you out. I'll collect towels and bags you can drop your wet uniforms into."

The O'Sullivans pitched in once more, putting the kettle on, grabbing towels, and finding dry outfits for Aretta and Macdara. Soon they were settled by the fire with dry clothes and loads of food in front of them. Since they had no clue how long it would take to restore the power, everything had been taken out of the fridge and cooked, so there was a heap in front of them—Irish breakfast, including, of course, brown bread, and rashers, and eggs, and potatoes, and black and white pudding, and sausages. Aretta took it in with big eyes.

"You're going to eat all that?"

"Macdara will," Siobhán said. He let out a rumble of a laugh and warmth flashed within her. She took a moment to find his hand and gave it a squeeze. He squeezed back and their hands parted.

"You should have a little to eat," Macdara said to Aretta. "We're going to need all the fuel we can get."

Aretta stared at the food, then shook her head. Siobhán hoped she didn't have an eating disorder, but if she did, now was not the time to discuss it.

"Take me through the evening," Siobhán said. "From the minute you entered the bookshop."

"By the time I arrived everyone else was there," Macdara said. "A nice crowd for the authors and for your birthday." His tone belied the disappointment at how the evening had ended.

"Right," she said. She was not going to indulge in a pity party at this moment, even if it was the last of her twenties. "And how long was the power on?"

"I'd say about twenty minutes. Your brood was setting the table with the cake, I was back and forth between the front windows, the lookout I suppose I was, and—"

"You were wanting to dig into my birthday cake," Siobhán interrupted.

"It looked like a good one, alright," he said with a sigh. "Bridie made it herself." Bridie was one of the best bakers in town. Siobhán could practically taste the fresh cream.

"Was anyone arguing, or did either of you notice anything odd?" Siobhán asked, pushing the thought of her birthday cake away.

Macdara shrugged. "Nothing out of the ordinary."

She looked to Aretta, who pondered the question. "Each author seemed to have a cluster of fans around them. Darren Kilroy was chatting with Padraig and Oran by the register. And yes, despite the unorthodox decorating, the cake looked scrumptious."

For a second Siobhán was puzzled by the comment, until an image of the cake flashed in front of her again: *BIRTHDAYS ARE MURDER*. Under normal circumstances it would have been humorous, but now it made her shudder. "Good observation skills," Siobhán said to Aretta. "What about Deirdre—she had people gathered in front of her as well?"

"Not as many as the others," Aretta said. "But there

was one man speaking with her—he seemed to be flirting. I was not specifically paying attention, and I'm afraid I have no familiarity with the locals."

"What did he look like?"

"Nothing stands out other than it was a handsome man. I barely glanced at them."

Siobhán nodded, jotted that down, and turned to Macdara. "Where were you when the power went out?" Aretta let out a small laugh. Siobhán raised her eyebrow.

"Sorry," she said. "'Where were you when the power went out?' You sound like an old-fashioned detective."

"You do," Macdara said, chuckling. She stopped him with a look. He cleared his throat and got back to business. "I was halfway back from the window," Macdara said. "You were taking your sweet time getting there."

Siobhán felt the heat rise to her cheeks. She was indeed. Even though she wasn't sure there was a birthday surprise in store, she was suspicious. And who didn't want to spend a little extra time looking good for one's own surprise party? And if she practiced her surprised look a few times in the mirror, well, that was to be expected as well. "I was trying to prepare our bistro in case the power went out," she lied. She turned to Aretta. "Where were you?"

"I was seated," Aretta said. "In the back row by myself. By this time, Darren Kilroy was seated a few rows ahead of me, and I had just caught sight of a man coming out of the bathroom before it all went dark." She hesitated, tapping her biro against her lip. "Wait. It was the same man I saw flirting with Deirdre." She sighed. "I wish I knew everyone's names."

"No worries," Siobhán said. "Did anyone scream?"

"I heard exclamations," Macdara said. "But everyone

knew there was a chance the power would go out, so there wasn't panic."

"A few thought the lights had been killed because it meant you were about to enter." Aretta stopped, then put her hand over her mouth. "The pun was not intended."

"No worries at all," Siobhán said. "You've been a great help." She tapped her biro on her notepad as she pondered it. "I wonder why no one heard a struggle. Or at the least, wouldn't Deirdre have screamed?" She thought of the thud she'd heard just after she saw the cake. Given the intricate staging of the body, that hadn't been Deirdre falling, otherwise there wouldn't have been time to prop her up with those hideous pages in her mouth, but had it been the killer trying to make an escape? Or had someone simply knocked into a bookshelf?

"Maybe she was sedated first," Macdara said after a beat.

"Talk me through it."

"Someone may have come up from behind, either injected her with a sedative, or perhaps had administered it earlier, then shoved the pages in her mouth just as the sedative was taking effect, allowing the killer to easily, and silently, suffocate her."

Aretta shuddered. Siobhán resisted the urge to give her a comforting pat; they were not yet close friends, and she did not want to seem patronizing. She knew that no matter how good your training, it was not easy to adjust to the grim realities of the job. She wondered if they were throwing Aretta in too soon.

"Maybe the pages contained traces of tree nuts," Siobhán said. Oran had posted a sign warning everyone about Deirdre's nut allergy. Had he inadvertently alerted the killer to the perfect weapon? "Darren Kilroy had a bag of peanuts on him the previous evening," Siobhán said. "He was sent out with them after Padraig did a search." She took note of it. They'd have to follow up.

"I don't know if a nut allergy kills that quickly," Macdara said. "I think we would have heard her go into distress, raspy breathing, something."

"If she was capable, she would have spit the pages out of her mouth," Siobhán said. "And wouldn't she have had an EpiPen on her?"

"Jeanie Brady will shed light on this," Macdara said. "But unless she says otherwise, I can't see this being an allergic reaction."

"Jeanie Brady?" Aretta asked.

"Our state pathologist," Siobhán said. "She's a gem." Siobhán turned back to Macdara. "This murder seems to involve a combination of planning, and striking when an opportunity hits."

"Premeditated, then adapted to the circumstances," Macdara said.

"What opportunity?" Aretta asked. "The power outage?"

"The power outage, and perhaps Deirdre's nut allergy," Siobhán said.

Aretta jotted down a note, then frowned, and when she looked up she looked at Macdara. Siobhán couldn't help but notice she had been doing this a lot. Was Aretta irritated by Siobhán? Or taken with Dara? Either way, this was not the time to worry about something so petty. "Did anyone hear Deirdre slump to the floor?" she asked instead.

Macdara lifted his head to the ceiling as he thought it through. "There was an electric whine just before the power went out, then a pop, like a crackle of electricity."

"Good," Siobhán encouraged. "Next?"

He took another beat. "The minute the lights were out, I heard several thumps. I don't know if any of them were from Deirdre. My assumption was that people were bumping into bookshelves, and each other. I think I heard books fall."

"I did too," Aretta said. "I'm pretty sure."

This was the problem with eyewitness accounts, or ear witness accounts, even if those witnesses were gardaí. No one had been expecting trouble. Their attention was on surprising Siobhán. Then they made certain assumptions when the power went out. Everyone but the killer was clueless as to what was really taking place in the dark. Was it part of the thrill? Carrying out this nefarious deed while surrounded by others? Planning an entirely different kind of surprise . . .

"What's she doing?" Siobhán heard Aretta ask.

"She's putting herself in the mind of the killer," Macdara said.

That snapped Siobhán out of it. "I am?"

"Do you deny it?"

"No. I just never thought of it in those terms."

"It's what makes you so good." He cleared his throat and lowered his voice. "It's also why I worry about you."

Siobhán would soak up the compliment later. "The power goes out. It's dark. Noisy. The perfect time to strike."

"Indeed," Macdara said.

"Do we know if the bookshop had cameras set up?"

Macdara shrugged. "I doubt Oran and Padraig even thought to install them, let alone had the time. We'll ask them. But we know who was there."

"Half the town," Siobhán mused.

"I know I'm new," Aretta said. "But I'm very interested in continuing with this murder probe."

"We can't let you into the crime scene," Macdara said. "But we can include you in our daily briefings."

"Perfect."

"But it will have to be on your free time as you have a full training schedule as a new garda," Macdara added.

"Understood." Aretta glanced at Siobhán. "Does that mean it will be your free time too?"

Was it? Did Siobhán have free time? "We can meet here at the bistro in the mornings after my run. I can do double duty and make my cappuccinos and yell at my siblings at the same time."

Aretta laughed. "I am an only child."

Siobhán nodded. "I'm jealous," they said in stereo. At the door, Aretta hesitated.

"The woman who passed away on the footpath," she said.

"Margaret O'Shea," Siobhán said. "I've been thinking about her too."

"In light of this, are you going to reexamine that case?"

Siobhán looked to Macdara. He nodded. "I guess we're in luck that the burial had to be postponed," he said. "We should have Jeanie Brady do a postmortem just to be safe."

Aretta nodded. "I think that is wise."

Macdara removed keys from his pocket. "I'll give you a lift home," he said to Aretta. He turned to Siobhán. "See you soon." He gave her a kiss. "Happy birthday," he said again. Siobhán said her goodnights and goodbyes and stood by the fire. She wanted Aretta to feel welcome. But she couldn't help but wonder if it was a mistake to allow her to tag along on a murder inquiry when she was still in training. There was something about this case that had Siobhán on high alert. She couldn't quite put her finger on what that something was. A feeling in her bones. That whoever this killer was, Siobhán had a sinking feeling they were already several chapters ahead.

Chapter 9

At two in the morning, when the power was restored, Siobhán O'Sullivan was still wide awake, cuddling Trigger, who was shaking so hard he was vibrating. She finally got him to calm down by reading him Joyce. Apparently, he had the sleep-reading gene as well. She dozed off in the chair, and before she knew it, her mobile was ringing. She picked it up, shocked it was already morning. It was Macdara. The crime scene photographer and forensic team were on their way to the bookshop. Siobhán tossed on her uniform and made a cappuccino that she drank in record time. She fed Trigger, peeked in on her still-sleeping brood, and stepped outside. The skies were dark and a sharp wind was blowing through, but the rain had stopped for now. The footpath, normally pristine, was strewn with branches, and green leaves, and the odd bits of tumbling rubbish. The air still smelled heavy with rain, and she had no doubt it would return. She headed for the garda station for their protective gear, and once at the bookshop she greeted Macdara. They donned the booties and gloves before entering. A quick glance above the doors proved there were no security cameras. "We'll have to check CCTVs of shops nearby," Macdara said. "The bookshop hasn't been here long enough to have security cameras." It was a shame, but of course they hadn't been expecting trouble this soon. That was the problem with trouble, it snuck up on you.

Siobhán and Macdara headed for the back wall. Oversized books were strewn all around the body. An enormous green umbrella lay in the middle of the books, and a lime-green biro was partially tucked underneath Deirdre's left leg. There was writing on the biro, but Siobhán wasn't able to make it out. Her eyes traveled to Deirdre's left foot, where a red rose was lying on the ground. Had Deirdre been holding these items, then dropped them? Or did the killer place the items at the scene? "Were Oran and Padraig collecting umbrellas by the door?" she asked Macdara. Oran, for one, did not seem like the type who would accept wet umbrellas in his new shop. Was the umbrella wet? She zoomed in on it. "The umbrella is dry," she added.

"The rain hadn't started when we arrived," Macdara said. "So, there was no need to collect the umbrellas."

"Right," Siobhán said. "I forgot." The rain had begun just before she reached the bookshop. "Do you think the rose is from Leigh Coakley?"

"It's a good bet," Macdara said. "We'll have to ask her."

Siobhán leaned in to see if she could read the titles on the books. "European history," she said. "No wonder the books are large and thick." She scanned the ground, spotting at least a dozen. Her eyes traveled to the shelves Deirdre was leaning against. Blank spaces stared out where the books should have been. Her gaze fell to poor Deirdre Walsh. She was wearing a long, flowered skirt, black boots, and a teal blouse. Her hair was shiny and straight, her makeup expertly applied. She had put an effort into looking good and it made Siobhán sad. Her gaze fell to the pages in Deirdre's mouth, cherry-red lips clamping the white paper.

"You should eat those words," she said.

Macdara turned to her with a puzzled look. "Pardon?"

"That's the gist of what Leigh Coakley said to Deirdre at the reading."

"Leigh said that to a visiting author?"

Siobhán nodded. "Deirdre riled her up by disparaging Nessa Lamb's new book."

"You're not seriously thinking of Leigh Coakley for this, are you?" He glanced at the rose as if wondering if its gorgeous red petals were poisonous.

Leigh Coakley had never committed any crimes. She arranged stunning bouquets for weddings, wakes, and birthdays. Led bake sales. Organized charity drives. Ran 5Ks. And had started the book group. She was bubbly and giving. It was like accusing the Tooth Fairy of murder. "I'm not leaning toward her. But you know as well as I do that in a murder inquiry everyone needs to be treated guilty until proven innocent."

Macdara sighed, removed his hat, scratched his head, and put it back on. "I'm still putting her in the Least Likely to Commit Murder category," he said.

"As you must. But I have a larger point. If Leigh is not the killer—"

"She's not—"

"Then the killer was in the room when she said it." *You should eat those words.* It could not be a coincidence.

"It's hard to imagine Leigh Coakley murdering anything other than her annual Christmas trifle," Macdara said, still stuck on the thought of one of their neighbors being a killer.

"And yet, here Deirdre sits, eating someone's words."

"Are you saying the killer is Leigh or someone might be trying to point a finger at Leigh Coakley?"

"The latter is what I'm mulling over right now, but we're too early in the investigation to proclaim absolutes. You know yourself."

Macdara frowned. "What kind of killer would go to the trouble to create such a complicated ruse? Sounds like a writer to me."

"Misdirection. Whoever this killer is—he or she is both calculated and impulsive."

"We've covered this," Macdara said. "He's a planned opportunist."

"Correct." *Or she.* She didn't need to point this out to Dara; this was no time to pick on pronouns. "Do you think Margaret's death is connected to this?"

Macdara rubbed his chin. "She was staying at the inn with the visiting authors."

"She wasn't the most pleasant person in the best of times, but why on earth would anyone harm an old lady?"

"Maybe she knew something. Saw something?"

"Lorcan Murphy was seen trying to get into her room."

"He said he had the wrong room, and didn't everyone say he didn't even make it in the door?"

"That is what they said." But Margaret was always watching everyone. She had seen or heard something.

And it had gotten her killed. Siobhán's fists clenched at her sides. This was personal. Poor Margaret. Poor Deirdre. "We have to catch him," she said. "Or her." She forced herself to look at Deirdre again, the pages protruding from her mouth. "I want to know what book those pages are from," Siobhán said. The hardest part of investigating a murder inquiry was the waiting. They couldn't touch the body, or the pages, or any of the books that had rained down around Deirdre Walsh. They couldn't push on the bookcase and investigate the secret office. They could only observe and surmise until Jeanie Brady arrived. Her eyes traveled once again to the European history books littering the floor. Macdara followed her gaze.

"Do you think the killer planned the exact spot?" Siobhán mused out loud.

Macdara folded his arms and stared at the body. "Like some kind of message?" he said. "The European history section. Maybe they have a history together?"

"Wow," Siobhán said. "That would be diabolical."

"Indeed." He sighed. "But it's more likely where Deirdre was positioned when the lights went off. And the killer knew it."

"The killer could have stood in this spot and called her over. After all, none of us noticed the body right away." She chewed on her lip. "Aretta said she saw a man flirting with Deirdre. Then she saw that same man come out of the bathroom." They both looked to the door to the men's room just a few feet away.

"I should have been paying more attention," Macdara said.

"You couldn't have known," Siobhán said. "But she said he was handsome and flirting. Can you think of anyone who fits that bill?"

"Me?"

She laughed. "You're handsome of course. Are you telling me you were flirting with another woman on my birthday?"

He shook his head as his face reddened. "I meant *Me* as in—why are you asking me? I don't know who's handsome and who's not."

"Men," Siobhán muttered. "Course you do. You're just too afraid to say it."

He harrumphed. "I suppose Lorcan Murphy fits that bill."

"I was thinking the same," Siobhán said.

"You think he's handsome, do you?"

"I did when he was only killing fictional elves," Siobhán said. "But nothing makes beauty fade quicker than an evil soul."

Macdara straightened up. "He seems like a good egg to me. Even if he was the one flirting with Deirdre Walsh, that doesn't make him a killer."

"But it does put him at the exact spot of her murder shortly before it happened," she said lightly. Maybe they were both too close to the people involved to investigate. They had already formed opinions of them. But killers could be likable. Charming even. It was one of the things that made this business so tough.

"Do you have your smartphone on you?" Macdara asked.

"Of course." Macdara didn't own a smartphone. He liked to quip that he would stick with his dumb one for the rest of his life. That didn't stop him from asking Siobhán to use hers for a multitude of purposes, her least favorite looking up scores for eejit sports games.

"See if you can get a picture of the pages," Macdara said. That wasn't a bad idea.

She pulled her camera up, zoomed in, and snapped.

"Can you zoom in on them?"

"I think I know how to work me own phone," she said lightly. He laughed. She fiddled with her phone some more until she had enlarged the photo. "*Musings on a Hill*. Nessa Lamb's book." Macdara gave a low whistle. "If the killer is going for misdirection, the pages in her mouth could be a ruse too," Siobhán said. "But we'll have no choice but to follow the trails, even if they lead us on a wild goose chase."

"I see what you did there," Macdara said, chuckling.

"What did I do?"

"Goose? Lamb?"

"Unintended."

"Even funnier." Humor was the salve that got them through the dark world of investigating murders.

"If Nessa Lamb is the killer, would she be bold enough to advertise it this way?"

"You would think not. But maybe. If that's exactly what she wanted us to think." They were dealing with writers. Craftsmen of story. It was putting her on edge. Siobhán had never felt so unsure of her investigative skills.

"Let's get the crime scene photographer in here, then the forensics team," Macdara said.

They called in the photographer, a lovely young woman out of Cork City, and after engaging in a polite chat stepped back as she began her work. "What do you think of Oran and Padraig?" Macdara asked Siobhán.

Siobhán hesitated. "My first instinct is to rule Oran out."

"Why is that?"

"Who would go to all the trouble to open a bookshop only to murder one of their visiting authors one day after they arrive?"

"Why indeed." He paused. "You specifically said Oran. Not Padraig?"

"I like both of them. But . . ." She thought of Padraig's wet coat. What if he'd run out to the adjacent building, used the supposed door connecting them, opened the secret bookcase in the blackout, murdered Deirdre, then pretended to be coming back in? She floated the theory to Dara. "He seemed out of sorts when he returned." Then again it was pitch black, and everyone turned to stare at him. He was also about to faint. That could set a person off his game.

"He left shortly after the power went out," Macdara said. "I'm not sure he had enough time to do all that. We'll have to test it out."

Siobhán nodded. "I don't want it to be him, but we do have to investigate all the suspects."

"We don't want it to be any of them, it appears." He gazed around the bookshop. "What about the fainting incident?"

"It looked genuine. Oran said it's happened before. And why else would they have smelling salts at the counter?"

"Indeed," Macdara said. Siobhán knew he could see what she did. Oran and Padraig had put a lot of love into the shop. Their passion rang clear. It was almost unthinkable that one of them would ruin it for the other. On the other hand, it was nearly the perfect murder if it was one of them. For who would believe such great lengths had been taken to throw suspicion off one of them? Siobhán wished none of this was happening, that she could simply go back to arguing with Oran over his elitist selection of books. "I'm inclined to agree with you," Macdara said. "Who goes to the effort to open a new shop just to risk the business by murdering someone shortly after it opens?"

Siobhán considered it. "Padraig seems to have less influence over the shop. Perhaps he isn't on board with this move." Either way, they were going to have to dig into Oran's and Padraig's personal lives. Many people wondered how Siobhán could deal with the grisly business of murder. What they didn't realize was that it was poking into the lives of the living that troubled Siobhán the most.

"Are you saying Padraig might have killed to get out of owning the bookshop and living in Kilbane?"

"It sounds extreme, but if he had an additional motive to kill Deirdre, I don't think the bookshop would be a barrier." Would her death drive up her book sales? Siobhán shared the thought.

"What are you thinking?"

"Aretta wondered if Deirdre could have killed herself. What if this was a twisted way to sell her books?"

"That sounds like someone with a severe mental illness."

"She was a writer," Siobhán said. "I'm not trying to be smart, but she wouldn't be the first writer in poor mental health."

"Everything is possible. But unless we discover she has a history of suicide attempts, I don't think it's probable," Macdara said. "And if it's Padraig, how would Margaret fit the picture?"

Siobhán shook her head. "We don't know yet if Margaret's death is connected. It could just be an unfortunate coincidence."

Macdara flipped through the pages of his notebook, then closed it. "Jeanie Brady can't arrive soon enough."

"I agree. Deirdre mentioned she was releasing a memoir. Would she kill herself before it's published?"

"Did she have a copy of the memoir with her?"

"Not that I'm aware." They scanned the room, but until they could start touching things, it would be impossible to find out if Deirdre had brought this manuscript with her. "Either way, we're going to need to get our hands on it. She said it was explosive. Could someone have killed her to stop a secret from coming out?"

"We certainly need to find out. Hopefully it's either here or in her room."

"That's true." Her room. They couldn't do much at the crime scene, but they could start interviewing suspects and go through Deirdre's room at the Twins' Inn. "We're also going to have to notify next of kin. I don't think the others in attendance know her well. I hope we'll find contacts in her phone."

"If not we'll check her social media sites."

"Speaking of her phone . . ." Siobhán looked around the crime scene. "No handbag. No phone."

"Unless the phone is in her pocket," Macdara said. He held up a finger. "I'll make a call." He strode outside. Under some circumstances, they could get permission to pat down the body and remove possible objects from the pockets such as a phone. Hopefully they would be granted that permission. Notifying the family was a difficult but imperative task. Then again, it was likely that Deirdre was on social media, and hopefully one way or another her loved ones could be quickly tracked down. Dara returned.

"We can pat her down," he said.

"She's not wearing a raincoat," Siobhán said. "Maybe the umbrella belongs to her."

"That will have to wait until we can process the entire crime scene," Macdara said. "I'm assuming there's a coat room, or designated area where they all hung them."

Macdara approached the body, careful to step over the books on the floor, and quickly patted her down. "There is something just underneath her left thigh," he said. He pointed.

Siobhán leaned in. "They look like reading glasses."

"Good catch," Macdara said.

"There's also a biro," she said, pointing out the lime-green pen.

"I was hoping it would be her mobile phone." Macdara didn't make a move to remove the eyeglasses or the pen. That would have to wait until the body had been removed and they came back with evidence bags. Macdara took a step back. "That's all we can do for now."

"No handbag, no phone, no room keys," Siobhán said. "Pages stuffed in her mouth. It's a murder."

"Technically someone could have robbed those items off her after she was already dead, but I'd say those chances are slim."

"Do you think missing items increases the likelihood that our killer is a woman?" Siobhán asked.

"How do you mean?"

"I doubt anyone memorized what Deirdre's handbag looked like," Siobhán said. "But any female could have been holding one without scrutiny. However, I certainly would have noticed if a man was suddenly holding a handbag."

"True, but in the dark and confusion it could have been set in a corner or slipped under a chair."

"Then retrieved when we asked everyone to step outside?"

Macdara looked around as if envisioning the scene. "Yes. Even hidden under a raincoat."

"Do you think Deirdre was in possession of something valuable?" That didn't quite add up for Siobhán, but she knew they had a lot to learn. Her eyes landed on the lime-green biro once more. There was some kind of writing on it, but she couldn't make it out, not even when she zoomed in with the camera on her phone. Her fingers itched to pick it up. Did Deirdre drop it, or the killer? She pointed it out to Macdara.

"I can't make it out either," he said. They turned to the photographer.

"All finished," she said, lifting up her camera. Siobhán was itching to pick the biro up, test it for fingerprints, grab a hold of something that would point them in the direction of a killer. But procedures were there for a reason, no matter how mental it made her.

"I'll make sure to e-mail the photos straightaway," the photographer said before she left. Digital cameras had sped up the investigative process, and Siobhán was grateful for that. At least it wouldn't be long before they could examine the photographs and forensics could now collect fingerprints and put markers near objects that might turn out to be evidence.

"Shall we head to the Twins' Inn?" Siobhán said.

"I'm afraid we might be waking them up, but yes. The sooner we get into Deirdre's room, the better."

"Don't forget Margaret's room as well."

Macdara nodded. "Good thinking. I'll give them a bell so they can at least change out of their jammies, and put those hounds in the back garden."

The wolfhounds were beautiful, but protective of the twins. If someone had murdered Margaret, it made sense that they would want to do it away from two enormous wolfhounds.

"I never officially got to say happy birthday," Macdara said as they headed for the exit. "I have a little something for you too." They had just passed the table with her birthday cake. The word *MURDER* was starting to bleed.

"Save it until we catch the killer," Siobhán said.

Macdara's eyes lingered on the cake. "I must admit, I may never eat cake again."

"Who are you trying to fool? If that cake wasn't part of a crime scene, you'd be digging into it right now."

Macdara sighed. "Maybe a wee bite," he said, as he put his arm around her and gave her a squeeze. "But Bridie loaded it up with icing just for you."

Chapter 10

The Twins' Inn had received a welcome facelift since its days as the Kilbane Inn. The formation hadn't changed of course. All the rooms were located on the same level and arranged in a horseshoe shape. Next door, a small house with a gorgeous garden served as the owner's dwelling. The house had been given a fresh paint, the old white replaced with a bright yellow, and extended to the facade of the inn. The purple trim really made both the house and the inn pop. In front of the inn, what used to be a bare patch of dirt was now an extension of the garden, bursting with spring flowers. It was downright cheerful. The twins, attractive and lively women in their thirties, were identical. They leaned into it, even wearing their wavy brunette locks in the same shoulder-length cut, with feathered fringes. They often dressed alike too. Today, despite the warning phone call, they were in matching jammies with thick pink robes and bunny slippers. One of them was named Emma, the other Eileen. Neither had a husband or children, something, given their youth and good looks, the villagers often remarked on. Siobhán could never tell them apart. They were waiting outside the office clutching fat mugs of tea as Siobhán and Macdara approached. The bunny slippers were jarring given the tears brimming in their eyes. Once they drew closer, Siobhán was able to read the writing on their mugs: *GOOD THINGS COME IN PAIRS*.

"We loved her," the one on the left said. "We loved Deirdre Walsh."

"Loved her," the other agreed. They each placed a hand over their heart and shook their heads.

"Would you like a cup of tea?" one said. "We just put the kettle on."

Siobhán and Macdara politely declined. "You've read Deirdre's work?" Siobhán asked.

"Not yet," the one on the right said. "But she gave us a signed copy of *Melodies*."

"She only gave us one copy," the other bemoaned. "It happens a lot."

"We can share," the other said.

"We're not joined at the hip. Why does everyone want us to share?"

Siobhán took in their matching outfits, matching hair, matching mugs, matching bunny slippers, and tears, and kept her gob shut.

"It hardly matters now," the first said.

"We are actually two separate people."

"I'm sorry," Macdara said. "I have trouble keeping you two apart. Can Emma stand on the left and Eileen on the right?"

The pair stared at him, their faces perfect for poker. Finally, they grinned. "Done," they said in unison.

"If you ever find me dead," Emma said, knocking her head, and turning to her twin.

"She's the one who did it," they said in stereo while pointing a finger at each other.

"She had it coming," Emma said.

Macdara laughed, then got down to business. "We're going to need to access Deirdre's room."

"Do you have a warrant?" Emma asked, innocently fluttering her eyelashes and taking a sip of her tea.

"We have shiny gold badges," Siobhán said, pointing to hers and then to Dara's. "See? Twins."

Emma shook her head. "I was hoping for a court order. We have to be very careful of our celebrity clientele."

"Even the dead ones?" Macdara blurted out. He was getting frustrated with the twins.

Their faces morphed back into blank canvases. Siobhán wondered if it came naturally, or had they practiced the look. "What the detective sergeant is trying to impress upon you is that we're trying to catch a killer," Siobhán said gently. "I'm sure Deirdre Walsh herself would approve."

"A judge would issue this warrant, no question," Macdara said. "I just don't see waking one up at this hour of the morning as the best move."

"And yet you woke the pair of us up without a bother, didn't ye?" Eileen chirped.

"Deirdre's things might help us find her killer," Siobhán repeated.

"Not without a warrant," Emma said. "We said the same to that agent."

"Agent?" Macdara stepped forward.

"Darren Kilroy?" Siobhán asked.

Emma's eyes widened and she nodded. "Dat's the one. He was mad to get in her room."

"Mad how?" Siobhán asked.

"It wasn't that he was rude per se," Eileen said. "But he was insistent."

"Desperate, I'd say," Emma added.

"What made you think this?" Siobhán asked.

"He was pacing up and down in front of her room, sweating," Eileen answered.

Macdara stepped forward. "When was this?"

The twins regarded one another. "Half ten, was it?" Eileen asked Emma.

"Twas."

"We had just finished *Judge Judy* and were nearly turning in."

Emma nodded. "We love *Judge Judy*."

"'I love the truth. If you don't tell me the truth you're gonna be eating your shoes,'" Eileen exclaimed.

"What?" Siobhán's gaze once again fell to the bunny slippers as if they could provide clarity.

"It's a *Judge Judy* quote," Eileen said. "Don't you watch *Judge Judy*?"

"I've been a bit busy lately," Siobhán said.

"'I eat morons like you for breakfast,'" Emma said. "'You're gonna be crying before this is over.'"

"Dat's a good one," Macdara said. "Now. Could you imagine waking Judge Judy up this hour because the pair of ye are too stubborn to let us in Deirdre's room?"

"Wake Judge Judy?" Eileen exclaimed. The twins shook their heads and crossed themselves.

"I'd rather die," Emma said.

"Dat's exactly how I feel about waking up a judge at this hour," Macdara said.

"He should have his own show on telly then," Eileen said.

"So he should," Emma agreed.

This was going pear shaped. Siobhán placed her hand on Macdara's arm. "Could we get back to Darren Kilroy for a moment?"

"Right, so," Macdara said.

"We would never wake Judge Judy up," Emma said. "Do we have *stupid* written across our foreheads?"

"And Judge Judy lives in America," Eileen added. "I think we're safe."

"Darren Kilroy?" Siobhán said, a little louder. "You were saying?"

Eileen nodded. "Right before we went to bed, we encountered him out here."

"How did he take it when you wouldn't let him in?"

"He said he understood," Emma said. "But he insisted that she had something that belonged to him."

"And he was sweating something awful." Eileen shuddered.

"And what is that something he wanted from her room?" Macdara asked.

Emma turned to Eileen. "Was it a book?"

"A manuscript on her laptop, isn't that what he said?" Eileen replied.

"I think you're right. I wasn't really paying attention. I was still thinking of that eejit who interrupted *Judy*. Now. She shut their gob, didn't she?"

"Ah, she did, so. She certainly did," Eileen said.

Macdara removed his mobile phone from his pocket

and stared at it as if the weight of the world was on him. "Only one thing worse than waking a judge up in the middle of the night. . . ."

He wandered away without finishing his sentence.

"What's the one thing worse?" Emma called after him.

Eileen tilted her head. "Not waking a judge up?"

"No," Siobhán said, not envying Macdara. "Waking the missus up first."

The twins blinked in stereo, then stared down at their bunnies.

"What room is Darren Kilroy in?" Siobhán asked. The twins once again stared at her without replying. Siobhán wondered if they were capable of reading each other's minds. She'd about had it with them as well. "You want a court order for Deirdre's room—fine. But if you don't tell me—"

"Room four," Emma spit out.

"But if you're going to go waking him, let us get back into the house first," Eileen said. The house was actually a small cottage situated next door to the inn.

"Go on, so," Siobhán said. "We'll be seeing you again with the court order." The twins hustled their backsides home.

Room #4 was at the apex of the U, and Siobhán headed for the door. The lights were off. Darren Kilroy was probably asleep. Macdara was correct. Waking people up was not always smart. Sometimes it worked to a garda's advantage: hit the suspect while he or she was sleepy and hope the truth stumbled out before they were awake enough to remember to lie. That was the best outcome. The worst: some people weren't the nicest when awoken from a deep sleep. Siobhán imagined that went double for cornered killers and she wasn't eager to find out which camp Darren Kilroy was in. She paused in front of his door before banging on it with her stick. If she was going to disturb his peace, she wasn't going to be wishy-washy about it.

Seconds ticked by before she heard him stir, followed by a crash, followed by cursing. By the time Darren came to the door, glasses askew, what hair he had left sticking up, robe pulled tight across a swollen belly, Siobhán's tension eased slightly. He seemed to be in the confused-bumbling category, so if she acted quick maybe he'd blurt out the truth before he could think better of it. Or before she threatened to make him eat his shoes.

"Sorry to wake you," she said. "May I come in for a quick chat?"

"Here? Now?" he said. Beads of sweat broke out on his forehead.

"Time is of the essence," Siobhán said, pulling her notebook and biro out of her jacket. She spied a kettle on the table next to the telly. "I'd love a cup of tea," she added. She didn't want a cup at all, but it would give Darren something to focus on and, if he was the nefarious sort, hopefully it would keep him from trying to spin lies to her questions.

Darren sighed and moved to the side to allow her to step in. "Of course." He ambled over to the kettle, flicked it on, and fiddled with the cups for a minute. "I suppose I know what this is all about." He stared at the kettle as if he was talking to it and not her.

A watched pot never boils. . . . Siobhán couldn't help the random thoughts that flittered through her mind. "Oh? What's this all about then?"

"I was trying to gain entrance into Deirdre's room. I didn't think it warranted being roused out of a deep sleep by the gardaí."

She wondered if by his phrasing, *gardaí*, plural, instead of *garda*, singular, he knew that Macdara was waiting just outside. If so, his entire shtick about being woken up was a lie. Had he been peeking through his curtains and knew full well they were outside? "Do you want to tell me why you were trying to get into the room of a murder victim?" She didn't mean to disrespect Deirdre Walsh by reducing her to a murder victim, but she wanted to keep Darren Kilroy on edge. He was trying so hard to appear calm and collected.

He met her eyes for a brief moment. "She has a manuscript on her laptop. I told her I'd take a look at it." They both jumped when the kettle shrieked. "Tea?" he said when they'd recovered from the fright.

Siobhán nodded. "With a drop of milk and a cube of sugar."

"I don't think they have actual cubes."

"Just a pinch then."

He shook a packet. "Half?"

"Perfect."

He set about making the tea, then handed her the cup. She loathed drinking tea out of paper cups. She set it down. "You seem like an intelligent man."

He sunk into a desk chair and crossed his arms. "I sense a *but* coming."

"A woman is just murdered and hours later you're trying to get into her motel room."

He blinked. "That sounds horrid."

"Indeed."

He swallowed. "I know it might sound selfish of me. She said it could be her big hit."

"You said you weren't interested in memoirs."

He stopped moving. "You have a good memory."

"Comes with the job."

"I did say that, didn't I?"

"Emphatically."

He nodded, and Siobhán had the feeling he was trying to buy time. "I'll admit. She appealed to my sense of curiosity. I spoke with her after that panel. She gave me a little more insight as to the contents of this explosive memoir."

"Do tell."

"Must I? It involves other writers. I was horrified, actually, when I found out what she was writing."

"And yet, there you were, trying to get into her room to get your hands on it."

"I know how it looks. But I am, at the end of the day, a businessman And . . ."

"Popularity can go up when a writer dies," Siobhán said, keeping her voice light.

He let out a breath, as if she'd just said the magic words. "I truly wasn't thinking of it like that—more so I wanted to honor the last request she ever made of me." He lowered his head. "I could have been kinder to her when she was alive."

"You weren't kind to her?"

"Don't put words in my mouth." He stopped, then gasped. "That was the wrong choice of words. Given what was done to Deirdre. It was ghastly. Don't you see?"

"I agree. It was ghastly."

"I can't sign either Nessa Lamb nor Lorcan Murphy if they had anything to do with this."

"I think that's wise."

"You have no idea what it's like to be an agent." He shook his head. "I just can't believe any of this is happening."

"What is it like to be an agent?" He was the type who spoke more freely if he felt one was on his side.

"Bombarded. That's the word. Constantly bombarded by desperate writers. They always want a piece of your soul."

That sounded very dramatic to Siobhán but perhaps it came with the territory. "And yet you voluntarily came and even agreed to sign one of them."

He nodded, then rubbed his chin. "I did."

"Why did you?"

"Because I wanted to meet Nessa Lamb. Whereas most writers are desperate for agents, Nessa is being courted by us. I really think I could take her career to the next level. It's the Holy Grail of being an agent. Lifting a writer from the abyss into the light." He rubbed his chin. "But what if . . . what if *she* did this?"

"Do you have any reason to suspect Nessa Lamb?"

"No!" He jumped up. "I swear. No reason at all."

Interesting. He didn't just pull her name out of a hat. And his overreaction proved that he was hiding something. She'd pull back a little, then go in once more, see if he flared up again. "It's true I don't know much about the publishing world. But Nessa Lamb as I understand, and as you've confirmed, is being courted by publishers whereas Lorcan and Deirdre are not. Is that correct?"

Darren nodded. "You've done your homework."

"I would hardly call being courted by agents and publishers lifting one from the abyss, would you?"

He blinked. "I suppose not. I guess you're trying to get me to admit that I'm simply looking out for my own interests."

"Are you?"

"Every agent worth his salt would do the same. The Forty under Forty article has caused the industry to scurry after her. She probably has loads of offers." He scratched his head. "At least she did."

"What do you mean?"

"If it gets out she's a murder suspect, do you really think any of them are going to stand by her?" He sighed. "I have to know. I have to know for my own peace of mind that she did not murder Deirdre Walsh."

Siobhán intended on keeping Darren Kilroy under pressure. He was talking now, words spilling out of him like a faucet turned on full blast. She didn't believe that his reason for breaking into Deirdre's room was to get a manuscript he'd had no interest in prior to his death. And right now he seemed fixated on Nessa Lamb.

"Do you think it's fair that you'd already made up your mind who you wanted to sign before you even arrived?" She wondered if Lorcan or Deirdre had any inkling. Then again, that would only have been a motive if it was Nessa who had been killed. Unless . . .

It was dark that evening. What if the killer had accidentally murdered the wrong author? Or was that too much of a stretch? It also meant, given there were only three of them, that Lorcan Murphy was the killer.

"Was I leaning toward Nessa?" Darren said. "Absolutely." He opened his arms. "But I was willing to change me mind if either Lorcan or Deirdre showed me something brilliant."

"I see," Siobhán said. "Why not wait until we finish our investigation and then approach the estate about Deirdre's memoir? Why the rush to get into her hotel room?"

Darren pulled a handkerchief out of the pocket of his robe and dabbed his forehead. "Of course, of course that's the sensible thing. But now it will be tied up for ages. I just happened to be passing by Deirdre's room and I thought if the manuscript was in there, why not have a quick look, and yes, I'm afraid that's how the twins found me, just giving the door a slight jostle to see whether or not it was locked."

Attempted breaking and entering? The twins hadn't mentioned that. Were they too star struck? They should have called the guards. "I don't think you're telling me the truth."

He threw open his arms. "How can I convince you?"

"Tell me the real reason you wanted to get into her room."

"If you see a manuscript on her laptop—her WIP—"

"Her whip?" What kind of case was this going to turn out to be?

Darren belted out a laugh, then slapped his hand over his mouth. "Sorry. Work-in-progress. WIP. Her memoir. That should prove that I'm telling the truth."

"We all heard her mention her memoir, so what would that prove?"

"I don't know what else to say."

"You're asking me to turn over a manuscript from a crime scene?"

He blinked, then picked up his tea, which was sitting cold on the nearby table, and stirred it slowly. "I suppose that's out of the question."

"Course it is," she said. "This is a murder probe."

"Right, so." He set his tea down, went to the closet, and returned with his billfold. Was he thinking of offering her a bribe? She'd never been bribed on the job before. She certainly wasn't going to take it, but she was curious to see how he would do it. He fumbled into it and produced a business card. "Can I give you this? Perhaps you could pass it on to the executor of her estate?"

"No," she said. "We're not messengers." Macdara had been tasked with contacting the next of kin and, given they hadn't been allowed to enter her room, guards were currently poring through her social media to locate family members.

"Apologies." He dropped the billfold on the table. Glanced at it. Glanced at her. Sweat began to pour down his face. The dabbing increased. "If you understood the publishing industry . . . How vicious it can get." He paused. She did not respond. Silence was a powerful motivator. It often made folks nervous, and they would then start rambling, often lies, but if they rambled enough, sometimes, they would accidentally let the truth spill out. The challenge then was to parse it from the lies. "She came up to me that evening. While we were waiting for you. Happy birthday, by the way. I don't know whether to say that or not."

"Not a bother. Go on, so."

"As I stated, she said she had a memoir that was going to be explosive." He swallowed again. "As you mentioned, I'm here to pick one of them to represent." He was taking his sweet time.

"Yes."

He nodded. "And as you already know, unless Lorcan or Deirdre showed me something to stop me in me tracks, I was going to pick Nessa Lamb." He glanced at the notebook in her hand. "Like you, I'm a note taker." He stood, and pointed to his bedside table. There, a notebook resided. "I made the mistake of writing it in my notebook."

Siobhán felt shivers up her spine. "Wrote what in your notebook?"

"That I was favoring Nessa Lamb."

"Show me."

He licked his lips. "That's just the ting. I can't show you. I dropped that particular notebook. Guess who picked it up?"

"Deirdre Walsh."

He nodded. "I'm afraid she read it." He hesitated.

"And?"

"First. It doesn't look good. I was supposed to be impartial, give them this week, read their works, all of that good stuff before I made my decision."

"What did Deirdre say to you?"

He looked at the ceiling, then finally made eye contact. "She said I couldn't sign Nessa Lamb."

"Couldn't?"

Darren swallowed. Nodded. "She said she had proof that Nessa Lamb plagiarized *Musings on a Hill.*"

Chapter 11

Siobhán didn't know what she was expecting, but this was a surprise. If it were true, a bombshell. "What kind of proof?"

He threw open his arms, then let them flap by his side. "That's what I was trying to find out."

No reason justified trying to break into a dead woman's room before the gardaí could get there, but at least this one held a ring of truth. "If Nessa Lamb didn't write *Musings on a Hill*, did Deirdre say whose work she thought Nessa had plagiarized?"

"No." He paused as if considering whether or not to say more. "We were interrupted by Lorcan Murphy."

"Lorcan?" Siobhán asked. Was he the handsome man Aretta had seen flirting with Deirdre? No offense to Darren Kilroy, but he didn't fit the description.

"Yes. He joined us, and the two of them started talking, and I slipped away. Shortly after, the lights went out."

"Where were you standing?"

He didn't hesitate. "By the register." This matched Siobhán's memory as well. At least the part about Oran standing by the register. She became lost in her thoughts as she visualized the bookshop. When she didn't respond right away, Darren seemed to grow paranoid. "Ask Oran if you don't believe me. He was standing behind the register. He'll remember."

The register was only a few feet away from where Deirdre's body was found. Had Lorcan and Deirdre moved over to the bookshelf with the secret passage after Darren left? "Did you catch any of their conversation?"

Darren frowned. "No. But please don't read into it. They certainly seemed friendly."

"Don't you worry," Siobhán said. "It's your job to read into things, not mine." She smiled. He tried to smile back but his lips failed him.

"That's why I wanted to get into her room. I can't sign Nessa Lamb if she's plagiarizing. It would ruin my reputation, my career." He began to pace. "Not to mention the reputation of my other authors."

"Such as Michael O'Mara."

Darren stopped pacing. "Yes. He's one of my most prolific authors. I have a duty to protect him." He shook his head. "I'd rather face a slew of his fire-breathing dragons than face an angry Michael O'Mara any day." He slumped onto the edge of the bed. Siobhán was tempted to ask him if the poor dragon was going to get his fire back in the next installment, because even though she hadn't yet read the books, she really wanted to know, but she forced herself to focus on the matter at hand. "What if Deirdre was making it all up?" Darren continued. "Trying to cast doubt on Nessa to slice the competition?"

"Have you spoken about this to anyone else?" If Nessa Lamb had learned that Deirdre was accusing her of plagiarizing . . . Siobhán could only imagine how it had made her feel. It was, quite frankly, a motive for murder.

Darren shook his head. "I haven't mentioned it to a soul. That would be slander!"

"And where is this supposed notebook now?" She was inclined to believe him, but she didn't want him to know that, so she was keeping her language skeptical.

"I assume you're going to find it either on the floor near Deirdre or on her person. She was still in possession of it when the lights went out." Siobhán was now eager to fetch this notebook and made a reminder note in her own. "You said you don't know much about the book business?" Darren Kilroy said.

"Not much."

"It's cutthroat."

"Many businesses are."

"Yes. You run a family bistro, don't ya?"

"Yes." He'd done his homework too. The question in her mind was . . . why?

"There was quite the crowd in the bistro after Deirdre was discovered." He shuddered. "Not just the people from the bookshop, but it appeared many in your village were drawn out by the event."

He wasn't wrong, but her skin prickled at the observation. "Your point?"

"It's simply a fact. Tragedy can affect sales. Good or

bad. In the case of the macabre—I didn't make this up—Deirdre's book sales will probably skyrocket. For a very limited time. I know that sounds horrible, but she for one would be thrilled. The real reason I wanted into her room was to see if she was telling the truth about Nessa Lamb. But it's also true that she was eager for me to read her new work, and yes, I thought I'd kill two birds with one stone, and get ahead of the competition." He gasped, then placed his hand over his heart. "I didn't mean to say kill."

"Don't sweat it." Given that he was literally sweating, they were both tripping over their words. "But if Deirdre's not alive to choose who publishes it, what difference does getting a hold of her memoir make?" They would need to find out if Deirdre had a will and who the beneficiaries were.

"My first objective, to be quite honest, was to determine whether or not she had proof of Nessa plagiarizing her hit novel. Aside from that, I wanted to read Deirdre's memoir first, and if I was in love with the manuscript I would have dealt with the executor of her estate, whoever inherits the rights to her work, plead my case. I was truly—partially—trying to honor the only thing she ever asked of me."

And profit off her death. Cutthroat was right. "I'm going to ask that you remain in town for the duration you were already scheduled. The rest of the week."

Apparently, he wasn't expecting this. "What?" he cried. "Why? I've told you everything."

"I'll be asking all of our suspects to remain." She emphasized the word *suspects*. "It's what? Four more days?"

He counted off on his fingers, then nodded. "I don't understand. You can take my business card. Reach me by phone. Dublin isn't that far away—I could come back if you needed me."

"If you were planning on being here anyway, why the rush to return to Dublin?"

"Michael O'Mara has been contacting me nonstop. He's a bit on the needy side. This would be the perfect time to make the trek to Bere Island before returning to Dublin."

"You can speak with him on the phone instead."

Darren stood up. "I don't believe that you can force me to stay."

"Probably not. But if you leave against our wishes it will force me to move you to the top of my suspect list."

"I see. Will you at least . . ." He hesitated.

"Let you know if we find proof of Nessa plagiarizing?"

"Yes."

"I suppose I could do that." She wasn't sure she could, or would, but she was willing to let him think she would in order to get him to stay in town. "And I may not know the book business—but I'm a heat-seeking missile when it comes to the murder book."

He swallowed again, and nodded. "I shall remain."

"Thank you." She smiled. She had a feeling she and Judge Judy would be besties. "We'll be contacting you when we've scheduled formal interviews at the garda station."

He showed her to the door. "May I ask one favor?" he said.

"Go on, so."

"You won't mention to anyone about my notebook, or Deirdre's accusation? If there's a killer on the loose . . ."

"Course I won't. We collect evidence, we don't give it out." She opened the door and exited his room. She heard the locks engage and a thud, as if he'd thrown his body against the door. She'd rattled him. Was it the fear of an innocent man worried a killer could come after him? Or a killer, worried he was going to get caught?

Chapter 12

When Siobhán exited Darren's room she found Macdara waiting by the office to the inn. "Any luck?" they asked each other in stereo.

"Let's chat on the walk," Macdara said.

Siobhán glanced in the direction of Margaret O'Shea's room. Crime scene tape had been put across the door. It was a necessary but unsettling sight. "What about Margaret's room?"

"In the morning I'm going to have guards accompanying the twins into the room for a first look. See if anything is out of order. We'll take it from there." Siobhán nodded. They would know the state of her room better than anyone else, and as long as access was restricted, evidence, if any, should be safe for now. They began the walk back to the bistro. Although the clouds in the sky

were still heavy, the surrounding greenery comforted
Siobhán. The air smelled fresh. Broken tree limbs were
scattered on the ground and flowers bent their heads.
Beauty and destruction, hand in hand. In the distance,
cows had come out to graze. Up ahead she could hear the
squeal of children stomping in puddles. A collie with
dirty paws shot past them, followed by a young lad bouncing a stick on the ground. She took a moment to absorb
the world around her before filling Macdara in on her en-
counter with Darren.

"Plagiarizing," Macdara said. "That's quite the accusation."

"I know. And if true, quite the motive for murder."

"You think?"

"Imagine if Nessa Lamb did plagiarize *Musings on a
Hill.* The publicity would be vicious. Let alone the cash
prize she just won—maybe even criminal. It wouldn't
just be the ruin of her career, but her reputation, her free-
dom. I can see someone murdering to protect such ramifi-
cations from befalling her."

"When you put it that way, so can I," Macdara said.
The collie with the dirty paws returned and dropped an
equally muddy ball at Macdara's feet. He bent over and
chucked it into the neighboring field, laughing as the dog
tore after it, dirt flying in his wake.

"Either Deirdre was lying in order to get an agent or . . ."
Siobhán left the rest unsaid.

"Or she was about to ruin Nessa Lamb's career and
reputation."

Siobhán nodded. "There's a third possibility."

"Darren Kilroy could be lying."

"Indeed." A horse with a cart, driven by a Traveler, passed by. The dog, dirty ball in its mouth, followed the cart.

"I suppose we'll have our answer to that when we gain access to Deirdre's room," Macdara said.

"That's the perfect segue. Did you reach the judge?"

Macdara nodded. "I got an earful. But he's faxing the warrant. I say we get a few hours of sleep and we'll be back to the room."

Sleep. The minute he said the word, Siobhán could feel the exhaustion in her body. "Darren was reluctant to stay in town," she said. "We'll have to make sure to appeal to the rest of them."

"Letting them know they'll be under a hotter light if they try to leave is a good start," Dara said. "We'll get on that tomorrow, and set up interviews."

Siobhán slept until half nine, which she hadn't done in years. For once she skipped her run; with the adrenaline and lack of sleep it was not a good idea. Instead she made brown bread and a full Irish breakfast for Macdara and herself. She could only eat half of hers but Macdara was happy to finish it. Shortly after, his phone rang. The search warrant had come through and they were free to enter Deirdre's room.

The twins were waiting for them by Room #10. "We didn't see any signs of a struggle or theft in Margaret's room," one of the twins said.

Macdara nodded. "I heard. We'll be keeping it a crime scene until the state pathologist can determine the cause of death."

The twins pursed their lips, but didn't argue. They turned their attention back to Deirdre's room. It was the last room, no neighbor to the left. Emma and Eileen argued over who would open the door until Macdara snatched the key. They stood waiting. "We can take it from here," Macdara said. He and Siobhán had their booties, gloves, and aprons in a plastic bag and wanted to wait until the pair left to put them on. They intended to do an initial look-through before bringing in the forensics team. They would not remove any of Deirdre's belongings, but they would be able to see if there were any clues that would help shape the investigation. Especially any evidence that Nessa Lamb had plagiarized her acclaimed book.

The twins sighed, then turned in unison and headed off. "Drop the key back to the office," one called over her shoulder.

Macdara opened the door. A slightly stale smell wafted out, but they entered to find it neat. The makeover brought about to the exterior of the inn by the twins had extended to the interior as well. A cheerful light yellow paint was on the wall, and paintings of the Irish landscape hung over the bed. A small white sofa had colorful throw pillows, and new carpeting completed the transformation. A stark cross (the only decoration supplied by Margaret O'Shea) still hung by the door, but surrounded by the rest of the cheer, it felt welcoming. The bed was made, most likely by Deirdre as it looked slightly rumpled, her luggage was open on a nearby dresser, and all the clothes inside were neatly folded. The bedside table held reading glasses, a bottle of paracetamol, and a glass of water. The bathroom held a makeup bag, toothpaste, mouthwash, and toothbrush.

"Where's the laptop?" Siobhán said out loud as they scanned the room.

"Notebooks, pens, books—they have to be somewhere," Macdara agreed.

"No sign of her handbag, keys, or phone either," Siobhán said.

They began opening cupboards, drawers, even the hot press, mini refrigerator, microwave, and shower. There was no laptop, books, or notebooks. No handbag, or phone, or keys to the hotel room. Macdara made a phone call and she heard him ask the evidence room to call with a list of items retrieved from the bookshop. "She's a writer and there's not a single book or notebook or biro in her room?"

Siobhán shared his frustration. "We'll have to ask the twins if they've been in, or the cleaning staff. . . ." She let it hang.

"From the way they behaved, they did not let anyone in, and this is not a bed that's been officially made."

"We need to find out the last time they or any staff member entered this room," Siobhán said. "But assuming it was before she was killed—that only means one thing."

"Somebody found a way to get in."

"Yes. Because somebody has her handbag with the key."

"That's one possibility," Macdara said. "And we'll check the CCTV. But they still risk being seen."

"What are you thinking?"

There was no adjoining room. Nothing amiss with the locks on the door. The lone window in the main room was shut and locked, nor did it appear disturbed. "The problem with inns," Macdara said, "is that over the years there can be a number of keys floating around. We'll have to find out if the twins changed the locks since they took over from Margaret O'Shea."

"But that would open our suspects up to the locals," Siobhán said. "What are the chances of the killer randomly coming across keys to the room?"

"Let's check the bathroom window," Macdara said.

The bathroom window, situated above the commode, was large enough for a person to climb through if he or she was determined. But try as they might, they could not budge it open.

"Let's check this from the other side," Siobhán said. They hurried out, and moved around to the back of the building. It abutted a stone wall and beyond it a farmer's field. Cows were out grazing, but once they noticed Siobhán and Macdara, several ambled over to see what the fuss was about. "Even the cows are nosey in this village," Siobhán said.

"Cheeky bovines," Macdara said.

Given all the rooms were on the ground floor, the window would be accessible via a leg up if the windows were easy to open. The window was just out of Siobhán's reach. The grass did seem slightly disturbed underneath, compared to the other windows, but there were no apparent footprints. However, dropped on the ground was a lighter, and biro. The lighter was red, the biro had writing on it. Gloves firmly on, she picked it up and read the writing splashed across it in black: *Michael O'Mara, THE DRAGON FILES*. "This looks like the same font on the lime-green biro in the bookshop," Siobhán said. "Author swag."

Macdara gave her a look. "Author swag?"

"I've been Googling," she said.

"Course you have," Macdara replied. "They must be Darren's biros. Or 'author swag,'" he added. "We'll have to ask if he passed them out to folks at the bookshop." They turned their attention back to the window.

"Someone may have dragged a chair up to it," he said. "We'll need to do the same." He glanced at the window. "I have a strong feeling this is how someone entered."

"Someone? Or the killer?"

"We could have a thief and a killer," Macdara said.

Siobhán sighed. That was the problem with investigations—possibilities were endless. "Was it just luck that he or she found it unlocked?"

"I was wondering the same thing."

"The alternative is that the thief, or killer, gained access to her room while Deirdre was alive, asked to use the restroom, and unlocked the window."

"Wouldn't that have seemed odd to her if one of the other participants asked to use her restroom? It's not like it would have been a far walk for any of them to return to his or her own room."

"Unless they were meeting for longer."

"Or having a romantic tryst."

This is often how they worked best, bouncing ideas off each other, working up a variety of scenarios.

"Let's try your phone camera again."

Siobhán was irritated she hadn't thought of it first. She brought her phone out, and zoomed in on the window. She could make out chips of paint around the frame and said so.

"Do they look fresh?"

"How would I know?"

Macdara sighed. "I don't see any on the ground, but will make a note for forensics."

There was something else. Little round pieces of silver around the circumference of the window caught her eye. . . . "Nails," she exclaimed. "This window has been nailed shut."

Chapter 13

No other window had nails or cracked paint. The twins confirmed that they had not nailed the window shut. All the windows did have a lock, but they could only be engaged from the inside. They did not hear hammering the other night, but they admitted that from where their cottage was situated related to the rooms, they may not have heard it anyway. Macdara and Siobhán were going to have to question the others. Further investigation was needed, but Siobhán felt confident in assuming the killer— or someone—had indeed entered Deirdre's room sometime after her murder and removed her laptop, notebooks, biros, and books. The twins also confirmed that the cleaning staff had entered Deirdre's room the day before but there had been a DO NOT DISTURB sign on the door all day the day of the murder.

"Why is it not there now?" Macdara asked.

"It is," Eileen said.

"No," Siobhán and Macdara said.

"I swear it was there," Eileen said.

"She's right," Emma said. "It was."

The killer had also disturbed the DO NOT DISTURB sign? Was there any logic to that? Or had someone else swiped it?

"We need to talk to your cleaning staff," Siobhán said.

Emma let out a laugh. "Sorry. But you're looking at them. We do everything."

"But you specifically said the cleaning staff had not entered the room," Macdara said.

"It's still us," Eileen said. "When we clean, we're the cleaning staff."

"What about security cameras?" Siobhán said.

"We can pull the ones from the front of the inn, but there is nothing at the back." Siobhán figured as much. The farmer's field wouldn't have one either.

"Please pull them right away," Siobhán said.

"E-mail the link and passcodes to the garda station," Macdara added.

The twins bobbed their heads in agreement.

"Do you have any empty rooms?" Macdara said. "We'd like to try getting into one the way we think someone did to Deirdre's room."

They were given the keys to Room #2. The decorations were identical to Deirdre's room, with slightly different landscape paintings. Siobhán entered the bathroom, stood on the toilet, and checked the window. "Locked," she said. She moved the lever. "But easy to unlock." From the doorway, Macdara took notes. She reached and lifted the window. It opened, but made a loud squeak. "Close the door and stand in the room. See if you can hear that," she said, shutting the window. Macdara stepped out and closed the door to the jax as she shut the window. Seconds later, he called out, "I can hear it."

"Hold on." She jumped down and turned the water in the sink on full blast. She returned and lifted the window. "Now?"

"Not that time."

She shut the water off and returned to the room. "All set." They retrieved the desk chair from the room, went around to the back of the building, and placed it under the window. Macdara went to steady the chair.

"We have to assume the person worked alone," Siobhán said. "It's not a far drop if I fall." She stood on the chair, then reached up to lift the window. "It won't open," she said. "If this is the method, the person left the window open."

"Hoping no one would notice and shut it?"

"It's a safe assumption. Even if Deirdre noticed her window open she may have assumed the person was trying to air out the bathroom."

"Excellent point."

"I'll open the window. Let's at least see it through, see if it's physically possible to climb inside from back here."

Macdara hurried around to the front of the building. Soon the window squeaked open. He returned to the back as Siobhán threw her arms into the window, grasping the inside ledge to try and haul herself up. She managed to lift her chest up and over the window. Her arms burned. She was going to have to start doing more pull-ups. "If it's not someone close to my height, this wouldn't have been easy," she said. "The person needs strength if he or she isn't tall."

"Either tall and strong, or short and strong," Macdara said. "Extremely helpful, Garda O'Sullivan." *Cheeky.* Was it her imagination or did he stress O'Sullivan? "Is it wrong to say I'm enjoying the view?" Macdara added.

"Your view is going to be a boot in the face if you say it again," she responded. She was halfway in, sliding face down over the commode. There were so many things they never prepared her for at Templemore Garda College. She slid in until she could rest her hands on the floor and pull the rest of the way in. The tank on the back of the toilet slid off with a bang, splashing water and barely missing her poor head as it thunked to the floor.

"You alright, boss?" Dara called, the humor in his voice gone.

"Fine," she said. "Do you tink that would have been heard in one of the neighboring rooms?"

"No," Macdara said. "Only from back here with the window open."

She hauled herself up off the floor. "Let's see how easy it is to get back out."

"They could have left through the front door," Macdara said.

"Too big a risk," Siobhán said.

"At night? When most folks were at the bistro?"

"Is that when you think this was done?"

"It's a good guess."

"Then why wouldn't they just enter through the front as well?" Siobhán demanded.

"That is always a possibility," Macdara admitted. "But

given the window was nailed shut and we found a lighter and a biro, I think our window theory has some merit."

"That's why I want to try exiting this way." She stood back on the toilet seat. It slid beneath her. "Perhaps we're looking for someone with both circus skills and surfing skills," she said.

Macdara laughed. "That ought to narrow it down."

She poked her head out the window. "If I go face first, I'm going to do a face-plant," she said. "But it's not possible to go feet first."

"Don't do it," he said. "The person either exited through the front door after making sure no one was around, or maybe they brought pillows out to soften his or her landing. Either way, we should check our suspects for scrapes and scratches, and ask the twins to check all the pillows in our suspects' rooms."

"Or, as we said, it's the killer who broke into the room and he or she stole Deirdre's key at the signing."

"Either way none of this was very helpful," Macdara said. "Good work."

He brought the chair back, then they locked the door, returned the key, and asked the twins if they had cleaned any of the rooms since the murder. They shook their heads. "Please gather the rubbish from all the rooms, mark the bags, and keep them. We'll be picking them up."

The twins flinched, but to their credit they didn't try to argue. This had never been part of the dream. "While you're collecting the rubbish please check the pillows and call us immediately if any of the rooms have signs of dirt or grass," he said.

"Including Deirdre's room?" Emma asked.

"No," Siobhán said. "The door is now covered in crime tape, as well as the back window. No one, including the two of you, are allowed in the room. When the forensics team has finished its work, we'll let you know." They had just started to leave when Eileen called out.

"Nessa Lamb's room has dirt and grass," she said. "She likes to go to the cemetery."

Siobhán and Macdara stopped. "How do you know?" Siobhán asked.

"She inquired about the cemetery, said she wanted to walk there. I think she's done it every day she's been here."

"What about her pillows?" Macdara asked.

Eileen shook her head. "I just noticed her runners by the door. They were muddy."

"Got it. Let us know what else you find, and do not mention any of this to any of the guests. And please call as soon as the rubbish is collected. But do not let any of the guests know."

The twins saluted. Siobhán found it kind of cheeky but Dara simply laughed. Siobhán was relieved when they hopped in the guard car. "Do you want me to drop you at the bistro first?" Macdara asked.

Their day had barely begun. "Why?"

"Because you're covered in toilet water," he said.

"Do you still love me?"

"Definitely," he said. "I just don't want to be anywhere near ya."

By the time Siobhán had showered, changed into her second uniform of the day, and reached the garda station, she entered to hear Macdara recounting Siobhán's escapades to an enthralled Aretta. "Circus and surfing," she heard Aretta exclaim. Their howls of laughter came to an abrupt stop when they noticed her in the doorway. Siobhán glared for a moment, relishing the horrified looks on their faces before joining in on the laughter. Aretta placed her hand over her heart as if checking to see if it was still beating.

"Why did you crawl through the window and not the detective sergeant?" Aretta asked. "Is it because you're a lower rank?"

Siobhán opened her mouth to say it was because she was taller, which of course she was not. Stronger? Nope. Smaller? As Dara pointed out, the window was of average size. "She has former circus training," Macdara said. The laughter resumed. This time the glare was real.

"I almost forgot," Aretta said, retrieving a notebook of her own from the pocket of her uniform. "A resident stopped by today to report a lurker."

"A lurker?" Siobhán said. What now?

Aretta nodded, reading from her notes. "He was a big fella, with red hair that looked as if it needed a wash." She stopped reading and waited.

"And?" Macdara asked.

Aretta shrugged. "That's it."

"We don't arrest people for poor hygiene," Siobhán said. "Where's the lurking part?"

Aretta glanced at her notes again. "I'm not sure. She was talking at rapid speed and said she was in a hurry to do her messages, but she thought we should look into it."

"Who reported this?" Macdara asked.

"Leigh Coakley."

"Leigh?" Siobhán said. Another one of their suspects. Was she purposefully trying to throw shade somewhere else? "Thank you." She took the piece of paper from Aretta. "We'll follow up."

Aretta stood. "I'll start scheduling those interviews."

"Great," Macdara said. "Start with Lorcan Murphy. And schedule it for my flat."

"Your flat?" Aretta asked.

Macdara nodded. "I live in the attached building. I'd like to make him feel more like a witness than a suspect. He's liable to reveal more that way."

Aretta glanced at Siobhán. "Absolutely," Siobhán said. "It has nothing to do with the collection of westerns on his shelf written by Lorcan Murphy."

Chapter 14

Macdara's flat, situated in a stone building semi-attached to the garda station, had a simple charm that made Siobhán's heart squeeze. It was an old stone building with timber beams. A large one bedroom, with the main room and kitchen revolving around a fireplace. Macdara was rather neat, and bookshelves dominated the far wall. He had a collection of his favorites: westerns. He grew up watching American cowboy shows on telly. Other than his westerns, Macdara was a history buff and Seamus Heaney fan. Leather chairs and a sofa faced the fireplace. Besides being neat and orderly, the place had a very masculine vibe, apart from a collection of cookbooks displayed on his counter given to him by his mammy. At times Siobhán was dying to buy a nice rug or painting, or plant to brighten the place up, but she wanted to respect his space.

She was welcome to spend as much time here as she liked and she had a key, but with the young ones and family business at home, they weren't here all that often. Macdara set about putting the kettle on and even placed a tin of biscuits on the table as they waited for Lorcan Murphy.

"He could be guilty, you know," Siobhán said, watching him fuss. "Lorcan Murphy."

Macdara's head shot up and his eyes narrowed. "I am aware."

Siobhán gravitated to Macdara's bookshelf, where she picked up one of his titles: *The Dusty Ride*. The cover depicted a man on a horse from the back, riding down a dirt road, kicking up dust.

"Fascinating," she said. She turned to the first page and read out loud. *"Deek Bolls wasn't the sharpest man in Wyken County, but according to the ladies in town he had the quickest draw."*

Macdara tried to suppress a chuckle but it turned into laughter, and then a snort. "It's the same wit that made *Dead Elf on a Shelf* popular," he pointed out.

Siobhán gave Macdara a look before placing it back on the shelf. He was over in a flash, removed the book, and put it back in a different spot.

"They're in order," he said. "Paws off."

"Do you have his *Dead Elf on a Shelf* books?"

"Not yet."

She couldn't help but laugh. Another look. "Sorry."

A knock sounded on the door, and Macdara hurried to open it. Lorcan Murphy stood in the doorway, hat in hand, like an awkward teenager picking up a girl for a first date.

"Come in, come in," Macdara said, pulling out a chair

at the table. She couldn't help but notice the seat Macdara saved for Lorcan Murphy faced the bookshelf. Macdara wanted Lorcan to see his collection. This fanboying was a fascinating new side to the man she was going to marry. Did this mean she was going to play bad cop? She stood in the corner, arms folded across her chest, accepting her role. Macdara offered Lorcan tea, which he accepted, already diving into the tin of biscuits, and humming while he ate.

Macdara took a seat across from Lorcan without even acknowledging Siobhán. He placed a recording device on the table and grinned at Lorcan. "Even though we're in my home, this is still an official interview. This session is being recorded, do you understand?" Lorcan nodded, then looked away from the recorder as he chewed his biscuit like a nervous little gerbil. "I'm going to need you to verbalize your acknowledgment," Macdara said.

"Yes," Lorcan said. "I have been made aware that you're recording my every word." He belted out a laugh. "Every writer's dream," he said with a wink.

"I'd love to talk to you about your westerns," Macdara said. "Let's get our standard questions about the night of the murder out of the way."

"Absolutely," Lorcan said. "We need to find her killer."

"We?" Siobhán couldn't help but blurt out.

"I don't mean to imply I can do your job, Garda," he said. "Perhaps it's a hazard of the job."

"In what way?" Siobhán asked.

Lorcan grinned. "My cowboys get into a lot of scrapes with bad guys." When she didn't laugh, he cleared his throat. "Not to mention the ladies." He winked. She stared. He frowned and looked to Macdara. "I just want to be of service."

"Have you known Deirdre Walsh long?" Macdara asked.

"I've known her for a few years. She's a regular at Irish writing events." A startled look came over his face. "*Was* a regular."

"Can you be more specific?" Siobhán said.

She noticed Macdara's shoulders tense.

"You want me to name every event?" Lorcan asked with half a laugh, looking to Macdara for clarification.

"Whatever you can remember," Macdara said.

"I've seen her at conferences in Dublin, book readings in Galway, book signings. I had never spoken to her until about a week before the invitation to Kilbane. Oran and Padraig had posted about this opportunity at a bookshop in Dublin. The notice was posted on a bulletin board in the vestibule. To be honest, Deirdre was in the process of removing the notice when I stopped her."

"She was trying to keep the opportunity away from other writers?"

"I'm afraid so."

"What did you do?"

"In an odd way, I have her to thank for this opportunity."

When he didn't elaborate, Siobhán spoke up. "How so?"

"I usually walked right past the bulletin board. I wouldn't have spotted it at all had she not been trying to hide it."

"How did she react when you confronted her?" Macdara asked.

"At first, she made excuses. She said she thought the event had expired and she wanted to make room on the board. That was the first lie. Then she said as an indie author she had a right to try to even the playing field. That's when she recognized me." Lorcan stopped gnawing on biscuits and leaned back in his chair. "After that she was quite friendly. She put the notice back on the bulletin board and she asked if I wanted to have coffee or tea at the café next to the bookshop."

"Did you?" Siobhán asked.

Macdara turned in his seat and gave her a look. He was irritated at her for taking over. She couldn't help it. There was something about his "open book" act that she didn't like. Or maybe she was so on guard because Macdara was letting his down.

"I did not. But I did snap a photo of the notice she returned to the bulletin board and said maybe I'd see her there." He opened his arms. "And I did."

"Had you read any of her works?" Siobhán asked.

"No," Lorcan said. "If I read the works of all the writers I met, there wouldn't be any hours left in the day."

"Do you know anything about her personal life?" Siobhán asked. "Does she have a partner?"

"I have no idea. But she was always alone at the events, if that's of any help to ye."

Deirdre was a beautiful woman. Did she date at all? Had she ever been married? At this point in the investigation they'd only been able to locate a brother living in Australia. Aside from arranging for her body and belongings to be sent to a funeral home in Dublin when they were finished with their investigation, it didn't appear as if there was going to be any family involvement. It was inexplicable to Siobhán that Deirdre's brother wasn't rushing home, not only to sort out her funeral, but to demand justice. It's what she would have done. But she'd long ago realized that not everyone behaved in the manner she would like. Perhaps they had not had a close relationship, but blood was blood and she found it terribly sad.

It was possible she had a lover somewhere wondering why she wasn't answering her mobile. Or a best friend. Did she have a best friend? Siobhán had a feeling that even if they tried to get their hands on her phone records it would take forever for them to arrive. Even pinging the mobile phone to see if it was still emitting a signal would be a huge help. Time was not on their side. Not when a murderer was free.

"Take us through the night of the murder," Macdara said.

Lorcan's tongue darted to the side of his mouth. "There's not much to tell. I arrived at six on the dot. I thought I was early, but the others were already there."

"Please name the others," Siobhán said.

"Certainly. Oran and Padraig McCarthy. Darren Kilroy. Nessa Lamb. And Deirdre Walsh." He waited until Siobhán gave a nod. "Oran mentioned before we began the readings and signings that it was your birthday." His eyes flicked to Siobhán again. "Happy birthday. I know it's of little importance given the circumstances, but I did want to give you this." He reached into a satchel at his feet and held up a wrapped present. It appeared to be a book. She hoped it was one of the elf ones.

"Lovely," Siobhán said, genuinely touched despite the fact that he could be a cold-blooded killer. "Thank you."

He beamed and set the gift on the table with a nod. "Let's see. I was standing by the counter speaking with Oran when the public began to arrive. Darren Kilroy was at the counter as well, speaking with Padraig. Nessa and Deirdre were standing near the chairs." He paused, then shook his head.

Macdara leaned forward. "What is it?"

"I don't want to start rumors, or accuse anyone of anything."

"We just want the facts," Siobhán said.

"It was my impression that Nessa Lamb and Deirdre Walsh were having a heated argument."

"Go on," Siobhán said when he hesitated.

Lorcan bowed his head. "I feel as if I'm doing something wrong by telling you dat."

Little did Lorcan Murphy know, Siobhán and Macdara had a pretty good inkling of what that heated argument could have been about. Maybe Darren had been telling the truth. Had Nessa Lamb learned that Deirdre was accusing her of plagiarism? This didn't bode well for Nessa Lamb.

"Did you catch part of their conversation?" Macdara asked.

"No. But Nessa was gesturing quite boldly and her face was red. I only noticed because she's usually so quiet and reserved."

"Did you ask her about it?" Siobhán asked.

"Not that evening." Lorcan sighed, then rested his head in his hands. "I loathe this."

"We need to hear everything," Macdara said.

"After Deirdre's body was discovered I joined Nessa at Naomi's Bistro. I asked her about what I had seen." He sat back and folded his arms. Then shook his head. "She lied to my face."

Siobhán stepped forward. "How do you know?"

"She said they were talking about birthdays. Does she take me for a fool? Who turns red faced and waves their arms around for a discussion about birthdays?"

"Some people are sensitive about getting old," Macdara said. He didn't dare look at Siobhán. She, on the other hand, glanced around his kitchen wondering where he kept the frying pans.

"Let's rewind to the night of the murder," Siobhán said. "After you observed the supposed argument, then what?"

Lorcan drummed his fingers on the table. "I'll be as precise as possible, but I can't promise one hundred percent accuracy. I wasn't expecting to have to recall every detail of the evening."

"Just do your best," Macdara said.

"Oran and I were interrupted by Padraig McCarthy. He wanted to talk to Oran. Something about going home to fetch something . . . a torch? Batteries? Something to do with the storm."

Oran and Padraig were renting a townhouse a short drive away. Under normal circumstances it would have been considered a short drive. But under such conditions? Would he really have driven home just for torch batteries?

What if that story was a lie? What if the "storm" was Deirdre Walsh? Did Padraig have a reason to want her dead? He could have slipped into the secret room, waiting . . . but he was dripping wet when she saw him. There was no doubt he had been out in the storm. He could have gone out the front, snuck around to the back in order to spring out from the secret passage from the other direction. Then in the chaos and dark, reappeared in the front of the store, thus giving himself an alibi. But why? Did Padraig have a motive to kill Deirdre Walsh? Lorcan Murphy was still talking. Siobhán had drifted off imagining the scenario and forced herself to concentrate.

"By this point Deirdre was standing alone by the women's restroom. I headed over to say hello."

"Is that the reason?" Siobhán asked. "Or was it to find out what she and Nessa had been arguing about?"

He opened his arms. "I suppose a little of both. She looked dejected."

"Go on," Macdara said.

"There isn't much to it. I said, 'How ya,' she said she was fine." He glanced at Siobhán. "She grumbled about having to postpone our readings because of a birthday party. Wondered why they couldn't do it on their own time. I'm sorry."

"Not a bother," Siobhán said. She supposed she couldn't blame Deirdre for feeling that way. It was supposed to be their night. Then again, who didn't like free cake?

"Shortly after, the lights went out. At first I thought the young lad—the one with the loud voice who was all hyped up, running to check the front windows—"

Ciarán.

"—at first I assumed someone had turned the lights off because the birthday girl was spotted. But then you didn't arrive. And people were asking each other if they'd turned out the lights, and someone announced the power was off. Then I heard noises from the front of the shop— the front door opening, because now you had arrived, and you know everything that happened after that."

"You didn't hear any other noises?" Siobhán asked.

"I heard too many noises. Mostly people chattering. Maybe a thud. I don't know for sure. Could have been books falling, could have been Deirdre. But I can't say for sure."

"Thank you," Macdara said. "You've been very helpful."

"What about author swag?" Siobhán asked.

"What about it?" Lorcan said. "I have a few bookmarks if you'd like one." He pointed to his gift. "There's one with your book."

"Was anyone passing out author swag at the event?"

"The event never took place, so I couldn't say."

"What about the previous event? Was any author swag passed out then?"

"Oh," Lorcan said as if suddenly remembering. "Yes. A biro. With Michael O'Mara's name splashed on it. Darren Kilroy passed them out."

Macdara got out of his chair and headed for his bookshelf. "I'm sure you've noticed, I have all your westerns."

Lorcan glanced at the shelf and grinned.

Macdara pulled out a book and waited. "If you have that biro on you now, I'd love an autograph."

"I don't," he said, patting his pockets anyway. His grin faded and his attention turned to Siobhán. "Does the biro have significance?"

Macdara put the book down and returned to his seat. "I suppose I wanted to get my hands on one," he said with a laugh. "I'm a big fan of the fire-breathers."

He was not. Macdara Flannery was back in the game.

Lorcan Murphy tugged at his shirt collar. "I suppose it's back in my room. I'll have a look later if you like." Macdara stared at him. Lorcan wiped his brow. "Or ask Darren Kilroy for another. He had loads of them."

Loads. If that was true, it wouldn't help narrow down their suspects. "How many is loads?" Siobhán asked.

Lorcan frowned. "Honestly, all these questions about a

biro. He had a number of them clutched in his hand. That's all I know."

"What color was your biro?" Siobhán asked.

"I think it's blue."

"You think?" Macdara asked.

"I thought writers liked to observe the details," Siobhán added.

"It's blue to me," Lorcan blurted out. He sounded angry. For some reason they had touched a nerve. Was it his biro under Deirdre's leg, or had he lost his biro underneath her window? "Tritanomaly," Lorcan finally said. "Look it up."

"Why look it up when you can elaborate?" Macdara asked.

"It's one of the four types of color blindness," Lorcan explained. "I have trouble differentiating blue from green and yellow from red."

Interesting. That meant either the one at the crime scene or under Deirdre's window could be his biro, but given his condition, he could claim it wasn't. They were going to need proof that he was telling the truth, although it would take quite a bit of premeditation to have that excuse on-the-ready.

"Did you use the jax at all that evening?" Siobhán asked. The men's restroom was located next to the shelves where Deirdre was found. Aretta saw a handsome man flirting with Deirdre. Siobhán had a suspicion it was Lorcan Murphy. Which put him right next to her near the time of her murder.

"Is there a witness who says I did?" he asked.

"I know these questions can feel intrusive," Macdara said. "But please try and answer them in a fulsome manner."

Macdara was bringing out his fancy words for the author. *Adorable*. She for one wasn't sure what to make of Lorcan Murphy. She wanted to like him. But just that fact put her on high alert.

"I did use the restroom." He swallowed. "Fine," he said. "I did something terrible and I'd like to make a full confession."

Chapter 15

"Should we take this to the garda station?" Siobhán said before Lorcan Murphy could begin his confession.

"It sounds as if we should," Macdara said, pushing back from the table and standing. Lorcan stood as well and put his hands up. "It's not what you think. She was already dead."

The hair on the back of Siobhán's neck tingled. "Tell us everything." She didn't want to wait for the station now. She didn't want to give him time to rewrite this story, whatever it was.

Lorcan was eager to talk. "I went to the restroom right after speaking with Deirdre. Before the lights went out. I was in there when the lights went out. I tell you, it was quite disconcerting."

"I can imagine," Macdara said. "Go on."

"I don't like the dark, okay? It's somewhat of a phobia. There I was, instantly shrouded in black. I panicked. I was at the sink, and had to feel along the wall just to find the door. Then I came out, feeling along the walls again, and I knocked books down. I don't know how many. And then . . ." He swallowed again, sweat appearing on his forehead. "I bumped into something. Kicked something with my foot. Something soft." He gulped. "I think it was Deirdre."

Macdara sat up straighter. Siobhán moved in. "Why do you think she was already dead?" she asked softly. It was time to switch to good cop.

Lorcan ran his hands through his hair. "Because I wasn't expecting a person to be there, and my boot struck her. When I realized it was a *person,* of course I was aghast. That must have hurt. Or so I thought. I apologized. She didn't reply. I'll be honest—it frightened me. I convinced myself it was just someone being rude. Can you imagine?" He shook his head. "I'm sorry. I was the one who knocked over the books, and if they find a bruise on Deirdre's leg that's probably from my boot. I don't know if they are able to discern whether bruises are postmortem, but I swear to ye, I accidentally kicked her and she didn't make a sound."

"Why did you leave this out of your story?" Macdara asked. He glanced at the tape recorder in the middle of the table. Despite his fondness for Lorcan Murphy at least he had the sense to bring it.

"Because it's too horrible to think about. Kicking a woman when she's down is one thing. Kicking her when she's dead is just a whole new level of horror."

* * *

Macdara stood near his front door, clutching his signed book to his chest. Lorcan Murphy had just left. "What do you make of all that?" he asked, a tinge of hope in his voice that she would declare him innocent.

"I did not expect the part about him kicking her," Siobhán said.

"Neither did I." He shuddered.

"But I don't trust writers," she said. "They're too good at making things up."

Macdara sighed and placed the book back on his shelf. "I don't see why he would lie about knocking books down and kicking her."

"If he's telling the truth, then someone killed her within seconds of the lights going out. As if the killer was waiting to strike and had it worked out perfectly." Siobhán headed for the door. "I need some air," she said.

Macdara looked at the clock above his sink. "We could get some lunch. Curried chips?"

"No wonder I'm marrying you," Siobhán said with a wink. "We should ask Aretta if she wants to join."

Macdara held the door open. "I would love to have lunch with Aretta, but I was hoping that you and I could be alone. Maybe talk about the wedding?"

They stepped outside. It was gray and drizzling. They began to walk toward their favorite chipper. Siobhán knew this conversation was coming, but she was still dreading it. "I have been giving our wedding date some thought," Siobhán said. "As you know, I just turned twenty-nine."

"We are going to properly celebrate your birthday when this is all behind us," Macdara said, placing his arm around her and pulling her in.

"Not a bother." She took a deep breath. "What if we –"
Siobhán's phone dinged. "Hold on."

"What if we?" Macdara said. "What if we what?"

It was a text from James.

WHERE ARE YOU?

It took her a second to figure out what he was on
about. When she did, she was mortified. "My parents'
wedding anniversary," she said, placing her hand on her
forehead as if to check if she was feverish. "It completely
slipped me mind. We planned a group visit to the cemetery."

"Understood. Do you want me to join?"

"I always want you to join," she said. "But I think we
need to do this alone." She kissed him. "Take Aretta to
the chipper. She needs to know where to get the best curried chips in town."

"I completely understand." He kissed her and gave her
a squeeze. "I'll save you a basket of chips."

"Don't bother, they don't last, you know yourself. I'll
have to get my own basket tomorrow."

Macdara nodded. "I'll enjoy them for you then, how's
that?"

"I don't even want to think about it," Siobhán said
with a laugh. "Enjoy away."

"Say hello from me." They kissed again, and Siobhán
hurried off for home. When she reached the bistro, she
found her brood waiting on the footpath. They were all
dressed as if going to mass and each of them held a white
lily. James had one for Siobhán. "They're gorgeous," she
said.

"They're from Blooms," Gráinne replied.

Leigh Coakley's shop. They would be continuing the

interviews of their witnesses (suspects) soon and that included Leigh Coakley. Siobhán hoped they could quickly eliminate her as a suspect. The world would be much darker if their cheerful local florist was a calculating killer.

"I want to change," she said. "I'll be back in two shakes."

"Make it one," James said as she flew into the house. She quickly took off her uniform and donned a lovely spring dress and flats, took her hair out of its tight bun and shook it loose. It was getting long again and, unless Gráinne cut it off whilst Siobhán was sleeping, this time she figured she would keep it that way. Once outside she took her lily from James and they began their procession to the cemetery. Ciarán and Ann walked ahead, Gráinne and Eoin were in the middle, and Siobhán and James held up the rear. She hadn't had a proper chat with her older brother in months. He'd been spending most of his time in Waterford where Elise had a new job.

"Have you set your wedding date?" she asked him.

He glanced away, kicked a rock with a shoe, and shook his head. "Have you?"

She mimicked his head shake. "We were just about to discuss it when you texted."

"Saved by the ding." James started to laugh, a low rumble, then Siobhán began to laugh with him. Soon, they were howling, drawing looks from the other four. "Elise is right," James said. "We're hopeless."

"I was thinking of mine in a year's time," Siobhán said.

"And what does Dara think about that?"

"I'll let you know when I actually get the words out of me gob."

James put his arm around her. "I want to wait until I have a better job." He was working as a handyman in Waterford. "I think I want to fix and sell houses."

"Really?"

He nodded. "Not any houses. The older Irish farmhouses."

"That sounds promising." James had always been handy and loved working outdoors. At least before his drinking took over. She would be happy to see him get back to it.

"There's not much money in it at first," he said. "Maybe ever."

"What does that matter as long as you're happy and can pay the bills?"

"Elise has bigger dreams for us," James said. "It's what she's used to." The pursuit of money had never been a characteristic of the O'Sullivans. Of course they wanted enough to get by. But apart from Gráinne's dreams of being a stylist to celebrities, most of them seemed content with well-enough. In her bones, Siobhán always felt that money corrupted people. In her opinion, greed was a deadly addiction. She thought of an old Irish proverb: *Money is like muck—no good till spread.* Or her mam's saying: "Your health is your wealth." But Elise Elliot was from a wealthy family, and Siobhán suspected this was at the heart of James's angst. "What does Elise think of you fixing up houses?"

James smiled and looped his arm around Siobhán. "I'll let you know when I actually get the words out of me gob."

One by one, starting with Ciarán, and going in birth order from youngest to oldest, the O'Sullivans approached the headstones of their parents: Naomi and Liam O'Sullivan. Had they lived, this would have been their thirty-seventh wedding anniversary. They all chatted with their parents, Ciarán telling them he was getting good marks in school, asking if they recognized his deeper voice, and telling them he was taking violin lessons, and he would come back soon to play them a song. Siobhán was secretly hoping "soon" meant after years of practice. Ann regaled them with all her Camogie wins, and told them about the new bookshop in town. Gráinne chattered away about her accomplishments as a personal stylist, beautifying the citizens of Kilbane one by one. When Eoin's turn came he focused on the bistro and the new dishes he wanted to add to the menu. Siobhán's ears perked up when he mentioned there was a new garda in town whose family was from Nigeria and that he was interested in learning if she had any dishes from Africa that she could teach him. He didn't mention his graphic novels. Did he think they wouldn't approve? Siobhán, not wanting to speak of murder, also told them about Garda Dabiri and the new bookshop in town, and how everyone had piled into Naomi's Bistro for comfort during the storm. James, the oldest and last to step up, talked about Waterford, and his desire to renovate older Irish houses, steering clear, as Siobhán had, of future marriage plans.

"I bet they're saying *happy birthday* to you," Ann said to Siobhán, taking her hand and giving it a squeeze. Siobhán squeezed back, resisting the urge to crush her sister in a never-ending hug.

"You're right," Gráinne said. "And we never got to celebrate." Siobhán was about to tell them it was alright, they'd do it another time, when Ciarán's newly deep voice started to sing.

"Happy birthday to you . . ." The rest of the O'Sullivans quickly joined in and, moments into their full-throated rendition, Siobhán had tears streaming down her face. When the song finished, she hugged and kissed every single one of them, noting how Ciarán rubbed her kiss off when he thought she wasn't looking.

They each laid their lily on the graves, and Siobhán included a small heart she had whittled. Kisses were blown and they began their walk out of the cemetery. They were nearly at the exit when Siobhán spotted a figure kneeling next to one of the headstones in the oldest section of the cemetery. It took her a moment to recognize Nessa Lamb.

"You lads go ahead," Siobhán said. "I'll join you in a minute."

"We're having cake and tea for Mam and Da," Gráinne said, disapproval in her voice.

Siobhán sighed. "Murder doesn't wait for cake," she said, thinking of her birthday cake.

"We'll see you later," James said, giving her shoulder a squeeze. "We'll save you a piece."

"But not if I eat it first," Ciarán said.

"I didn't expect to see you here." Siobhán had come up from behind, startling Nessa Lamb, who jumped at the sound of her voice.

"Oh. Hello," Nessa said when she recovered. She stood and gestured around her. "I love cemeteries."

"You do?"

Nessa nodded, her gaze traveling around the headstones, angels, and Celtic crosses. "Older ones, like this one."

"Yes," Siobhán said. "I do as well."

Nessa smiled. "I like reading the names, imagining what their lives were like." Her eyes traveled to the headstones for Liam and Naomi O'Sullivan. "I hope you don't think I'm being disrespectful."

"Not a bother." She gestured to her parents' headstones. "Give it a try."

Nessa shook her head. "I'm afraid that wouldn't be fair. I know they're your parents. I know your mam has a bistro named after her, Naomi's Bistro, and there are six of you, the O'Sullivan Six to be exact, and I know your parents were tragically killed in a motor vehicle accident by a drunk driver several years ago."

Interesting. Had Nessa Lamb been investigating Siobhán? Was she simply a curious writer, instinctively doing her job? Or the killer, trying to get a bead on the enemy? Nessa opened her arms, then dropped them. "I listen. People talk. It's a hazard of the job."

"We have that in common," Siobhán said.

"Oh?" Nessa said with a slight smile. "What have you heard about me?"

This could be the perfect time to mention the plagiarism, but Siobhán wasn't quite ready to play that card. Not until she sat down for her official interview. For now, she could hover around the subject. "I heard you didn't get along with Deirdre Walsh." She had also witnessed it herself at the first author gathering, but she wanted Nessa to think she was on her side.

Nessa shook her head. "I hardly knew her."

"Did you like her?"

"I know plenty like her," Nessa said, doing some skirting of her own. "Authors who wear the stink of desperation."

"Have you read her work?"

"I'd never even heard of her. It's a mystery to me how she was included in this group."

"Why don't I walk you back to the inn and we can continue this chat." Siobhán didn't want to remain here discussing the case any longer. This was a place she came to chat with her mam and da about her siblings, and the lighter side of life. Once again it crossed her mind that they didn't need an earful about murder.

"What's this?" Nessa pointed to the carving of the wee heart Siobhán had left on the headstone.

"I whittle. It's a skill I learned from my grandfather."

"I'm impressed."

Siobhán shrugged. "It's hardly a novel."

They walked in silence at first, and Siobhán watched Nessa take in her village. Planters filled with spring flowers were starting to appear around the town square. On Saturday mornings townsfolk often gathered to plant more, the local garden committee summoning volunteers with their favorite motto: *Many hands make light work.* In addition, King John's Castle with its passageway through the first floor of the four-story structure drew one's attention to the town square. In the background the steeple of Saint Mary's Church rose proudly, in front of them shop fronts awash in an array of pastel colors emitted a welcoming and friendly vibe. And in the other direction their ruined Dominican priory, affectionately shortened to *the abbey* by most in town, sat in the field with the river gurgling nearby, all of it encased within Kilbane's medieval stone walls. This was home, and always would be. "Have you wandered everywhere about town?" Siobhán asked, as she pointed in the direction of the abbey.

"At least twice," Nessa said. "You're quite lucky to have such architecture and history in one little village."

"We are indeed." This was the most she'd heard Nessa

speak and she wanted to keep her talking. "Where do you get your ideas?"

"Everywhere. Ideas are all around us, all the time. I pick a little here, a little there, and start to put it together, like a wee bird building a nest."

Interesting. It was a little bit like investigating a case. "Did Deirdre say anything to you about her new project?"

"The one dat was going to blow people's minds? Her memoir?" Nessa used air quotes with the word *memoir*.

"That's the one."

"No. Why? . . . Oh. You're looking for a motive. Yet another similarity."

"How so?"

"Characters need motives too."

"Oh?"

"Of course. Their desires drive the story."

"And if you were writing Deirdre Walsh as a character, what would her desire be?"

"That's easy," Nessa said. "Success at any cost."

"That sounds like a specific gripe," Siobhán said.

"You're astute," Nessa replied. She sighed. "I suppose you're going to hear this from someone so it might as well be me." She reached into her handbag and handed Siobhán a folded-up piece of paper. When Siobhán went to open it, Nessa put her hand on top of hers. "Would you mind waiting?"

"What is it?"

"I think it will be clear when you read it. I'll tell you all about it when I'm called into the station for my interview."

"Why don't you want me to look at it now?"

"Because I'll get too worked up. I'll meditate on it before I see you again, and hopefully I'll be able to keep my anger in check."

"That's why I whittle," Siobhán admitted, feeling a kinship with Nessa.

"It's that kind of detail that makes for a great character," Nessa said.

Siobhán nodded, not sure she fully understood. She supposed everyone lived life through the lens of his or her career. And some were more cheerful than others. But rage was one thing for an everyday citizen, and quite another for a murder suspect. Before she knew it, they had reached the Twins' Inn. Nessa waved goodbye and headed for her room. Siobhán turned and began the walk back home. The minute she was out of sight from the inn, she opened the sheet of paper. It was a one-star review of *Musings on a Hill.* The review was typed and short. It seemed to have been printed from a Web site:

Save yourself loads of time. This trash belongs in the rubbish bin.

Below, in black biro, someone had scrawled an additional sentence:

The Hills Have Eyes

Chapter 16

The Hills Have Eyes. Was it a comment on *Musings on a Hill?* Another reference to plagiarism? At the first gathering in the bookshop, Deirdre Walsh had brought up Nessa's one-star review and Nessa accused her of writing it. Did she? Did she also slip this printed copy to Nessa to rub it in? Siobhán waited until Nessa disappeared into her room at the inn, and she was still standing in the courtyard. She heard footsteps approaching from behind and whirled around to find Emma standing before her hoisting up a huge black bag. "Here's the rubbish from the rooms, only we've made a terrible mistake." Emma shoved the bag at Siobhán, giving her no choice but to take it. "Actually. Two terrible mistakes." Siobhán wished she had gloves. The bag was so full it was nearly bursting. It would be her luck to have it rip open on her way home. "I'm so sorry," Emma added. "Eileen is sorry as well. Two apologies, twice, for two mistakes. Is that making sense to ya?"

"No," Siobhán said. "What mistakes are you on about?"

"First mistake. We emptied all the trash into one bag. We forgot to say whose trash came from whose room. I'm really, really sorry."

Siobhán sighed. "Our directions were very clear."

"I know. They were very clear. We were so nervous that someone would figure out what we were doing that we collected it as fast as we could, and we . . . we . . . just forgot!" Emma threw her arms up, her voice squeaking.

"Don't get your knickers in a twist," Siobhán said. She didn't need people poking their heads out to see what was going on. "And the second mistake?"

"We can't send you the security tape from the night before Margaret died, or the morning Margaret was found—may she rest in peace—or the day of Deirdre's murder, or the day after the murder, or anything from this week at all."

"Why not?"

"Something went wrong. The entire week is showing a black screen."

"You're joking me."

"I'm not. It's all gone. Poof!"

"Has this ever happened before?"

"No."

"Did you call the security company?"

Emma nodded. "They said there's nothing we can do. The storm probably interfered."

"Probably?"

"They're pretty certain it was due to the storm."

"And let's say it wasn't due to the storm. Are they able to tell us if someone deliberately went into the system and deleted it?"

"I'd be able to tell you that. No. I'm almost certain of it."

"Certain someone did or certain someone didn't?"

"Certain someone didn't. Almost certain."

"I need you to be certain-certain." It made sense that the camera would have been affected the day the power went out, but Margaret's death was days before the storm wreaked that kind of havoc. She was hoping to see if Margaret left the inn on her own two feet.

"I would say that I am close to being certain-certain that no one got into our system because the person would have needed our password to do that."

"And your password isn't something obvious, is it?"

Emma started to blink rapidly. "What do you mean?"

"Like *twins* or *twinsinn* or *thetwinsinn*," Siobhán said.

Emma burst into tears. Siobhán could hardly comfort her while holding a bag of rubbish, so she put it on the ground with a sigh, then patted Emma's arm. "Alright, calm down, pet. Take a breath."

"Are you going to arrest us?" Emma was still blubbering. "We're absolutely gutted."

"Of course not," Siobhán said. Emma nodded, then wiped her face, blew her nose, and sighed as if she was disappointed. Perhaps they thought they'd find themselves in front of Judge Judy. "Thank you," Siobhán said. She didn't realize she was still holding the one-star review in her other hand until Emma pointed to it.

"*The Hills Have Eyes,*" she said. "Now that was a spooky film."

"What?" Siobhán folded the paper in so she couldn't read the rest, but was crushing it in the process.

"The American horror film?" Emma waited. "A remake of Wes Craven's film?"

"Right," Siobhán said. *Not a clue.* "What's it about?"

"A family's car breaks down in the desert and they're set upon by a group of cannibalistic mutants!" Emma's eyes flashed with excitement. "You didn't hear this from me, but Eileen nearly wet herself with that one."

"I swear I will never mention it as long as I live," Siobhán said.

"Are you planning on watching it?"

"I prefer movies that keep me knickers dry," Siobhán said.

Emma trilled out a laugh. "You should watch it with that handsome man of yours. Have you set a date for the wedding?"

Siobhán picked up her bag of rubbish. "I'd better get back to the station." She had a feeling the person who wrote *The Hills Have Eyes* was commenting on Nessa's book and not mutant cannibals in the desert, but she supposed they would have to examine all angles. But her gut said that that gruesome angle didn't fit this particular plot. Unless something in the film was a nod to the novel. These writers were going to make her mental! She suddenly had a lot more questions for Nessa Lamb. Did she know who wrote the cryptic note? Did she write it herself? Had she ever watched this horror film? Maybe the person was poking fun. Calling all writers cannibals? Some days she wished she'd never become a guard. She could have stayed with the bistro, feeding Irish people instead of investigating them. *Mutant cannibals.* Now that was a first.

Aretta sat in front of the rubbish bag, gloves on her hands, her eyes sparkling with the anticipation of discovery. Siobhán had forgotten what that felt like, when the job was shiny and new, when she was itching to use the skills she'd learned at Templemore. She hadn't intended on foisting the rubbish job upon her, but when Aretta walked into the station and spotted the bag, she asked for it. Notebook and biro by her side, she was set up in an interview room because they had the largest tables. Aretta had already divided the table into sections with names taped to each: Darren Kilroy. Lorcan Murphy. Nessa Lamb. Deirdre Walsh. And the last one simply had a large question mark, for the pieces of rubbish she couldn't attribute to any guest in particular. Siobhán had a feeling that most of the contents would fall into that category. She had helped Aretta cover the table in clear plastic, for no matter how excited Aretta was about the task, rubbish was still rubbish.

"My father never throws anything away that can be of use," Aretta said. "But you can learn a lot about a person from what they choose to discard. What a person deems worthless."

It was a novel thought. What would a person learn about Siobhán? She ate too many crisps and chocolates. That was hardly a secret. Perhaps one would learn that she was a runner from the number of laces she'd used up. She might be considered an underachiever from her endless to-do lists where she'd be lucky to mark a third of them as done. Or could that be interpreted as an over-achiever for having so many items on the list in the first place? Much could be debated about her endless receipts from the chipper. The reason for all the shoelaces would become clear then, wouldn't it? *Perhaps she wouldn't need to run if she just cut back on the crisps, and chocolates, and curried chips.* But, luckily, she always tossed the chipper receipts on site; really, when would she ever need to prove she ate yet another basket of heavenly curried chips? Perhaps Aretta was onto something and Siobhán was relieved her rubbish wasn't under scrutiny. "Don't forget they are all traveling," Siobhán said. "I think we'll learn less than we would if it was rubbish from their homes."

Aretta nodded. "We shall see."

Siobhán stood in the doorway for a moment, wishing she could feel the same sense of excitement. "Are you sure you don't want another hand?"

"I'm sure," Aretta said. "I'm tired of doing paperwork."

"Fair play to ya," Siobhán said. "Would you like a cup of tea?"

"I couldn't ask you to do that."

"It's not a bother, I'm offering."

"Yes, please." Aretta turned her concentration to the task at hand. Siobhán set about fetching the tea, then added a tin of biscuits, and when she returned, Aretta was lost in the process of sifting. She nudged the tea close to her when Siobhán set it in front of her, but she made no move to open the tin of biscuits. Siobhán was dying to ask her if she ever ate, and how much, and what she liked to eat, but she hadn't figured out a polite way to do it.

"Did you go to the chipper with Detective Sergeant Flannery today?"

"We did," Aretta said.

"Aren't their curried chips heavenly?"

"I prepared my own lunch today," Aretta said. "But I enjoyed the conversation."

"Lovely," Siobhán said. She wanted to ask what Aretta had prepared for lunch, but maybe if she had wanted Siobhán to know she would have elaborated. Siobhán was nearly out the door when Aretta called out.

"I nearly forgot. Leigh Coakley was in to see you."

What now? "Oh?"

"She wanted to know if you made any progress on that lurker."

Siobhán had forgotten all about the lurker. "I've been busy with mutant cannibals," Siobhán said.

This made Aretta stop and look up. "What?"

"I'm only messin'," Siobhán said. "Have you ever seen the film *The Hills Have Eyes?*"

Aretta shook her head. "Is it a documentary?"

"No. It's a horror film."

"I only watch documentaries." Aretta stated it matter-of-fact and went back to her sorting.

Siobhán nodded, as she searched her mind for documentaries she'd watched and could pontificate on, but the only one she could remember was one where some man gained three stone eating nothing but burgers and fries for a year. Given Aretta's tiny appetite she didn't think it wise to mention it. "Refresh my memory about this lurker? He was a big man in need of a wash with red hair. She saw him going through rubbish?"

"That's it." Aretta smirked. "Not unlike me."

Siobhán laughed. "I'd say a different goal entirely.

Unless our lurker was trying to learn about folks in this village."

"Doubtful."

"Indeed." A lurker hardly seemed like a top priority, but given they planned on speaking with Leigh anyway, and were hoping to do it without making her feel like a suspect, this might just be the perfect excuse to chat with her.

Leigh Coakley's interview wasn't scheduled until the next day. Siobhán headed home for lunch, mulling over the prospect of paying her an impromptu visit. She smiled as the bell to Naomi's Bistro dinged, announcing her arrival. The front dining room was filled with patrons, but in the back dining room she found Ann and Ciarán huddled at a table near the garden, thumb wrestling. From Ann's cries of pain, it seemed Ciarán was winning.

"Why aren't the pair of ye in school?"

"It's teacher's day," Ann said.

Siobhán had forgotten all about it. Teachers used this day to catch up on grading and planning. "Why don't you come with me to the flower shop. We'll get some plants and seeds and you can spend the afternoon doing some gardening."

"Yes!" Ann was keen.

"Can I ride bikes with Paul?" Ciarán asked. Paul was a skinny lad always zipping about town on his bicycle.

"Do you have any homework?"

"Finished it this morning."

"Good lad. Fine. Wear your helmet and be back in an hour."

"Two?"

"No more than two."

Ciarán bounced off. Ann watched him go. "He used to love the flower shop."

It was true. He would help pick out bouquets and always insisted on carrying them home, then helping arrange them in vases. "He's growing up," Siobhán said. "Finding his own way." She didn't like seeing the changes either, but it was the way of things. "Ready?" she asked, grabbing a ham and cheese toastie to go.

"As I'll ever be."

"Heya," Eoin said as they were about to exit. Siobhán turned. He was slightly out of breath.

"We're going to the flower shop," Siobhán said. "Need something, pet?"

"I was just wondering when we might expect Garda Dabiri next?" He was trying to sound casual. Ann slapped his arm.

"You love her!"

Eoin swatted her hand away and turned to Siobhán. "Well?"

Siobhán struggled not to smile. "Honestly, she doesn't seem to eat much, so I don't know."

"Tell her I'll make anything she likes. Maybe she has some suggestions for our menu." Ann made kissing noises. Siobhán placed her hand atop of Ann's blond head. "That's a lovely idea, I'll tell her."

Blooms had its own bell that announced Siobhán and Ann's arrival, a tinkling that sounded like wind chimes. Leigh's daughter, Agnes, just a year ahead of Ann, was at the counter staring into a laptop. She looked up and grinned when she saw Ann.

"How ya?" Agnes was a spunky girl, and despite not participating in any organized sports had an athletic look about her, short black hair in stylish layers. The biggest difference since Siobhán had seen her last was the silver hoop in her left nostril.

"Hello, Agnes," Siobhán said. "You're looking well."

"Tanks." She pointed to her laptop and looked at Ann. "Have a look at dis." Ann hurried over to the counter to share in whatever secrets were on the screen.

"Is your mam in?" Siobhán asked.

"Mam," Agnes yelled at the top of her lungs. The back curtain fluttered and soon Leigh Coakley emerged, wiping her hands on her apron, bits of green leaf stuck to her.

"Ann," Leigh said with a bright smile. "Lovely to see you."

"You as well, Mrs. Coakley," Ann said perfunctorily.

"Would you like to join me in the back?" she said to Siobhán. "I have to get an arrangement finished for the memorial."

"Memorial?" Siobhán asked, following Leigh past the cooler stocked with colorful flowers and through the curtain and into the back room. "What memorial?"

Leigh stood in front of an easel where she was working on a circular wreath awash with white roses and lilies. "They're having a gathering at the bookshop for both Margaret and Deirdre as soon as they're able to reopen."

They were expecting word from Jeanie Brady any minute now to be granted permission for the body to be moved to Butler's Undertaker, Lounge, and Pub. And given Jeanie would also have to do an examination on Margaret's body, it would be a while before either of them had official funerals. A memorial was a good idea, but Siobhán did not like the fact that she was the last to know.

"I see." Siobhán felt the sting of rejection, even though she understood it came with the territory. Either way they were out of their minds if they thought she would stay away. "Garda Dabiri said you came to the station to see me," Siobhán said.

"Yes," Leigh said. "That reminds me. I have a welcome bouquet for her. Will you bring it back with ya?"

"Fair play to ya. Course I will."

"Thank you."

"She said you mentioned a lurker?"

Leigh nodded. "He was going through my rubbish bins the night before the murder. I wouldn't have mentioned it, as the poor thing looks as if he's living on the streets, but given what happened to poor Deirdre, I thought—well, what if it's him and I say nothing?"

"What if it's him?"

Leigh swallowed. "The killer," she whispered.

"What can you tell me about him?"

"He was a big man. Burly. Dirty and baggy clothes. I couldn't see his hair because he was wearing a cap, but he had a red beard streaked with gray. In his sixties if I were to guess."

"Could it have been a Traveler?"

"I wondered the same, but then I saw him again this morning passing by the caravan park on my power walk. The Travelers didn't say a word to him, so no, he's not with them."

As Leigh placed roses on the wreath, Siobhán looked around the tiny work space. At the edge of a table near the window was a paperback book. She nudged over and picked it up. *The Dragon Files: The Flamethrower,* by Michael O'Mara.

"It's his latest," Leigh said without even turning to her. "His best yet."

"I haven't read him yet," Siobhán said.

Leigh's spine straightened. "I certainly hope Oran McCarthy comes to his senses and realizes what a mistake it is not to sell his books." She snipped away at stems. "Imagine if I only sold one variety of flower in the shop!"

"I am in agreement with you there."

"Michael O'Mara lives on Bere Island. I always thought of taking a little trip, but it hasn't happened yet. Not that I would approach him or anything. I've heard he's become a recluse."

"Oh?"

"Rumors are he's drunk most of the day. I tell you, you wouldn't know by reading him."

"Rumors aren't facts," Siobhán said. "Perhaps he simply likes to keep his own company and tis only cups of tea he's tippin'."

"You could be right."

"Speaking of Michael O'Mara, were you able to pick up one of his biros?"

"The ones Darren Kilroy was passing around?"

"The very same."

Leigh reached into her pocket and pulled out a yellow biro with the megastar's name splashed across. "Please don't tell me you'll be taking it as evidence."

"No, you can keep it." Leigh visibly relaxed, then handed Siobhán a white rose.

"Tanks." She twirled the rose in her hand. "Did you bring roses for all the authors the night of the murder?"

Leigh frowned. "No."

"What about the day before?"

Leigh shook her head. "I brought a bouquet for Oran and Padraig. You saw it yourself."

If Leigh was telling the truth, where had Deirdre's red rose come from? Just then, a vision of Nessa Lamb emerging from the limo rose to mind. She was carrying a bouquet of red roses. Siobhán tapped a note to herself on her phone to ask her about them. She couldn't recall seeing a discarded bouquet at the crime scene. Then again, the day she saw Nessa with the bouquet was also before the murder. Was it possible one of the roses from either Leigh's or Nessa's bouquet dropped and remained on the floor? She had a feeling that Oran or Padraig would have noticed it and picked it up. It seemed like a little thing, but Siobhán had learned that often the little things could lead to big revelations. "I'm going to need a list of all the orders you've received since the authors arrived in town."

Leigh stopped snipping and gazed intently at Siobhán. "I don't suppose I can ask why."

"I wish you wouldn't."

"When do you need it by?"

"Can you bring it to your scheduled interview tomorrow?"

"Not a bother. Now, when will I be doing your wedding flowers?"

Siobhán was on her way back to the station when Macdara called. "You're not going to believe this," he said.

She stopped, bracing herself. "Try me."

"The techs processing Deirdre's room called. They want to know why we didn't list her laptop among the evidence to bag."

"Because it wasn't there."

"Exactly."

"You're saying . . . it's there now?"

"Meet me at the inn?"

"I'm on my way."

Chapter 17

Twenty minutes later Siobhán and Macdara stood in front of Deirdre's room, suited up in booties and gloves. The laptop in the middle of Deirdre's bed wasn't the only new addition to the room since they'd last entered. On the bedside table were three of Lorcan Murphy's westerns, two of *Dead Elf on a Shelf*, Nessa Lamb's *Musings on a Hill*, and no less than five installments of *The Dragon Files,* by Michael O'Mara. On the other bedside table sat ten copies of Deirdre's latest book, *Melodies*.

A long period of silence ticked by as Siobhán and Macdara stared at the books and the laptop.

Siobhán was the first to break the silence. "Do you think whoever stole these didn't realize we had already been in the room and so they put them back?"

"The crime scene tape on the door hasn't been disturbed," Macdara said.

"Good point." Unlike some motels, this one did not have any adjoining rooms. They checked the bathroom and confirmed that the window was still nailed shut.

"We never followed up on this," Siobhán said. "We should check at the hardware shop to see if any of our visitors bought nails or a hammer."

"I don't think our killer would be that obvious," Macdara said.

"But sometimes they are."

"I'll add it to the list," Macdara said as they returned to the main room. "But that window was nailed shut the last time we visited. And the crime scene tape hasn't been disturbed." He folded his arms and scanned the room again. "How did the killer get in?"

"It's a mystery." Siobhán picked up one of Lorcan's books. It was not signed. She quickly went through the rest. None of them were autographed. "Let's assume these belong to Deirdre. Why did she bring all of these here?"

"Oppo research?" Macdara suggested. "Look what I found," he said, gesturing to piles of notebooks near the laptop. "The killer is trying to bury us in red herrings. I do not like this one bit."

Cunning. They still had to process this new information, treat it as evidence, and the killer knew that. Was he taunting them? Or simply a professional at throwing up smoke screens? "Is the laptop password protected?"

Macdara opened the screen. "Tis." Siobhán gravitated to the notebooks; there were three of them. She opened the first. There, in neat handwriting, on the very first page, Deirdre had jotted down passages from other authors' books:

LORCAN MURPHY

The dust had barely settled when Rob Brant crested the hill on his purebred stallion, spurs jingling in the hot sun.

NESSA LAMB

The breeze is cool and the long night stretches in front of me. I've seen clouds before, but there's something about the muted swirls above my head that keep me transfixed. It's as if they're speaking directly to me, or maybe I'm going mad.

MICHAEL O'MARA

Gitana inhaled, hoping if he blew as hard as he could, his fire would return with a vengeance. Instead, he exhaled nothing but toxic vapors. Not even a little spark, nor did he feel heat in his belly. Just a cold lump where the heat once raged. He was a has-been, a loser, a waste of a dragon.

LORCAN MURPHY

I woke up to discover the Elf had indeed moved, because instead of being perched on the shelf with that irritating little smile, the wee thing was face down on me plate with red sauce all around him and a giant cleaver stuck in his back.

Siobhán jumped when she realized Macdara was be-hind her, reading over her shoulder. "What in the world?" he said.

"If this turns out to be Deirdre's handwriting, it looks as if she's copying passages of their work."

"I can see that," he said. "But why?"

"Do you think . . . was it actually Deirdre who was plagiarizing?"

Macdara frowned. "Given what little commercial suc-cess she's had, if she was, I'd say she plagiarized the wrong author."

"Maybe she planned on choosing one of these next," Siobhán said.

Macdara considered it. "Perhaps she's just writing down her favorite passages from each?"

"Perhaps. But she didn't seem like a fan of anyone else's work but her own."

"It's probably a fascinating character study, but how does it help us find her killer?"

"I don't know," Siobhán said, putting the notebook down with a sigh. "Any Michael O'Mara biros?"

Macdara looked around. "I don't see any here."

"Then the one near her body may have been hers."

Macdara entered the bathroom once more. After a mo-ment, he called out to Siobhán. "Look at this."

On the back of the toilet was an unopened pack of cig-arettes. Benson and Hedges, a common brand. "Another red herring?" Siobhán asked. "They were not there be-fore."

"We have to treat it as evidence," Macdara said. He marked the pack with evidence tape. The forensics team would have to return and bag all of the new objects. "Did you ever see Deirdre smoke?"

"No. But I only saw her at the bookshop and of course she wouldn't have been smoking there."

"She could be one of those who sneak one here and there. If so, she didn't have a chance to open this pack."

Siobhán returned to the main room, strode over to the closet, and put her nose to Deirdre's dresses. Then she did the same with the clothes in her luggage bag. "I don't smell a trace of smoke." She was about to close the closet door when something on the upper shelf caught her eye. A black leather handbag. "Her handbag," she said. She opened it. In its depths sat a small makeup bag. No wallet, phone, or keys. This may not have been her preferred handbag. "This wasn't here before either." Siobhán had never had a case where a murderer returned evidence. "Whatever the killer was worried about us finding has no doubt been removed."

"Is there a motel key?" Macdara asked.

Siobhán carefully went through the handbag. "No."

"The killer still has it. At least we know how he or she got into the room. The twins are going to need to change the locks." Macdara scratched his chin. "Why did the killer want to return her things?"

"Either because he or she removed incriminating evidence—"

"Or wanted to plant it," Macdara finished.

"Can we even trust that all these items belonged to Deirdre?"

"I suppose we can't." Macdara sighed. "Did we ever find out if any of our other writers smoke?"

"I hear the writers have been hanging out at Butler's Pub," Siobhán said. "We should check with John."

John Butler, the owner of Butler's Undertaker, Lounge,

and Pub, would have no problem squealing on his clients as long as there was something in it for him.

"The plot thickens," Macdara said.

"What's good for writers is bad for guards," Siobhán added with a sigh.

"That's all we can do here for now," Macdara said. "We'll have tech process the additional evidence and send the laptop to our experts. In the meantime, why don't we have Aretta meet us for lunch at O'Rourke's and see if she's had any luck processing the rubbish."

"Riddle me this, Batman," Declan said, leaning over Macdara. He and Siobhán were seated at O'Rourke's poring over the lunch menu as if they didn't already know what they were going to order. "We've got actual writers in town, and none of them have shown up at my fine establishment to drink." O'Rourke's was a mighty fine pub, and Declan the best of publicans. A large man with a gaptoothed grin, Declan O'Rourke was a walking encyclopedia when it came to trivia, ranging from the opera to old westerns. And if you were smart enough to compliment his Laurel and Hardy memorabilia in the window, you might even get a free pint. He heard more confessions than Father Kearney and could settle a dispute with a single glare from down the bar. The writers should be here; O'Rourke's was the best *craic* in town, but the village had numerous pubs, and for some reason the writers had gravitated to Butler's. The most likely reason being it was close to the bookshop. Anyone who got to know Declan, his boisterous voice, his big laugh, his quick wit and banter, would have been happy to become a regular.

"Rumor has it they're hanging at Butler's," Macdara said.

Declan crossed his arms and looked out the window. "Why?"

Macdara shrugged. "They're writers. They like death stakes."

"Do the bookshop owners drink? Haven't seen them in here either."

"Neither have I seen them at the bistro," Siobhán said. "You know how it is when you open a new business." Siobhán soaked in the dark wood, the smell of ale, already looking forward to a good feed. She glanced at the bar, where most times she'd find her best friend Maria working away, but she'd gone on a proper holiday with her new boyfriend. Maria promised they'd properly celebrate Siobhán's birthday when she returned. She was going to have to get in line.

The door opened and they all turned to see a smiling Aretta enter. She approached with a folder in her hand.

"Garda Dabiri, meet Declan O'Rourke," Siobhán said.

"One passion fruit mocktail coming up," Declan said.

Aretta's smile widened and she nodded.

"Apparently they've met," Macdara said.

"A mocktail," Aretta replied, "is a cocktail without the alcohol."

Given she looked as if she had just imparted wisdom on to them, Siobhán and Macdara played along and nodded.

"I prefer my tails without any mock," Macdara said. "But I'm on duty." He lifted his mineral as Aretta sat down next to Siobhán. Macdara and Siobhán ordered bacon and cabbage, but Aretta remarked that she'd already eaten. Siobhán didn't believe her, and was starting to become increasingly curious, nearing obsessed about Aretta's eating habits.

"My brother Eoin might have a little crush on you," Siobhán said. The minute it was out of her mouth, she felt guilty. And when she saw a look of shock on Aretta's face, and noticed Macdara bending his head so low she thought he was going to duck underneath the table, she felt even worse. "I think he just wants to show off his culinary skills," Siobhán said. "And if you have any recipes to share, he's always looking to expand."

"I will take that into consideration," Aretta said solemnly.

"Grand." Siobhán wished she had a sock so she could stuff it in her own gob. Luckily their drinks arrived on, and then their food, and each fell into silence as they took a few minutes to enjoy it, especially since the next portion of their discussion would be rubbish. Literally.

"First, I found a number of receipts," Aretta said, laying copies of three receipts out on the table once their plates had been cleared away. Macdara looked forlorn, and Siobhán knew he was thinking about dessert. "One for batteries, another from Annmarie's gift shop, a twenty-euro item, and the last is from Mike's fruit and veg market. I did not find any for nails or a hammer, and I called Liam's hardware shop as you requested, Detective Sergeant Flannery, and he did not recall any of the visiting authors buying a hammer or nails."

"Do the other receipts list the specific purchases?" Siobhán said, picking up a tinge of excitement in Aretta's voice.

"Mike's Fruit and Veg listed the purchase," Aretta said. "Nuts. A large variety pack."

Macdara whistled. "If Deirdre's nut allergy caused her death, this could be huge."

"I also stopped into Annmarie's gift shop," Aretta said. "She informed me that Lorcan Murphy had purchased a teddy."

"He has a daughter," Macdara said.

"This is good work," Siobhán added.

Aretta simply nodded her head at the compliment. "I also recovered the packaging from the batteries, but no packaging from the nuts. Most everything else fell into normal rubbish that I could tell, although everything is documented in my report."

"Most everything else?" Siobhán asked.

"There are a few more interesting bits," Aretta said. "First, there is this." From her satchel she removed a torn piece of paper, with writing scrawled in all capital letters in thick black ink:

WHAT ARE YOU DOING HERE?

Chapter 18

"It's a photocopy," Aretta pointed out. "But it is an exact replica down to the tear. The original is in the Evidence Room."

Siobhán felt a tingle that often accompanied a shocking discovery. If only the twins had separated the rubbish according to each room, like they had requested. Now there was no way of telling not only who sent this note, but perhaps more informative, who received it.

"What are you doing here?" Macdara repeated, as if just uttering the words might help him figure it out.

"This may not be a smoking gun," Siobhán said. "But it's definitely loaded." Macdara gave her a look. She grinned. "I can read westerns too."

"Will you use a handwriting expert?" Aretta asked.

"Unfortunately, we don't have sophisticated experts like they do on telly," Macdara said. "We'll send it up to

Dublin of course, to see what they can do about it, but we won't be given priority and it won't be done quickly, I can promise you that."

"We can compare it to the handwriting in Deirdre's notebook, although one is all capital letters, and the other is cursive."

"It's hard to tell from this photo," Aretta said. "But there was tape on the corners of the note."

"As if someone taped it to the door to their room?" Macdara asked.

Aretta nodded. "Maybe there are traces of paint chips on the tape that we could match to the doors?"

Siobhán understood Aretta's desire for forensic evidence. It was taught at Templemore and glorified by shows on telly. But the truth was that small villages did not have the capabilities to get that fancy, nor, as Dara had pointed out, were they given priority. "I think we can safely assume it was taped to the door, or somewhere the recipient would see it," Siobhán said. "I don't think verifying that fact would be worth the time and effort."

"And money," Macdara added.

"What else?" Siobhán asked.

"There is one more note. It does not appear to be the same handwriting." Aretta put her hands up. "I do not claim to be an expert." Her eyes danced with excitement. Siobhán was starting to think Aretta might make a good scribbler; she was definitely building up to something and enjoying the slow tease. She pulled the second note out of her satchel and slid it across the table. Siobhán and Macdara leaned in.

I DON'T BELIEVE IN GHOSTS

"What in the world?" Macdara said.

"Is it a dialogue?" Siobhán wondered out loud. It was true that unlike the first note, this was scribbled fast and loose, and the handwriting at a glance did not appear to come from the same person.

Aretta raised an eyebrow. "A dialogue?"

"What are you doing here?" Siobhán said. "I don't believe in ghosts." She twirled a strand of hair around her finger before remembering she was in public and stopped. "Or . . . I don't believe in ghosts . . . What are you doing here?"

Macdara and Aretta simply looked at her. Siobhán placed the two notes next to each other:

> *WHAT ARE YOU DOING HERE?*
> *I DON'T BELIEVE IN GHOSTS.*

She stared at it for a moment, then switched the order:

> *I DON'T BELIEVE IN GHOSTS.*
> *WHAT ARE YOU DOING HERE?*

"If it's a dialogue, the meaning is lost on me no matter what order they go in," Macdara said.

"Are any of them writing about ghosts?" Siobhán mused. "Lorcan perhaps?"

"Why him?" Macdara's back was up. He was still enamored with Lorcan Murphy. Heavens, if he was guilty he could still write his books from jail, could he not?

"It's not that far of a leap from elves to ghosts, is it?" Siobhán asked.

"Perhaps it was a euphemism. Such as ghosting," Aretta said.

"Ghosting?" Macdara said.

"It's slang for when you stop texting or calling someone you once dated," Aretta said.

"Kids these days," Macdara said with the shake of his head. He took Siobhán's hand. "I promise I'll never ghost ya."

"Tanks a million," Siobhán said, withdrawing her hand. "I'll reserve the option." She gave him a playful kick to the shin so he would know she was joking and turned back to Aretta. "We need to find out if Deirdre was in a romantic relationship with one of our other suspects."

"Or perhaps a lover had followed her here and we haven't met him or her yet," Aretta said, jotting down a note. "Are you thinking about that lurker?"

"Lurker?" Macdara asked.

"Sorry," Siobhán said. "So much has been going on. Leigh Coakley has spotted a stranger in town. She said he was going through her rubbish bins. Big burly man with a red beard."

"Could he be a Traveler?"

"She said she saw him pass by the Travelers' caravans and they did not seem to be interacting."

"When did you learn all this?" Macdara asked.

"I popped into the flower shop today, before I came here," Siobhán said. "I didn't get any sense that Leigh had anything to hide. But I did learn they plan to have a memorial at the bookshop as soon as it's no longer a crime scene." She studied the notes again. "What if this lurker is Deirdre's secret lover?"

Macdara sighed. "So you're saying Deirdre Walsh's lover is a burly man who rummages through rubbish?"

Aretta laughed. Siobhán gave him another kick underneath the table. "Anything else?" Macdara asked.

Aretta shook her head. "Those are the main items. The rest, as I mentioned, I put in the category of mundane rubbish."

"The notes and the nuts," Macdara said. "I'd say it was a good haul indeed." A familiar figure walked past, and Siobhán caught a flash of a green suit pass by. Darren Kilroy. He was on his mobile phone, headed toward the patio.

"I have an idea," Siobhán said. "Why don't we hold the interviews with our suspects here?" The back section of the pub was quiet and far enough away from the counter that the regulars wouldn't be able to eavesdrop.

"Because you want your friend Declan O'Rourke to have customers?" Aretta asked.

"And we want to put them at ease," Macdara said. "Let them feel helpful. They're likely to let their guard down."

"We're dealing with professionals," Siobhán said. "They lie for a living. We need every advantage we can get."

"In fact," Macdara said, "I'd like to try something. Let's speak with them as a group before getting them one on one."

"What does that do?" Aretta asked.

"If one of them is lying, they'll have to adjust to information given by the others. Then one on one they may start tailoring those adjustments, or calling another out on a lie."

"Can you give our suspects a bell and ask them to come here?" Siobhán said. "Darren is on the patio. I'll let him know."

Aretta rose and nodded. "I made the right choice coming to Kilbane. You might be a quirky pair, but so far I am learning a lot." She headed off to make the calls.

"Quirky pair?" Siobhán said, staring after her.

"She was looking at you when she said it," Macdara said with a grin.

If Darren Kilroy was worried about anyone overhearing his conversation on the phone, he should have told his mouth that. Siobhán could hear him way before she ever breached the exit to the outdoor area. She wondered if she would find him smoking, but the only thing in hand was the phone. Today he was wearing a light green suit with a white bow tie dotted with green polka dots. She wondered if he had always dressed so stylish, or had it been since the money started rolling in from Michael O'Mara's books?

"I can't tell you exactly how much longer; they've asked us to stay put for a few more days." His back was to Siobhán, and although it hadn't been her intention to listen in, she didn't do anything else to alert him of her presence. Most people had a sense of when they were being watched, unless of course the other conversation was so intense that it overrode those instincts. This seemed to be the case here, and although there was nothing alarming in his words, it made her wonder whom he was speaking with. "No. No. No. That is not a good idea. Not now."

Interesting. His Spidey senses must have clicked in for he suddenly whirled around and spotted Siobhán. She waved. "I have to go." He clicked off without waiting for the other person to respond. She wished she had the power to summon his phone records, but she didn't have enough evidence to get that kind of request approved. Not yet anyway.

"I didn't mean to startle you," she said, hoping there was an easier way to get him to reveal what that was all about.

"I hope this is over soon," he said. "I have other clients and every single one of them thinks I only work for him or her. Writers are fragile, fragile flowers."

"Was that your most famous client?" She wondered what Michael O'Mara was like. Living every man's fantasy, making a fortune writing about dragons. She made a mental note to Google him.

"If it was, he has nothing to do with this case, and I'm sure you understand that I have a duty to protect the confidentiality of my authors."

"I see." She waited a moment, treating him to a long stare. He concentrated on his phone, but she could tell he was making a conscious effort not to be intimidated. "Do you smoke?"

"Not anymore."

"How long has it been?"

"Twenty years."

"Fair play."

"Why do you ask?"

"I'm sure you understand I have a duty to protect my investigations."

"I do indeed." He started to walk past her.

"Don't wander too far. We're going to be conducting the interviews here."

"Here?" He sounded startled. *Good.* She wanted them on their toes.

"Will that be a problem?"

"Not at all," he said. "I shall remain here." He wiped his brow with a handkerchief that matched his bow tie as he left the patio.

Aretta entered the patio as Darren made a hasty exit. She turned and watched him disappear. "Was it something you said?" she quipped.

Siobhán laughed. "You're going to do just fine at our station."

Aretta grinned. "Lorcan Murphy and Nessa have arrived."

"Great." Siobhán suddenly recalled that she had yet to tell Macdara about the third note, the piece of paper Nessa had given her with the one-star review and handwritten scrawl. *THE HILLS HAVE EYES*. How could she have forgotten? And as memory served, despite being capital letters it did not look like the handwriting on either of the notes found in the rubbish. Were they looking at three notes written by three different people, or three notes written by one person, but carefully disguised to look like three? Or was it something obscure that Nessa herself had written? Siobhán was going to have to ask her about it before she submitted it to evidence. She touched the pocket of her uniform and confirmed it was still there.

Lorcan Murphy was thrilled they were holding the interviews at a pub. He sat in front of a pint and fish and chips. "Declan," Siobhán said. "Could you remove these items until after the interview?"

"Sorry, luv," he said, taking the pint and plate away as Lorcan stared after it like a dog who'd just had a meaty bone snatched. Another figure hovered nearby. Nessa Lamb.

"Please," Siobhán said. "Have a seat."

"I thought this would be one on one," Nessa said.

"We decided to shake things up a bit," Siobhán replied. "Sit."

Nessa perched at the edge of the booth, barely making eye contact with Lorcan Murphy. It took another five minutes for Darren to arrive. His face was flush. "Sorry, sorry," he said. "I had to grab a bite to eat before my blood sugar crashed."

"Lucky one dat," Lorcan said, throwing another glance in the direction his food and pint had gone.

"Sit."

Darren looked around, then instead of sitting by Lorcan, he pulled up a chair from a neighboring table. Lorcan's head was buried in his smartphone and suddenly he looked up and belted out a laugh.

"What?" Nessa Lamb asked when no one else did.

"The *Irish Book Reviews* said someone should check to make sure I have a pulse," Lorcan said with a grin.

"You know that's not a compliment, don't you?" Nessa asked.

He shrugged. "Any time your name is mentioned as an author it's a good ting."

Nessa shook her head and crossed her arms. "Unless you're being investigated for murder."

"We're not seriously suspects, are we?" Lorcan said, as if it had never occurred to him.

"Does this answer your question?" Nessa held her smartphone out for the others to see. It was a local newspaper out of Dublin, and the headline read:

LAMBS AND ELVES TO THE SLAUGHTER
Nessa Lamb, writer of *Musings on a Hill,*

is a person of interest in the murder of indie author
Deirdre Walsh, along with Lorcan Murphy, known
for his gruesome Dead Elf on a Shelf series.

"My word," Darren Kilroy said. "That's abominable."
All heads swiveled to Siobhán and Macdara.

"That didn't come from our office," Macdara said. "I
promise you that."

"This is a cruel business," Lorcan said. "They didn't
even mention my westerns." He shook his head. "Gruesome? They're missing the point entirely!"

"I didn't kill Deirdre Walsh no matter what anyone
thinks," Nessa said. She placed her phone down and shivered. "The sick thing is—my sales have skyrockcted since
this article came out."

"I'd better check mine," Lorcan said, rubbing his
hands together.

"Aretta, will you pass around the sheet?" Macdara said.

Arctta nodded and slid a sheet with the An Garda Síochána letterhead across the table. Darren was the first up.

"What's this?" he said, pushing up his glasses.

"We just need you to write your name in capital letters," Siobhán said. "Easy-peasy."

"I see." Darren's biro hovered over the line. It was not
one of his author's biros. Perhaps he saved the swag for
events. He signed his name in capital letters and passed it
to Lorcan Murphy. Lorcan produced his own biro from
his blazer, a simple black one.

"I thought you already had me autograph," he said
with a grin to Macdara.

"Print please," Macdara said. "In capital letters."

Lorcan scrawled it as fast as he could. Was he trying to

hide his identity? He flung it over to Nessa. She stared at it.

"I know why you're doing this," she said. "You showed them the one-star review with the note."

Macdara and Aretta's heads swiveled to Siobhán. She stared back, hoping they wouldn't say anything in front of the others. Let Nessa think it was her note they were following up on.

"We won't be doing anything," Siobhán replied. "But our handwriting expert will." Once again she counted on Aretta and Macdara not contradicting her, and she was relieved when they did not disappoint.

"You have an expert handwriting . . . person?" Darren asked.

"Forensic document examiner," Aretta said. "That's her official title." Siobhán suppressed a grin. She caught on fast.

"Given Nessa has already referred to this, I think everyone should see it." Siobhán slid the one-star review to the middle of the table. Although Macdara and Aretta were not obvious about leaning in to read it, Siobhán could see they were doing their best to study it inconspicuously.

Lorcan frowned as he read it. "'Tis terrible," he said. "But we all get one-star reviews. It would be more unusual if you didn't have any."

Darren reached into his suit for a pair of eyeglasses, put them on, leaned in, and read silently, lips moving. "*The Hills Have Eyes,*" he said. "The horror film?"

"I think this was written by Deirdre," Nessa said.

"Including the written note?" Siobhán asked.

Nessa tilted her head. "I don't know. I had never heard of this movie—*The Hills Have Eyes . . .* ?"

"Mutant cannibals," Siobhán said confidently. Macdara coughed, trying to squelch his shock. "Perhaps she was alluding to the competitive nature of writers?"

Darren took off his eyeglasses. "Could it be a threat?"

"It's obviously a threat," Nessa said.

Or someone accusing her of plagiarism.

"Why do you think it was Deirdre?" Siobhán asked. She really wanted Nessa to bring up the plagiarism accusation unprompted.

Darren let out a sound, something between a groan and a gasp. "I think I know what it means," he said. "And it's all my fault."

Chapter 19

All heads swiveled to Darren Kilroy, whose hand shook as he pointed to the one-star review. "I know the site the review was posted on. I mentioned that site in a blog post. A writer had asked me if I look at reviews when considering a new author."

"And what did you say?" Macdara prompted when Darren stopped talking.

"I said I give them some weight, especially if a book has numerous one-star ratings. But I never would have paid attention to such a vile comment. It says more about the person who wrote it than the author. I'm afraid I must disagree with Ms. Lamb."

"Disagree?" Nessa said.

"I don't think Deirdre Walsh wrote this. She was a smart woman. She would have known it wouldn't move the needle in her favor."

"She posted it anonymously," Nessa said.

"How did it come to be in your possession?" Aretta asked.

"It was taped to my door at the inn," Nessa said. "The morning of the murder."

Given none of them knew that Margaret's death was now being investigated as a murder, Siobhán knew Nessa was referring to Deirdre's murder. Another note taped to a door at the inn. An order formed in Siobhán's mind, whether right or wrong:

> *WHAT ARE YOU DOING HERE?*
> *THE HILLS HAVE EYES.*
> *I DON'T BELIEVE IN GHOSTS.*

"Mr. Kilroy's right," Lorcan said. "We have no proof this was Deirdre. She was the one who was murdered. Quite frankly it strengthens *your* motive."

Nessa Lamb glared at Lorcan across the table. He held her gaze.

"Please," Darren said. "Mr. Kilroy makes me think of me father. Call me Darren."

"Do any of you write ghost stories?" Siobhán asked, her eyes ping-ponging between Nessa and Lorcan.

Nessa shook her head and looked at Lorcan.

"Ghost stories you're after?" Lorcan asked. "I can't say I have."

"What about you?" Macdara asked Darren. "Do you have any authors writing ghost stories?"

"No," Darren said with a chuckle. "I've got me hands full with dragons."

Lorcan leaned across the table. "I tink elves would fit nicely into your portfolio then, don't ya?"

"Michael O'Mara might see you as competition," Nessa said. "Whereas mine couldn't possibly be considered competition. He wouldn't have to worry about blurring the lines. I hear O'Mara can have quite the temper."

"I heard it's a miracle he can hold a biro these days," Lorcan said. "Is he still blacking out in public?"

This was going pear-shaped. "What is wrong with you two?" Nessa said. "Don't you see what she's getting at?" Nessa reached her hand across the table but stopped short of touching Siobhán. "I see what you're saying. You're right. Maybe Deirdre didn't leave that review."

"What leads you to believe that?" Siobhán asked. Given Siobhán didn't even know what she was getting at, she was eager to see what Nessa would say.

"I was the one getting death threats. It was dark in the bookshop. Deirdre was a victim of mistaken identity. It was I the killer was after. All this time. It was I."

Soon after they concluded the impromptu interview. Siobhán, Macdara, and Aretta stood out on the footpath. Siobhán apologized for leaving them in the dark about the one-star review and accompanying note.

"I know we don't have an official forensic examiner," Aretta said. "But do you mind if I study all three notes to see if I can identify similarities?"

"I don't see the harm," Macdara said. "Especially now that we have their handwriting samples."

They were about to part when someone cleared their throat behind them. They whirled around to find Darren Kilroy waiting.

"Yes?" Siobhán said.

"I can't help wondering why you asked us about ghosts," Darren said.

"I'm afraid I can't share that information at this time," Siobhán said.

"Perhaps you would be alright if I offered some then," Darren said. He glanced around as if to make sure they were alone.

"Go on, so," Siobhán said.

"Given Deirdre was accusing Nessa Lamb of plagiarism, maybe she discovered something else instead."

They waited as he eagerly searched their faces for a reaction. "Out with it," Macdara said finally.

"What if Nessa Lamb's book wasn't plagiarized but it wasn't exactly written by her?"

"I don't understand," Siobhán said.

"Ghostwriters," Darren said. "I've represented several in the past. What if *Musings on a Hill* was written by a ghostwriter?"

Eoin was near the window chatting with customers at a table when Siobhán and Aretta entered the bistro. Aretta, still jotting down something in her notebook, didn't notice Eoin's gaze on her, nor the intensity of it, but Siobhán certainly did. Come on. He had plenty of young girls after him, did he have to set his sights on her new work mate?

"How ya?" Eoin called, his eyes lingering on Aretta.

"We are well," Aretta answered with a bright smile, oblivious that this wasn't his normal grin. "And you?"

"I'm better now that you walked in."

Siobhán rolled her eyes and headed for her cappuccino maker. Her brother had always had more confidence than all of them rolled into one. "Would you like one?" Siobhán asked Aretta.

"No thank you."

"Would you like tea? Water? A mineral?" Eoin asked.

Aretta shook her head as she edged closer to Siobhán. "Your employee is very friendly," she said.

"He's my brother," Siobhán said. "Chef, artist, and all cheek." Eoin, meanwhile, had gravitated toward them and was in earshot. "Eoin, meet Aretta. Aretta. This is Eoin."

Aretta nodded and waved. Eoin grinned and waved back. "I'm the most talented and handsome of the O'Sullivan Six if you were wondering," he said with a wink.

"I see," Aretta said. "That is good to know." When she turned back, Siobhán noticed Aretta was wrestling with a smile, trying and failing to put it down.

"I actually have a favor to ask," Eoin said.

Aretta tilted her head. "Of me?"

"Yes. I hope you don't mind. I've been on a mission to expand our menu. I've been practicing French dishes for a while and I was wondering if you have any Nigerian recipes you'd be willing to share with me?"

Aretta smiled brightly. "My father is the cook of the family. Perhaps on his next visit I can introduce you and I will leave it up to you to wrestle his culinary secrets from him."

"Oh," Eoin said. "Absolutely." Siobhán nearly burst into laughter. Aretta had handled that beautifully. Although Siobhán knew Eoin was genuinely interested in the recipe, she also knew which Dabiri he wanted to learn it from. "In the meantime, I am going to practice," Eoin said. "I am thinking of starting with pepper soup and fried bean cakes."

"I will offer my sampling services when you are ready," Aretta said, flashing him another grin. Eoin's face reddened in seconds. He grinned back, nodded, and disappeared into the kitchen, whistling away.

"What do you think of Nessa Lamb's claim?" Aretta asked when the machine from heaven stopped its frothing noise and the Irish Romeo was out of sight. "Or that of Darren Kilroy?"

"Nessa certainly threw a plot twist into the investigation with her conviction that she was the intended target," Siobhán said. She gestured to the back dining room and garden beyond. The sun was slicing through the dark clouds, a rare sight the past few days. "Shall we go out in the garden?"

"Yes," Aretta said.

The scent of lavender and mint wafted over Siobhán as they stepped into the back garden and she mulled over the questions Aretta had just posed. Nessa *could* have been the intended victim. But it was Deirdre Walsh to whom Leigh Coakley had said, "You should eat those words." And it was Deirdre with the nut allergy. Siobhán shared her thoughts. Aretta nodded. "Anything is possible. That's the problem with possible."

"Is there no way to find out for sure?" Aretta began to walk around the small garden, taking in the flowers and herbs. "This is well organized."

"You can thank my brother Eoin for that," Siobhán said.

"He is passionate about being a chef?"

"He is. He truly is."

"Perhaps I could teach him to make pepper stew."

Siobhán nodded, trying to keep her reaction neutral. Eoin would be over the moon. "He's also an artist. You can find his graphic novels at Gordon's Comics."

"The same shop where you wanted to speak with the owner because he threatened to sue the bookshop?"

"Yes," Siobhán said. "But I do not have any reason to believe that Chris Gordon is anything other than harmless."

"Are you going to try and find out if Nessa Lamb was the intended victim?"

"If there are traces of nuts on the pages stuffed in Deirdre's mouth, then it would not be probable that Nessa was the target. Everyone knew Deirdre was the one with the nut allergy."

"And if there's not?"

Siobhán sighed. "Then I suppose it moves closer to probable." But if Nessa was the intended target, and Deirdre obviously wasn't the killer, then who would want Nessa dead? Lorcan Murphy? Arguably, he was the most successful of the authors in terms of income. He didn't seem desperate to have Darren Kilroy as his agent. He could be faking it. But was jealousy of book deals and literary awards really a motive for murder? Jealousy in love, sure. But books? She supposed each profession had their mad actors. But weren't writers supposed to channel their frustrations onto their characters instead of each other? Siobhán's mobile rang, startling both of them. Macdara's photo flashed on the screen as it rang.

"Good news," he said. "Jeanie Brady is on her way, and should arrive in the morning, but our photos did the trick. She's given permission for the body to be moved to Butler's."

That was good news. Finally, they could get their hands on the crime scene.

Chapter 20

Oran and Padraig McCarthy were waiting for Siobhán and Macdara by the entrance to Turn the Page. A black hearse, no doubt one from Butler's carrying Deirdre's body, pulled away just as Siobhán and Macdara showed up. Siobhán crossed herself and sent a little prayer to the heavens for Deirdre Walsh. Then she turned to Oran. She couldn't help but feel a little smug that the roles of who was allowed into the bookshop were reversed. Maybe she should require Oran to quote from the An Garda Síochána handbook to gain entrance. Not that they would be allowed in today, but they would need to explain to them how to access the secret room.

"We'll show you," Oran said. "Do you have extra protective gear?" He stared at their booties, gloves, and gown.

"You'll have to tell us instead," Siobhán said. "From out here."

Oran chewed on his bottom lip. Padraig patted Oran's elbow, then turned to them with a smile. "Anything at all."

"How do we open the bookshelf?" Siobhán said.

"The secret door," Padraig corrected.

Oran's mouth twitched.

"What?" Siobhán asked.

"It's a secret door," Padraig repeated.

"Promise me this will stay between us," Oran said. "We went to a lot of trouble having it built, and if a secret door isn't secret anymore, then there's really no point at all in having one, is there?"

"No," Siobhán said. "What was the point in the first place?"

"Just a bit of fun," Padraig said.

"How's that working out for you?" Siobhán said.

Oran stared at Siobhán. "Has anyone ever told you you're a difficult person?"

"Not in such polite terms," Siobhán replied.

Macdara cleared his throat. "I'd like a better explanation for why you think you needed a secret door."

Oran sighed. "It was a lark at first," he said.

"A lark?" Macdara asked.

Padraig nodded. "Yes. As in, we had too many glasses of Cabernet one night and were daydreaming about the shop and said, 'Wouldn't it be fun to have a secret bookcase that opened into our office.'"

"I never knew Padraig would actually follow through with it. But that's the kind of man he is," Oran said.

Oran stopped to smile at his husband, and Padraig smiled back before turning to Siobhán. "When you face the bookcase you'll see a red leather book on the farthest upper-right-hand corner. You'll see a little notch that marks the spot."

"Red book, farthest upper-right-hand corner." Siobhán jotted it down. "Title?"

"You can't miss it," Padraig said. "It's not a real book, it's a mechanism. Red leather."

"Pull it out and push on the case," Oran added. "It will swing inward."

"What if someone randomly decided to pull the book out?" Siobhán asked.

"That wouldn't do anything," Padraig said. "The book would only pull slightly out, then seem as if it was stuck. There is no title on the spine, and it blends in on the book-shelf."

"But you have to give the shelf a hard shove on the right-hand side precisely where you find the notch," Oran said. "We thought the chances of someone discovering it on his or her own were slim."

"Yet the lads who built it are aware, aren't they?" Macdara said.

A look of worry came over their faces. "Do you think they told someone, and that person is our killer?" Padraig's voice squeaked.

"Deep breaths," Oran said. "Can't have you fainting on the footpath."

"What's in the secret room?" Siobhán asked. She didn't want Padraig to faint on the footpath either, so she kept her voice light and veered away from the accusation that a stranger had accessed their secret door to commit murder. Although it was a troubling possibility.

"It's our back office," Oran said. "You'll find a safe where we intended on keeping rare books. A desk. Inventory and boxes we haven't unpacked. And a bookshelf shoved against the door to the alley."

"Why?" Macdara asked. Siobhán remembered them mentioning this in previous conversations but it never hurt to get a suspect to tell a story again. Often little inconsistencies could be dead giveaways that a lie was being spun.

"When we rented this building, the owner didn't have a key to that door," Oran explained. "We intended on changing the locks, but until then we didn't want to take the chance that someone had the key and might sneak in."

"Did anyone ever try to break in while you were there?"

"No," Padraig said. "But there's always rubbish outside the door. Cigarette butts and whatnot."

"I understand Darren Kilroy brought biros with Michael O'Mara's name on them to pass out to everyone," Siobhán said. Oran frowned, but Padraig nodded. "Were there any extras?"

This time they both frowned. "I believe they were all snatched up," Padraig said. "If you really want one you can have mine."

"What color is it?"

"Red."

"I'll keep it in mind," Siobhán said. "Why don't you two head to Naomi's Bistro while you wait," she added. "My brother Eoin is the chef. Tell him your lunch is on me."

"We've been meaning to try Jade's," Oran said quickly.

Jade's was the Chinese restaurant at the other end of the street. She couldn't argue with that—their food was delicious. But what did they have against her bistro? One day, she would get to the bottom of it, but for now she put it out of her mind as she stepped into the bookshop.

It was strange to be back in a place that first brought her so much excitement, and just as quickly, a deadly shock. Macdara and Siobhán would go through the scene first and then the forensics team would collect any evidence and dust for fingerprints before turning it back to Oran and Padraig. Siobhán was horrified that her cake was still there, drawing annoying little fruit flies. It would be boxed up and sent to Jeanie Brady, probably not the sweet surprise she'd want it to be. The chances that it was poisoned and Deirdre had just happened to lick the icing were small. But still, it had to be done. They stood in front of the shelf, staring at the books scattered on the floor. Siobhán glanced up at the top shelf. She could reach the red book on her tiptoes.

"If one accessed the secret room from this side, they would have to be tall," Macdara said.

"They're all history books," Siobhán said. "Long and heavy."

"What are you thinking?"

"Someone could have fashioned a stepladder."

"I hate it when you blow my theories out of the water," Macdara said.

"I'm anxious to see if the door to the alley is still barricaded," Siobhán said. "If not . . ."

"It opens up our suspect pool to the entire village."

"I'm afraid it does."

"Go on, so," Macdara said. "I know you want to do the honors."

Siobhán stepped up to the bookshelf, stood on her tiptoes, and removed the red book. Then she found the notch, leaned into the right-hand side, and gave it a shove. The entire case swung open with a creak. Books jiggled on the shelf, but none of them fell. *Impressive.* Even though she was expecting it, Siobhán emitted a squcak of excitement and she heard Macdara chuckle behind her. She stared into a dark abyss.

"We forgot to ask them where the light switch was located," she said. "Do you have your torch?"

"I can run and get one, but I didn't think to bring it either," Macdara said. "Paw around for it."

It took her several attempts, but she finally located a switch and soon lights flickered, then stayed steady, revealing, as promised, a back office. Unlike the pinewood floors of the bookshop, this back room was made of stone walls and a concrete floor. It was colder in here, with a slight odor of mildew. Cobwebs gathered in the corners and the lights emitted a soft whine. The safe Oran and Padraig mentioned was in the corner next to a large desk piled with papers and books. There were numerous cardboard boxes piled against the right wall. A large bookshelf had been shoved against the back door, just as Oran and Padraig said. But instead of being shoved all the way against the door, it stood on a diagonal with a foot gap between it and the back door. There was enough room for a person to squeeze in from the alley. Siobhán and Macdara stared at the door. Specifically the lock. It was not engaged. Macdara cursed, something he rarely did on the job.

"Anyone could be the killer," Siobhán said as he turned the knob on the door and it yawned open. "Absolutely anyone."

"Technically," Macdara said. "But a random person did not go to this kind of trouble to murder Deirdre Walsh."

"Someone needed not only the motivation, but access and knowledge of the bookshop," Siobhán said. "Would Oran or Padraig be so obvious?"

"Maybe they would. Hoping we would think it was preposterous they would do something so obvious."

Siobhán exhaled. "If one or both of them is guilty, this was planned far in advance, starting with this secret door."

"Let's check out the boxes and the desk, and then the alley," Macdara said with a nod.

The boxes, all twelve of them, held books. They were stacked up against the back wall, and given some of them looked old and rare, unless he was the one who opened it, she was pretty sure Oran was going to be outraged that the back door was open. The desk was crammed with the usual office detritus, and folders. A particularly thick one was labeled: *DESIGN*. It held wallpaper swatches and sketches, and sheets ripped out of magazines. Siobhán felt a twinge of pity for the pair. This had been their dream shop. It was obvious that months, maybe even years had gone into imagining it. And the final product had been spectacular. She hoped they were innocent and could keep the shop going, put this behind them. But right now, justice mattered the most. "Do we need any of this?" Siobhán asked.

"Anything financial in nature we'll have to take," Macdara said. "It could go to motive." Siobhán nodded and placed evidence stickers on the folders that contained financial information. She held up a business card. CONSTRUCTIVE BUILDS.

"I bet this is the contractor who built the secret door," Siobhán said.

"Good work," he said. "We'll contact them."

Once they were finished with the interior, they exited the building and came around to the back alley. The lock had not been damaged, it was simply unlocked, which meant either Oran and Padraig hadn't engaged it in the first place or noticed it was unlocked, or someone out there had a key. Or someone had picked the lock. Or they were lying. "What if Padraig and Oran do have the key?" she said.

"We can check with the landlord," Macdara said. "But walk me through it."

"Padraig left the bookshop that evening and returned soaking wet just as the lights went back on," Siobhán said. "What if instead of returning home, he ran around the back of the shop, entered, waited for the blackout, then snuck onto the floor and killed Deirdre?"

"But he forgot to put the bookshelf back in front of the door? And he left the door to the alley open?"

"There wasn't time to shut it. Once we discovered the body, we ushered everyone out the front and secured the building." She stared at the partially opened back door. "The guards secured this alley. They wanted to leave the door as they found it."

"I wish they'd brought it to our attention earlier," Macdara said. "It's possible someone could have snuck past them and entered our crime scene." He rubbed his face. "Whoever our killer is, I do believe this is the point of entry."

Siobhán scoured the alley. Cigarette butts, packets of crisps, and mineral cans dotted the landscape. They had bigger things to worry about than polluters, but Siobhán loathed anyone who would toss their rubbish anywhere but a bin. She pointed at the cigarette butts. "We should see if we can determine the brand. See if it matches the cigarettes found in Deirdre's room."

"Good thinking," Macdara said. He put an evidence marker near the cigarette butts. "I'm going to have the team collect the safe as well. Oran and Padraig claim it's empty. We'll need to verify that."

Siobhán nodded. "Hopefully they'll give us the combination."

"It won't look good if they don't. I have a department meeting," Macdara said, glancing at his watch. "Will you shake down Oran and Padraig for the digits to the safe?"

Siobhán grinned. "I thought you'd never ask."

"I swear it was closed and locked and the bookshelf was in front of it," Padraig insisted.

"Not a doubt," Oran repeated. "We never unlocked that door." He licked his lips.

"And yet the door is unlocked," Siobhán said. "Are you sure the bookshelf was flush against the door?" Siobhán had ambushed them at Jade's and was now sitting across from them in a booth, eyeing their stir-fry and spring rolls.

"Positive," Oran and Padraig said in stereo.

"I need to go through our boxes and make sure nothing has been stolen," Oran said, stabbing into a spring roll with his chopsticks.

"I'm afraid that is going to have to wait. When was the last time you were in there?" She glanced at the spring rolls again. Perfectly crisped on the outside. Were they ever going to offer her one?

"Opening morning," Oran said. "I haven't been in since."

"Neither have I," Padraig said.

"We're going to need the combination to the safe," Siobhán said. What if she just took a spring roll? Casually, as if it was totally proper? Anyone else would have offered them straightaway.

"Our safe, our books, our files," Oran said. "This is so invasive."

"So is murder," Siobhán said.

"Of course," Padraig said, taking out a biro and jotting down the combination on a napkin. It was one of Michael O'Mara's biros. Another green one. Siobhán had been hoping that only one of each color had been passed out.

"I thought you said yours was red," Siobhán said, pointing to the biro.

"It's mine," Oran said. "What is with you and the biros? Is there a problem?" Oran eyed the biro. "Is it poison?"

Siobhán arched an eyebrow. "Why would you think that?"

"Sounds like something from an old detective novel, doesn't it?" Oran said. "The poison pen."

"Yes, it does." Did he know a pen was found near Deirdre's body? How? It had been dark in the bookshop for the most part, and after the body was discovered and the lights came on, she couldn't imagine anyone breaking through his or her shock to notice a biro on the floor. It had mostly been hidden underneath Deirdre's left leg. Was Oran the killer, or was he just taking a stab in the dark?

Chapter 21

The next afternoon, Jeanie Brady was waiting for Siobhán outside Butler's Undertaker, Lounge, and Pub. She was a short and round woman in her fifties, with layered brown hair, full cheeks, and alert hazel eyes. A down to earth woman, she was astute, meticulous, and cared deeply about her profession. "Do you mind if we do a walk-about?" Jeanie said when Siobhán approached. "Me legs are stiff from the car ride, then getting straight to work."

"Not a bother," Siobhán said.

"There's a few heads in the lounge," she said. "From the way they're drinking I'm guessing it's the scribblers."

"I can't blame them," Siobhán said. "It's been a stressful few days." Although the weather had calmed down, there were remnants of the storm everywhere you looked. Branches that had fallen from trees, rubbish blown about, and puddles that had yet to evaporate. As they walked,

Jeanie Brady wasted no time in filling Siobhán in on her findings thus far.

"There were no traces of nuts on the pages," Jeanie Brady said. "And although official tests will take a while, in my professional opinion this death was not caused by a nut allergy." Did that mean the intended victim could have been Nessa Lamb? "But I did find an injection mark on the back of her neck, and I believe the killer held a gloved hand over her mouth and nose while the poison did its job."

"Poison? From the injection?"

"No." Jeanie stopped for a moment in front of the Kilbane Museum, a tiny stone building filled with Irish history and artifacts, and had a look in the window briefly before they continued on. "Tests will have to confirm it, but I believe the injection was to sedate her."

"That was Macdara's theory as well."

Jeanie nodded. "Although, once again, tests will have to confirm it, I believe the poison was on the back of a sample I found in her mouth."

"Sample?" Siobhán stopped. "Do you mean the book pages?"

"There was no poison on the book pages."

"Okay . . ." Jeanie Brady was working up to something and Siobhán had learned to give her room to do it.

"This was a cold and calculated murder."

"I agree, but take me through it." This time when they began walking again, Jeanie Brady picked up the pace. It gave Siobhán the urge to go running, but in the moment she'd settle for the brisk walk.

"The syringe with a sedative, the glove, the sample. It took a lot of planning, especially to strike that quickly once the power went out."

"You said gloved hand. How did you determine it was a glove?"

"I found a tiny fiber around the victim's mouth consistent with leather. Black gloves, it appears."

They had arrived at the field in front of the abbey, and were approaching the small bridge across the river. In the distance the abbey was a comforting sight. Every time Siobhán was near it, she couldn't help but imagine the monks who used to live there, brewing beer at the river, cooking in the kitchen, praying in the chapel, and perhaps watching the light shine in through the abbey's stunning five-light windows.

"Are any of your suspects interior decorators?" Jeanie Brady asked. There was a sparkle in her eye.

This had been the last thing Siobhán expected her to say. "Interior decorators?" She shook her head. "They're all writer types." She hesitated, remembering Padraig's folder dedicated to the bookshop. "Wait. One of the bookshop owners designed and decorated the shop."

"How do you know?"

"There's an entire folder labeled *Design* in their back office." *The office they wanted to keep secret.* As a lark? Or something more sinister?

"I need it. Immediately."

"Of course." Siobhán placed a call to Macdara and described the folder in the back office labeled *DESIGN*. She hung up, and turned to Jeanie. "They're going to pick it up now and it will be logged into the evidence room at the garda station."

"Let's go."

They turned and headed in the opposite direction. "Are you going to be examining Margaret O'Shea's body next?"

"Yes. But if she too was murdered by arsenic we'll be waiting on those test results."

"Arsenic?"

Jeanie nodded. "That's my best guess. It kills quickly and is readily available. And then there's a matter of the sample. . . ." Jeanie Brady pulled out her mobile phone and brought up a photo. She handed it to Siobhán, who had to squint to make sense of what she was looking at, adjusting the distance of the phone to her eyes. "That's right," Jeanie said. "You're getting older, I hear." Jeanie reached into her pocket again and pulled out an enormous bar of chocolate. "Happy birthday, luv."

Siobhán felt an unexpected thrill as she accepted the chocolate and tucked it into her own pocket for later. "Thanks a million. I can't believe this is the last of my twenties."

Jeanie Brady sighed. "Twenties," she said. "I barely remember them. But your thirties? Now that's living."

Siobhán grinned, then turned back to the mobile phone. "What is this?" It was a small section of decorative paper. It looked old, or faded. Yellow edges with swirls of light blue in the middle.

"That," Jeanie Brady said, "is what ultimately killed Deirdre Walsh."

"I don't understand."

"Wallpaper," Jeanie Brady said. "Deirdre Walsh was killed by poison—best guess arsenic—on the back of a sample of wallpaper."

Jeanie Brady wanted to stop in front of Turn the Page. They stood in front of the bookshop as Jeanie cupped her hands and looked in the window.

"I can just imagine that new book smell," she said, inhaling as she stood back up.

"I can take you inside," Siobhán said. "We can pick up booties and gloves at the station."

"Another day," Jeanie said. "Your photos of the scene were very clear, and if we went in I would just want to poke my nose into books."

"Are you a big reader?"

"I like nonfiction. True crime is my favorite." She laughed. "I know, I know. You'd think I'd want a break from my work. But I eat it up. Especially when the rich and famous are up to no good. I'm a little addict."

"I'm afraid you won't find any true crime books in there yet," Siobhán said. "They only sell literary fiction and history."

Jeanie scrunched her nose. "What kind of nonsense is that?"

"Oran McCarthy is very particular about his literature."

"That can't be good for business," Jeanie said, as they turned to head to the garda station. "Not that I don't appreciate good literature."

"Please," Siobhán said, as they passed King John's Castle. "I need to know more about this wallpaper."

"You and me both," Jeanie Brady said. "The book pages in her mouth hid it from view, but this little sample of wallpaper was found in her mouth underneath the tongue. If she was too groggy to respond, this was a very efficient place for the poison to quickly circulate through the bloodstream."

"Arsenic," Siobhán said. "In wallpaper."

"Arsenic is quick," Jeanie said. "Death within minutes. Sedating her first so she can't scream while the poison is delivered through the mouth makes sense. The gloves, the injection mark, and the wallpaper, as well as reports that no one heard her scream, all paints a sinister picture."

"Tells a story," Siobhán said, mostly to herself.

"Indeed," Jeanie said. "Indeed, it does."

"That means our killer needed to get his hands on a hypodermic needle, wallpaper, and arsenic," Siobhán said.

"I wish I could say that wasn't easy to do. But one can get almost anything on the Internet these days and I'm not even talking about the Dark Web. The *Guardian* newspaper proved this once by purchasing antique fly-paper infused with between two hundred and four hundred milligrams of arsenic from eBay."

"My word," Siobhán said as a shiver ran through her. Mankind was, and probably always would be, made up of light and dark. When they reached the front of the garda station they came to a stop. Jeanie's gaze stayed on the bookshop across the way. The sun was peeking out from beneath dark clouds. A brief respite from the rain. If it stayed out long enough, there would be rainbows. It was a good metaphor to cling to in dark times. After the dark, the sun will shine, and in between there will be rainbows.

"Let's talk about the items found near Deirdre's body," Jeanie said. "The umbrella, biro, and a red rose."

"Yes," Siobhán said. "We don't know whether Deirdre dropped them, or the killer planted them."

"I didn't always read true crime," Jeanie said. "I started with mysteries."

Another big reader. Siobhán was feeling like the lone one out. She was really going to have to rectify that. "Okay."

"Here's what comes to mind with the items." Jeanie counted off on her fingers. "First, the rose. Umberto Eco's *The Name of the Rose*." She held up a second finger. "Poisoned pens are a popular trope in many murder mysteries, and of course, most intriguing of all is the umbrella." She held up the third finger.

"The umbrella?" Siobhán said. "I would have thought it was the least intriguing. There was after all a big storm that day."

When Jeanie Brady turned to her, her eyes conveyed her excitement. "Have you ever heard of the Bulgarian umbrella?"

"No," Siobhán said. "Is it better in the wind?"

Jeanie laughed, then frowned, and wagged her finger. "Tis a good thing there's a bookshop in town. You can brush up on your reading."

Had Jeanie Brady not just given her a lovely bar of chocolate, she would have been tempted to knock her about with a brellie if she had one on her. "I can run home and Google it, which I've been doing way too much lately, or you could save me a bit of time and enlighten me."

"Indeed, I will. Twas developed by the Bulgarian Secret Service and perhaps assisted by the KGB. During the time of the Cold War, mind ya. Was only used as an assassination tool twice, I believe."

"Assassination tool? Did they knock someone over the head?"

Jeanie Brady sighed, her disapproval evident. "The pointy end had a hidden mechanism. Containing a tiny pellet of ricin." Siobhán felt a shiver run through her. "All the killer had to do was walk by, poke the victim right quick, and rush away." Jeanie acted it out for her, so immersed in her role as assassin that Siobhán was suddenly grateful the woman had been drawn to the good side of crime.

If the umbrella was the murder weapon, Deirdre could have been stabbed in the dark when no one was watching. "You'll want to test the tip of the umbrella for poison then, as well."

"I can have a look," Jeanie said, waving it off. "However, my initial guess, given the sedative and poison wallpaper did the job, is that the objects are more of a message. A story the killer is painting. *Showmanship.*"

"I've thought that all along," Siobhán said. "Our killer is very creative." This murder had been meticulously crafted. Siobhán doubted very much that the killer had accidentally killed the wrong victim. No. Deirdre Walsh was the intended target. Was Nessa Lamb the mastermind? Trying to throw Siobhán off the trail by suggesting the killer was after her?

"Let's go collect our evidence," Jeanie said, nodding at Siobhán as she held the door to the garda station open. "And I hear you have a new garda. I'd very much like to meet her."

Garda Dabiri and Jeanie Brady got on like a house on fire. They chattered away before the three of them sat in an interview room where they could spread out the contents of the interior-decorating folder organized by Padraig along with photos of the crime scene.

"They have good taste," Jeanie said as they separated the samples and photos of the bookshop.

"Wait until you actually step inside the shop," Siobhán said. "It's gorgeous."

Jeanie leaned closer to the photographs. "I don't see any wallpaper."

"No," Siobhán said. "Just samples in the folder. The walls have all been painted."

"Did the space have wallpaper previously?"

"That is a good question," Siobhán said. "I don't know."

Jeanie Brady pulled out the photo she'd e-mailed to the garda station of the wallpaper found in Deirdre's mouth. It was cream colored with blue swirls. It looked old and did not match any of Padraig's wallpaper samples.

"That sample looks familiar," Aretta said, tapping her forehead with her index finger. "But I can't quite place where I've seen it."

"Think about something else," Jeanie said. "It's the only way it will come to you."

"We have an interview scheduled for later this afternoon with the bookshop's landlord and the lads who built the secret door," Aretta said. "I can make a note for the guards to ask the landlord if he knows if the walls were previously wallpapered."

"Secret door?" Jeanie said.

Siobhán filled her in on the bookshelf that was actually a door to the back office. "Interesting," Jeanie said. "And *creative*."

Jeanie stretched. "I know there is more to go over, but I'm knackered and I need to go back to my room for a kip."

"You should just make it a good night's sleep," Siobhán said. She was feeling tired herself. Jeanie would also be attending to Margaret O'Shea's examination tomorrow. "Good work, everyone," she said. "We'll start fresh tomorrow."

They began to clear the table. Jeanie stood, reached into her handbag, and pulled out a hardback book. "I'm only disappointed I won't be able to get this signed." Siobhán caught the name Michael O'Mara on the spine.

"It's his very first," Jeanie said.

"I thought you only read true crime," Siobhán teased.

"I thought Michael O'Mara might be here," Jeanie said with a sigh. "My nephew is a fan." They left the interview room and headed for the exit.

"Are you staying at the Kilbane Inn?" Siobhán asked.

"No, I've taken a room above the comic book shop." Chris Gordon had rooms above his shop and often rented them out. Siobhán still hadn't had a good chat with him. His interview was scheduled for tomorrow.

"I'll walk you," she said.

"I'm heading that way too," Aretta said. "May I join?"

"Of course," Siobhán said. The rain was back, spitting on them as they made the short trek to the comic book shop.

"I've never seen that edition of a Michael O'Mara book," Aretta said, pointing to the one Jeanie held under her umbrella, trying to keep it dry.

"It's a first edition," Jeanie said.

"May I see it?" Aretta asked. Jeanie nudged close and handed it over. Aretta waited until they reached the overhang of the comic book shop, backed up against the wall, then gently opened the book. Moments later she gasped. Jeanie Brady leaned in.

"What is it?" Siobhán asked.

"In his latest books, Michael O'Mara does not have an

author photo. And I've been looking everywhere online. All I could find is a black and white photograph from when he was young. I was curious because someone mentioned he had a beard. And *look*."

Aretta turned the book around. The author photo was in color. He stood in front of a farmer's field, a big grin on his face. He was a burly man with a long red beard.

Chapter 22

"I don't understand what you two are so worked up about," Jeanie said, growing frustrated at being left out.

"We've had a lurker in town," Siobhán said. "A burly man with a red beard spotted going through rubbish bins."

"It's possible he was in town earlier," Aretta said. "Just as the visiting authors got into town."

"Wait," Jeanie said, taking her book back. "Are you saying Michael O'Mara—this Michael O'Mara came to Kilbane just to murder an unknown author?"

"Perhaps he felt threatened that Darren was about to sign a new author and came to see his agent," Siobhán said.

"Why would Michael O'Mara be threatened by an aspiring author?" Jeanie persisted.

"I've heard rumors that his problems with alcohol have been escalating," Siobhán said. "But if he is in town, I agree—as of yet—we don't have a valid explanation."

"Good luck with that," Jeanie said. "That's why I prefer working with the deceased."

"We need to talk to Darren again." Siobhán turned to Aretta. "Can you schedule him for a second interview tomorrow? Let's bring him into the interrogation room this time."

"Should I check with the Detective Sergeant?" Aretta asked.

"No," Siobhán said. "I'll let him know." Aretta looked as if this might not be the best plan, but she demurred. "Good work," Siobhán added. Aretta Dabiri viewed Siobhán as overstepping. It was becoming clear. Hopefully trust would build between them eventually. Aretta parted with them when they reached Gordon's Comics.

"She's lovely," Jeanie said.

"Yes," Siobhán agreed. "We're lucky to have her."

"Why would Michael O'Mara be digging through rubbish?" Jeanie asked before they entered the comic shop.

"That's an excellent question."

"Well, this is certainly an interesting twist," Jeanie Brady said. "If he is in town, maybe I'll finally get an autograph."

Chris Gordon was shelving comics when they walked in. He smiled at Jeanie Brady. "How is your room?"

"Excellent," she said. "I'm looking forward to a deep sleep."

He glanced at a large clock on the wall. It depicted Superman hanging off the hands. It was only half six. "This early?"

"It's been a long day," Jeanie said with a salute. "Good night."

"Night," Siobhán and Chris Gordon replied. He tucked his head back into the box of comics, while Siobhán stood watching him. After a few seconds, he stood and turned to her.

"Okay, okay," he said. "I'm sure Eoin told you I was upset about the bookshop opening."

"He did." She pretended to search her memory. "Something about you threatening to sue?"

"Stop looking at me like that. Once I met Oran and Padraig I was totally fine with it."

"Oh? When was that?"

"They came over at nine a.m. the morning they opened."

"You're not awake at nine a.m."

"I was that morning. I wanted to see for myself if anyone was going into the shop."

That sounded genuine. "Got an eyeful, did ya?"

He shrugged. "I was hoping some of the crowd would come in after."

"Did they?"

"Just a few."

"A few is more than none." He shrugged again. "What did Oran and Padraig say to make you suddenly like them?"

"They said they'd be willing to keep postcards advertising my shop at their counter, if I kept theirs on mine." He walked over to the counter and held up a business

card. It depicted the front of the bookshop with the title:
TURN THE PAGE.

Siobhán wandered over to the counter and took one for
herself. "Tanks."

"Are they going to close down now?"

"I hope not," Siobhán said. *Unless one of them is a
killer*. She left that part out in case Chris was looking to
start rumors.

"Why am I being asked to come into the station?"
Chris asked as she headed to the door.

"Because you felt threatened by the bookshop."

"You think I murdered someone just to shut them
down?"

"Did you?"

"Of course not. Siobhán. You know me."

"I'm just doing my job."

"That's finc. Just tell me. Tell me you know I didn't do
this."

"Just tell the truth and you'll be grand."

He sighed. "There's more drama in this village than in
these comics."

Siobhán laughed. "I certainly hope there's less." Once
again, she was almost to the door when he called out to
her.

"Hcy," he said. "Who's the new guy in town?"

She felt a prickle up her spine. "New guy?" she asked
innocently.

Chris nodded. "The big one with the red beard."

Later that evening, Siobhán settled in the dining room
in front of the fire, snuggled up with a mug of tea and her

laptop. She'd assigned Chris Gordon the task of writing down every spotting he'd had of the mysterious man with the red beard. As much as she was dying to hear the details, she wanted them on the record, and she wanted Macdara to hear them firsthand. But that didn't mean she couldn't do a little research of her own. She Googled Michael O'Mara. As Aretta had mentioned, the only author photo she could find of Michael O'Mara was in black and white, and in it, he was a young man. Jeanie Brady must indeed have a rare edition of his book. He lived on Bere Island and was known to be reclusive. Located off the Beara Peninsula, in County Cork, Bere Island had a population of around 220 people. In some ways that seemed perfect for a recluse, but it also meant that the small number of people probably knew everything about Michael O'Mara. It was no surprise that rumors swirled of his drunken escapades.

She pushed the CONTACT tab out of curiosity. There was a public relations firm in charge of handling his messages. Siobhán's mind filtered back to Deirdre's claim that her new book was explosive. A tell-all. Was it a stretch to wonder if she had something on Michael O'Mara? That certainly would have brought him to town. But why was he seen rummaging through rubbish bins? It was probably someone else. She was eager to hear what Darren Kilroy had to say. She would also let Nessa Lamb know that she had never been the target of murder. Would it calm her down? Or did she already know that because she was the killer? And then of course they had Leigh Coakley and Lorcan Murphy to consider. But unless they uncovered a motive, at this point it was anybody's guess as to which one of them was a calculated killer.

* * *

Darren Kilroy looked more relaxed than he had at their previous meetings, despite the fact that he was seated in Interrogation Room #1 in front of Macdara and Siobhán. He was dressed casually, in trousers and a work shirt, but no bow tie or blazer, or bright colors. "Does Michael O'Mara have a red beard?" Siobhán asked.

He cocked his head, as if amused at the question. "He does."

"Is he a big burly man?" Macdara asked.

"He is."

"Could you think of any reason he might be in town?" Macdara continued.

"In town?" Darren frowned. "You mean . . . here?"

"Yes," Siobhán and Macdara said in unison.

"If he's in town, I'd be the last to know," Darren said. "Michael O'Mara hasn't left Bere Island in years."

"Do you visit him there?" Siobhán asked.

"Not even once," Darren said. "Movies and telly love to show agents and authors having face-to-face meetings. When he's in Dublin we meet for dinner alright, but that hasn't happened in years. All of our correspondence is through e-mail or on the phone."

"We hear he's been on a decline the past few years, as far as drinking is concerned," Macdara said.

Darren sat back and crossed his arms. "What's the story here, lads? Why are you asking me about Michael O'Mara?"

"We believe he's in Kilbane," Siobhán said. "He may have even been here when Deirdre was killed."

He uncrossed his arms and placed his hands on the

table as if he was about to push off. "You can't be serious."

"We are," Macdara said. "We never joke about murder."

"Why on earth would Michael O'Mara . . ." He stopped midsentence. "No," he said. "It can't be him."

"What were you thinking just now?" Siobhán asked.

"Let me call Michael," Darren said. "I'm assuming he'll tell me he hasn't budged from the island, and you can bet some of the locals will be able to back him up, and we can stop going down this rabbit hole."

"I'd still like to know what crossed your mind just then," Siobhán said.

"Me too," Macdara said. "Indulge us."

"It's crossed my mind lately that Deirdre had a lover. Someone she was trying to keep on the down-low. But it can't possibly be Michael. Can it?"

"First, what made you think she had a lover?"

"It was at the inn, the day we arrived," Darren said. "She was outside talking to someone on the phone. I passed her as I was going to the ice maker." He looked to the right as if trying to recall the memory. "I don't think it was what she said, but the way she was saying it. A flirtatious tone. She said, 'I miss you.' That's it."

"She has a brother," Siobhán said.

"Believe me, this wasn't a tone you'd take with a brother."

Siobhán glanced down at her notes. Aretta had scoured Deirdre's social media. There was no mention of a boyfriend, her status was set to single, and none of her photos showed off any romances. But she had been a beautiful woman. And successful enough, even if she wanted more. It seemed within the realm of possibility. What if she did have an affair with the mysterious author and had planned to spill secrets about him in her explosive new tell-all? And what if he found out? "If Michael O'Mara hasn't left Bere Island in years, how would the two of them have met?"

"That's what I'm telling you. It's not possible." He took out his phone. "May I call him? See if we can put this to bed?"

"Why don't you put him on speakerphone," Macdara said.

"I can't do that," Darren said. "He'd go mental. He's my client and a man who values his privacy above most everything else."

In that case, would he murder someone if he or she threatened to divulge all his secrets? Someone like Deirdre Walsh?

"We'll wait, then," Siobhán said. "You can place your call in Interview Room Two."

"I was thinking I'd take it outside."

"Go on, so," Macdara said.

"He usually doesn't answer," Darren said. "But I'll make sure to let him know to call me back."

"We're also going to need his phone number," Siobhán said.

"Why?"

"People lie," she said. "Mobile towers don't."

"I'm going to need some kind of official request in that case," Darren said. "This is my reputation on the line." He hurried out.

Macdara turned to her. "What do you think?"

"I think we need to find out if Deirdre Walsh has ever been to Bere Island."

"When was the last sighting of this lurker?" Macdara asked.

"The morning after the murder," Siobhán said. "According to Leigh and Chris Gordon."

"And since?"

"Not a word."

Darren Kilroy appeared at the door. "I left a very urgent message. Hopefully he'll phone me back."

"What brand of cigarettes does Michael O'Mara smoke?" Macdara asked. Siobhán knew that Macdara didn't know if the man smoked at all, so he was taking a risk.

"Benson and Hedges," Darren said without hesitation. He then looked stricken, as if he'd said something he shouldn't have. "But that's a very common brand."

They didn't have results on the cigarette butts found under Deirdre's window or in the alley behind the bookshop, but the unopened pack of cigarettes found on the back of the commode in Deirdre's room had been Benson and Hedges.

"Did you ever see Deirdre smoke?"

"Deirdre Walsh?" Darren frowned. "No. But I must repeat. I did not know her that well. But the times I did run into her, no, I never saw her smoke, nor did I ever smell it off her."

"Benson and Hedges," he said when Darren took his leave. "It indeed looks as if Michael O'Mara either was or is in town."

"And whether or not they were lovers, it seems he has

some connection to Deirdre," Siobhán added. "Do you believe that Darren didn't know he was in town?"

"If he was secretly carrying on with Deirdre, it's possible," Macdara said. "I'll call the gardaí that handle Bere Island, see if I can learn anything more about Mr. O'Mara's whereabouts." They stood and stretched their legs. Macdara glanced at the clock on the wall. "I have the meeting with the landlord and the lads who built the bookshelf in the morning. We'll have to find out if any of them smoke Benson and Hedges as well."

"And ask them about wallpaper," Siobhán said. She had already filled him in on Jeanie's surprising findings.

"I wish I could get a warrant to search all of our suspects' rooms," Macdara said. "I wonder where the killer stashed the needle he used to sedate Deirdre."

"For all we know the killer threw it in the river. A needle in a haystack is one thing, but a needle in a village . . ."

"You're right, you're right. Wallpaper. Arsenic. There's something old-fashioned about that."

"Not to mention the umbrella, rose, and pen," Siobhán said. "I think Jeanie Brady is right. I think the killer was telling a story."

"Where does Margaret O'Shea fit into this story?" Macdara asked.

"I wish I knew. I'll be eager to see what Jeanie finds. Either she was at the wrong place at the wrong time—and could have identified Deirdre's killer—or she just happened to pick that morning to venture out on her own, and it was too much for her poor heart to handle."

"We're also going to need a sample of Michael O'Mara's DNA," Macdara replied with a sigh. "Now, why do I get the feeling that's easier said than done?"

"If Deirdre and O'Mara were romantically involved, that might explain why her mobile phone was taken," Siobhán said. "Perhaps she had photos of the two of them on it." A thought suddenly struck her. "The rubbish bins at Gordon's Comics," she said. "What if Michael O'Mara wasn't going through them—what if he was dropping something into them?"

Chapter 23

"Save the rubbish?" Chris Gordon said. "Of course I didn't."

"After you saw the burly man going through the bins, did you look in the bins?" Macdara asked.

"You two have an odd idea of me," Chris said. "No, I did not."

"Those bins would have been picked up that evening," Siobhán said. "If he put something in them, it's long gone." Secretly, she was a bit relieved. Going through rubbish bins was her least favorite part of the job.

"What do you think he left in there?" Chris studied them and Siobhán watched his eyes widen. "You think he's the killer?"

"You don't know what we think," Siobhán said. "And it's not your place to try and figure it out."

"I heard she was poisoned," Chris said. "Do you think he left poison in my bins?"

"Don't believe everything you hear," Macdara said. "We'll need to look at the images from your security camera."

"How do you know I have a security camera?" Chris asked.

Outside, above the door to the shop, Chris Gordon had installed a plastic Spiderman. He crouched above the entrance, as if waiting to pounce on the next soul coming through the door. "Because that thing's eyes follow me wherever I go," Macdara said, gesturing to the door.

Chris nodded, then grinned, until he caught Macdara's disapproving look and the smile vanished straight away. "Do you want to see them on my screens, or do you want me to send you a digital file?"

"Let's have a look, and see," Macdara said.

Chris nodded. "Follow me." He led them to a back room. It was basically an oversize closet, but Chris had filled it with large screens. Series and movies based on Marvel and DC Comics played on several screens. Another, the largest of them all, showed the footpath in front of the shop.

"My word," Siobhán said. "Is this live?"

"It is," Chris said. "State of the art."

And very stalkerish, but that was a discussion for another day, so Siobhán kept her piehole shut. On the screen they could see her neighbors Sheila and Pio Mahoney walking past, holding bags from Mike's Fruit and Veg Market. They appeared to be arguing. Siobhán caught Macdara's gaze. *This is creepy*, she thought, wondering if he thought the same. But right now, she was grateful for it.

"I'm not spying on people," Chris said as if he could

read her mind. "I'm trying out different window dressings to see which ones make the most customers enter the shop. It's not like anyone is doing anything personal as they pass by."

She supposed he had a point there. "Can you rewind to the morning the bookshop opened?" Siobhán said. "And let us have the room?"

"Would you like tea and scones too?" Chris said with a heavy dose of sarcasm.

"That would be lovely," Siobhán said with a grin. "You're a regular superhero."

In general, watching CCTV cameras was about as exciting as watching paint dry. That is until it wasn't. After a long period of nothing, suddenly Lorcan Murphy and Nessa Lamb came into view on the screen. The surprising bit was that Lorcan had his arm looped over Nessa's shoulders.

"I didn't know they were so close," Siobhán said.

Macdara shifted uncomfortably next to her. "I bet his wife doesn't either."

She'd forgotten. Lorcan Murphy was married with young ones at home. "Maybe they're just good friends." Just then, Lorcan and Nessa stopped, looked into each other's eyes, and kissed.

Macdara groaned. "You'd better not have any friends like that."

Siobhán gave him a soft kick and turned back to the screen. "Is it possible they're in this together?"

"That's quite a jump, isn't it? Shifting to murder?"

"As you've stated, that's not an innocent kiss. I think we can safely assume they're having an affair. Given we have a rather small suspect pool and one of them did it, I'd say it's actually an easy jump."

"What's the motive?"

"Maybe Deirdre knew about their affair? Maybe that's what she meant by her memoir being explosive."

Macdara groaned again, and rubbed his face. "Lorcan does make a nice little living from those elf books. I bet the missus would try and take him for everything if she found out about this."

"And if Nessa Lamb is plagiarizing her works—or she has a ghostwriter—and Deirdre was about to spill that news, then perhaps they teamed up to take down the enemy." Once Lorcan and Nessa were out of view from the screen, there was another long period of not much happening, other than townsfolk passing by on their way to or from somewhere else. Siobhán was about to end the video stream when something strange appeared. A figure, dressed all in black, streaked by carrying a large brown sack. "Did you see that?" She turned to Macdara, who was in the middle of a yawn.

"See what?"

"Stay awake, cowboy. You're going to want to see this."

They'd watched the clip five times. "Who in the world is that?" Macdara asked. "He looks like someone right out of one of Chris Gordon's comics."

"I know one thing," Siobhán said. "It's not Michael O'Mara." The figure was average size, and slim. "Let's get this video evidence to the station. You have the interview with the landlord and the construction lads."

"I'm going to need coffee," Macdara said. "Let's hit the shop first."

"Chocolate and crisps as well," Siobhán said.

As they arrived at the garda station, hands filled with caffeine and sugar, Aretta approached them, thrumming with energy.

"I have solved a part of this mystery," she said. Siobhán handed her a cup of herbal tea. Aretta peeked under the lid, then inhaled. "How did you know?"

"She observes," Macdara said with a chuckle. "What do you have for us?"

"I can show you," Aretta said. After dropping their goodies off at their desks, they followed her all the way back to the evidence room where Aretta led them to the shelf containing the items picked up from the bookshop. They all put gloves on from a container on the shelf, and Aretta picked up the evidence bag containing the umbrella. "Here." She pointed to the handle. There, in gold, were the initials *LM*.

"Lorcan Murphy," Siobhán said. "When it rains, it pours."

"Good work," Macdara said to Aretta. "Will you schedule a meeting with Lorcan Murphy and Nessa Lamb? And we'll place them in separate interrogation rooms. But keep the shade open when they're first seated so they can see each other." There was a window between interrogation rooms one and two. It was used for this exact purpose, letting witnesses get a glimpse of each other before the dark shade came down. It encouraged truth-telling as each worried about what the other might say.

"Is there news on Nessa Lamb?" Aretta asked.

"We caught them shifting on CCTV footage," Siobhán said.

"I take it, it wasn't a peck on the cheek," Aretta said.

"It definitely was not," Siobhán agreed.

"That is an interesting development," Aretta said. "People forget that we now live in a world where there are eyes everywhere."

The Hills Have Eyes. The title popped into Siobhán's mind. Was that what the note was referring to? Was Deirdre tipping them off that she knew about their affair?

"One more thing. The figure in black with the satchel you saw on Chris Gordon's tape?"

"Yes," Siobhán said.

"I know who that is."

"You do?" Shock was evident in Siobhán's voice.

"Why didn't you mention this before?" Macdara demanded.

"I think it's best I let you experience it for yourself," Aretta said. "Tonight. At the ladies' book club meet." She calmly stared at them. "I understand you prefer I just tell you, but believe me, I cannot think of a better way. And the meeting is tomorrow afternoon, so there really isn't long to wait."

"I'll go," Siobhán said. "Where are they meeting?"

"Since the authors have been staying at the inn, the book club has met there. The twins let us use their back garden." She hesitated. "Or inside the twins' cottage if it rains."

It felt as if it would never stop raining. "Looks like I'm joining the ladies' book club after all," Siobhán said.

"Try not to fall asleep," Macdara said. "Now let's turn our attention to Lorcan and Nessa's interview. I have an idea."

* * *

Unlike their earlier chats with Lorcan Murphy and Nessa Lamb, this time the pair appeared nervous to be officially summoned into the station. *Good.* Aretta followed their request to lead them to Interview Rooms #1 and #2 and she waited until they made eye contact through the window before pulling down the shade.

"You're making me a bit nervous," Lorcan said with a laugh. "I suddenly know how the poor elf on the shelf must feel."

"The original one, or the ones you kill off?" Siobhán couldn't help but ask.

More nervous laughter spilled out of him. "I've been a naughty boy, have I?"

"You tell me." She hadn't meant for the conversation to start so soon, so she shut her gob and placed the recording device in the middle of the table. He looked at it, and began to nibble on his lower lip.

"We'll be back in a moment," Siobhán said. "Can I get you anything?"

"Do you mean like a solicitor?" Lorcan asked.

"Do you need a solicitor?" Siobhán asked, treating him to a pleasant smile.

"How would I know?" he asked with forced cheer.

She leaned in. "Have you broken any laws?" He shook his head. "Do you intend to lie?" Another shake. "You'll be grand."

"I don't have anything to hide." He grinned, but his complexion had paled.

"Wonderful. Coffee? Tea? Water?"

"Water. Thank you."

"Sit tight." Siobhán exited, making sure he heard the slam of the door behind her.

Siobhán and Aretta entered Nessa's interview room. Nessa was in a chair, hands under her thighs, rocking back and forth. "Are you well?" Siobhán asked.

Nessa stopped rocking. "Fine," she said.

"Would you like a cup of tea?"

"No, thank you."

"Water? Coffee?" Nessa shook her head. "Would you like to call a solicitor?"

At this she stopped rocking. "Is that really necessary?"

"I'm required to ask." She gave a nod toward Lorcan's interview room. "Some folks prefer to have one present."

"Lorcan asked for one?"

"I'm afraid I could never tell you that."

"Water, please," Nessa said.

Siobhán placed a recording device on the table in front of her. "We'll return shortly," she said. They exited, also letting the door slam shut.

"They look very guilty," Aretta said.

"They do," Siobhán agreed. "Of something. It will be our job to figure out what."

Macdara was waiting for them in the hall. "Neither has officially requested representation," Siobhán informed him.

"Good. I'm off to meet with the landlord of the bookshop." He gestured to the interview rooms. "The pair of ye can do the honors." He nodded to Aretta. There were nods all around and then Macdara headed for the exit.

Siobhán turned to Aretta. "Ready to combine work with working out?" she said.

Aretta nodded and glanced between the rooms. "I will follow your lead."

"I'd also like you to stand by the door," Siobhán said.

"One sitting, one standing. It keeps a subject off kilter," Aretta said.

"Indeed it can," Siobhán said. "Ready?"

Aretta grinned. "I am more than ready."

Lorcan Murphy raised his eyebrow, then glanced at Aretta, who stood by the door, before focusing on Siobhán. "My relationship with my wife?" he asked. "What does that have to do with your investigation?" His voice squeaked. He looked to the dark window. "Is Detective Sergeant Flannery going to join us?"

"No," Siobhán said. "Please answer the question."

"We're fine," he said. "Happily married." He shrugged and tried to pull off a smile.

"Lorcan and his wife are getting a divorce," Nessa said. "I'm sure he's just told you the same thing." She made swirls on the table with her index finger. "It's the reason he's stopped writing."

Siobhán tilted her head. "I wasn't aware that he stopped writing."

"It's temporary," Nessa said. "Until the divorce is finalized."

"Because he's heartbroken?" Aretta asked.

"No. Because he doesn't want her to get any more of his royalties."

* * *

"It wasn't really a lie. I just didn't see how it pertained to your investigation. I still don't. But yes. If you must know, my wife and I are getting a divorce."

Siobhán took her time glaring at him, in case he thought about lying again. "And you've stopped writing because of it?"

Lorcan's gaze flicked to the window as if he couldn't believe Nessa was tattling. He slumped in his chair and nodded. "It's bad enough me future agent will get ten percent."

"Does Darren Kilroy know that if he signs you he'll have to wait until after your divorce is final to receive a book?"

"No. But it wouldn't matter if he did." Lorcan Murphy relaxed in his seat.

There was something to his tone. Siobhán leaned in. "Why is that?"

"It's true," Nessa said after glaring at the shade between the rooms. "Darren Kilroy was going to sign me all along."

"You sound confident."

Her eyes flicked to Aretta, then back to Siobhán. "What did he tell you?"

Siobhán gave Aretta a knowing look. "What do you think he told us?" Her tone suggested he had spilled a juicy secret.

Nessa looked to Aretta again. "Is this normal procedure? One question for me, one for Lorcan, with the pair of ye running back and forth?"

"There's no crying in the baseball. According to American movies anyway," Siobhán said, tossing the comment to Aretta, standing by the door.

"What?" Nessa said.

"I do not know much about the baseball," Aretta said. "Why would they cry?"

"I know nothing about the baseball either," Siobhán said. "They run around a diamond or some such. Personally, I think they should run *for* diamonds. Now that I would watch."

"That would be interesting," Aretta said. "I would watch that. Unless they are blood diamonds. I would not watch if they were blood diamonds."

"Nor I," Siobhán said.

Nessa's head bounced between them as they jabbered. Siobhán cleared her throat, getting Nessa's attention. "Despite not understanding the baseball, what diamonds have to do with it, or why they would cry in the first place, let's take Tom Hanks's word for it, shall we? There's no crying in the baseball."

"No crying in the baseball," Aretta echoed.

"I don't think it's *the* baseball," Nessa said. "I think it's just *baseball*." She folded her arms across her chest.

"But I do know murder inquiries," Siobhán continued. "And there's no normal in murder inquiries." Siobhán looked to Aretta once again. "Would you agree?"

"I would very much agree," Aretta said. "Nothing has been normal since I arrived at the Kilbane Garda Station."

"Now," Siobhán said. She turned her gaze on Nessa and did not let up.

Nessa finally exhaled and placed her hands on the

table. "Darren Kilroy was never going to sign Lorcan Murphy because he has already signed me."

A tingle started at the base of Siobhán's spine. She felt Aretta stand up straighter. "When did he sign you?" Siobhán asked.

"The morning we arrived," Nessa said. "We all met for breakfast. Afterward, he and I had a private meeting, and he officially offered to represent me."

The morning they arrived. He wasn't supposed to decide until the week was up. But if what Nessa was saying was true . . . Siobhán stood up and began to pace as she thought through it. Darren Kilroy signed Nessa Lamb that first morning. Did Deirdre Walsh learn of this? Did she then start a rumor that Nessa was plagiarizing or that Nessa had a ghostwriter? And if so . . . what did it mean? Did Nessa Lamb kill Deirdre Walsh to protect her career? Was Margaret O'Shea a witness to the whole sordid mess?

"Where were the two of you when Darren said he wanted to sign you?"

"At the inn," Nessa said.

"Where at the inn?" Siobhán persisted. *Close to Margaret O'Shea's room?*

"There's a picnic table in the courtyard," Nessa said. "We met there, he offered me a contract, and we had a verbal agreement."

A verbal agreement. Someone may have thought there was an opportunity to change Darren's mind. "Have you received the written contract?"

"He e-mailed it later that day. I'm waiting to have an entertainment lawyer look it over before I sign it." She paused. "And to be honest . . ."

"Yes?"

"Since this whole murder business I've been thinking it over. I don't know if I want to sign with Darren Kilroy now. What if it doesn't look good? What if everyone thinks I'm a murderer? What if *he's* a murderer?" She shook her head. "It's all ruined. Deirdre's death ruined everything."

"Breakfast the first morning?" Lorcan said. "Yes. The twins have a back garden with a picnic table. It was a grand, fresh morning." He stopped. "Why do you ask?"

Out in the hall, Aretta put her arm on Siobhán. "Are we going to need a third interview room for Darren Kilroy?"

Siobhán considered it, then shook her head. "It would start to feel like a circus."

"It doesn't already?"

"It appears to be working."

"Oddly, it does." Aretta held up a finger. "By the way, a baseball field is in the shape of a diamond."

"Pity," Siobhán said. "I'd much rather they played with real diamonds." She winked and Aretta laughed. It was the kind of laughter that filled the room.

"I like the Yankees," Aretta said.

"My brother Eoin used to wear a Yankees cap all day long," Siobhán replied. She left it at that. If a romance was going to develop, it would occur without any shoves from her. She also hadn't decided how she felt about it. Romance and work were such messy partners. Then again, she was hardly in any position to judge. "And don't worry," she said. "Because we are definitely going to have another chat with Mr. Darren Kilroy." But for now, they weren't quite finished with the pair they already had at the station. "Ready?" she asked Aretta.

"Or not—here I come," Aretta answered.

Chapter 24

"Darren Kilroy wasn't supposed to choose an author until the end of the week," Siobhán said. Nessa Lamb's hair was sticking to the side of her face. She started combing it back with trembling fingers. "Why would he sign you the very first morning?"

Nessa stopped messing with her hair and looked at her fingernails. "I may have told him that I was going to sign with another agent."

"Were you?"

She nodded. "I've had multiple offers since the Forty under Forty article. It wasn't a lie."

"But it was a manipulation."

"No. I was being open and honest."

"Did you mention this to him in front of Lorcan and Deirdre?"

"Of course not."

"Not that open and honest," Aretta piped in.

"Deirdre Walsh didn't have a chance. She has no book sales to speak of. No track record as a writer. And Lorcan Murphy's sales had slowed as well. There are only so many elves you can kill before everyone is sick to death of it." She barked out a laugh at her own pun, then stopped when she saw no one was laughing with her. She threw a guilty look to the shade. *Threw shade at the shade*, Siobhán thought. She pushed the pun away and focused on Nessa Lamb.

"Did Deirdre or Lorcan find out he had signed you?"

"No." Nessa looked as if she was about to say something else, but then stopped. Siobhán rose. Aretta opened the door. "Stop," Nessa said. "Please."

"Something wrong?" Siobhán asked, hovering over her.

"Back and forth, back and forth. You're making me dizzy!"

"I'm just having a hard time sitting still today," Siobhán said. "You're welcome to file a complaint with the Detective Sergeant."

"I only told Lorcan *after* Deirdre was murdered. Believe me. If Deirdre knew, I'd be the one who was dead."

Siobhán didn't leave but she remained at the door. "Why did Darren go through all of this then? Why pretend that everyone had an equal shot?"

"Oran and Padraig McCarthy. They go way back with Darren Kilroy. He did it to support their new bookshop." Nessa exhaled. "I assure you. I've told you the truth and nothing but. If anyone found out that Darren had signed me before the murder, they didn't find out from me."

"If one was standing in the courtyard of the inn while

you and Darren were discussing your representation, you don't think it's possible that someone overheard you?" Siobhán kept her voice light, but from the startled look on Nessa's face she'd driven the point home.

"It's possible," she said. "But then . . . why would that make someone kill Deirdre?"

"I don't know," Siobhán said. "Maybe Deirdre fought back. Maybe she started rumors." *Or maybe she told the truth.*

Nessa licked her lips. "What kind of rumors?"

"The kind that could ruin another author's career," Siobhán said. "The kind that kill."

"Yes," Lorcan said immediately, when the item was placed on the table in front of him. "That's my umbrella." He frowned. "Why is it in an evidence bag?"

"What did you do with it after you entered the bookshop that evening?"

He frowned, then looked up. "I carried it to my chair."

"And then?"

He shrugged. "I hung it on the back of the chair." He leaned in. "Did someone hit Deirdre over the head with me umbrella?" Siobhán, of course, did not answer. "Do you really think I would have remembered to take it with me after finding out Deirdre had been murdered, and you shouting at all of us to leave the bookshop?"

"I simply asked if it was yours," Siobhán said, keeping her cool, but imagining him as an elf that was about to get his.

"'Tis." He eyed the evidence bag. "But if it has anything to do with that poor woman's death, I never want to see it again."

"Tell me about the morning you accidentally entered Margaret O'Shea's room," Siobhán said.

Lorcan frowned again. "I don't know what there is to add. It was getting dark. I'd had a bit to drink, as did everyone else, in the back garden. And I opened the wrong door. Believe me. The lungs on that woman! I was the one it traumatized."

"Traumatized?"

He nodded. "You should have heard her giving out to me. Like I was actually trying to get into her room. It was humiliating." He rubbed his face. "Ask the woman who owns the flower shop."

Siobhán sat up straight. "Leigh Coakley?"

He nodded. "That's the one."

"What does Leigh have to do with anything?"

"After Margaret slammed the door in me face I whirled around and there she was, laughing at me." He squinted as if he was trying to see the memory. "What was it she said . . . ?" Siobhán wanted to know, so she left him room to work it out. "Something along the lines of . . . 'At least she's no longer focusing on me.'"

Siobhán and Aretta stood outside the garda station with mugs of tea, watching people wander in and out of the town square. There was a break room but Siobhán preferred being outdoors, taking in the fresh air. She was feeling thrown off by Lorcan's last comment about Leigh Coakley. It reminded her that Leigh was the one who had told Deirdre to *eat her words*. Now she'd been in some kind of argument with Margaret O'Shea the night before she died? Leigh had never mentioned anything of the sort to Siobhán. They were going to have to get to the bottom of it and the prospect didn't thrill her.

"I don't feel assured about Nessa Lamb," Aretta said. "Do you?"

"Pardon?"

"I do not feel assured that no one found out about her secret deal with Darren Kilroy."

"Neither do I. But, if Lorcan Murphy had learned earlier that Darren signed Nessa, and it inspired a murderous rage, wouldn't he have taken it out on Nessa? Or Darren Kilroy? Or Oran and Padraig for that matter? Anyone but Deirdre Walsh."

"Maybe Lorcan told Deirdre."

"And? Deirdre what? Staged her own death?"

"Maybe Deirdre began harassing either Nessa Lamb or Darren Kilroy, or Oran and Padraig for that matter," Aretta said. "And one of them took matters into his or her own hands."

"That's the right line of inquiry," Siobhán said.

"But?"

"But there's something about the planning of this that tells me the timeline you've just described is still too impulsive for this killer."

"Do you solve cases mostly on intuition?" Aretta had a blunt way of speaking, and her tone was friendly, but the question felt jarring. Did she?

Siobhán shook her head. "I back it up with evidence," she said. "And I try not to get too attached to any one theory early on."

"Including the theory that Nessa Lamb was the intended target?" Aretta asked.

"We don't have anything to suggest that Deirdre was a victim of mistaken identity."

"Nessa Lamb suggested it, did she not?"

"She did," Siobhán said. "The question is why."

"Either she's afraid a killer is after her, or she is the killer," Aretta said.

"Or she's protecting the killer," Siobhán added.

"Lorcan Murphy?"

"They are lovers." *Secret lovers.* And secrets could kill.

"If Deirdre was the intended victim," Aretta continued, "why wasn't she killed by nuts? Why did the killer use a sedative and arsenic instead?"

"An allergic reaction to nuts wouldn't have been quick or silent," Siobhán said. "Deirdre undoubtedly had an EpiPen in her handbag. People would have heard her gasping for breath. Our killer is smart enough to know that."

"But it's equally possible, isn't it, that she *wasn't* the intended victim?" Aretta paused, letting Siobhán ponder it. "It was after all, dark and confusing in there."

"And the killer only had seconds," Siobhán said. "Yes, it is possible. But I would not say it is *equally* possible." Her gut was not pointing toward mistaken identity. Maybe she did follow her gut. She could not teach this to Aretta, nor could she even completely defend it. And even though at first she felt prickly, having Aretta question her methods was good for her. She needed to keep open to all possibilities. And Aretta was intelligent and observant. They could learn from each other. But that didn't mean she was going to ignore her gut. And her gut insisted that the killer got his intended victim. Deirdre Walsh. Margaret O'Shea, on the other hand, was an outlier. Siobhán hoped Jeanie Brady would find hers a natural death. Otherwise, Siobhán had no idea what they were dealing with. But, in addition to finding a killer, as Guardians of the Peace their job was to make sure no one else lost their life. "I'll see if we can assign a garda to trail Nessa Lamb while she's here. Just in case."

"Looking forward to book club?" Macdara asked with a big smile. Siobhán stood in the door to Macdara's office, wishing she could squeeze his face until he stopped grinning.

"Can't wait," Siobhán said with her fingers crossed behind her back. The group would be discussing Nessa Lamb's *Musings on a Hill*. Siobhán had started it last night and fell asleep at page three. "I can't wait to learn if she ever gets off the hill."

Macdara laughed. "Any idea what Aretta wants you to see and what it has to do with the figure we saw on Chris Gordon's screen?" He stopped laughing. "I will regret giving her latitude if it turns out to be serious evidence in this case."

Siobhán nodded. She'd had the same thought. "I don't have a clue. What did you learn from the landlord or lads who built the secret door?"

"No wallpaper was ever on the walls. We've got one smoker in the group but Marlboro is their brand."

"Not Michael O'Mara's brand."

"Correct. And speaking of our possible lurker, one of them thinks he saw our lurker in the alley behind the bookshop."

"That's big news. When?"

"The day they were putting in the secret door."

"Before our authors even arrived."

"Correct." He pulled open a drawer and held up an evidence bag. "And one of the lads found this in the alley the other day. *After* the murder. They didn't realize it could be evidence." It appeared to be a small stick. Siobhán squinted and touched it. It was made of a hard metal.

"What is it?"

"An old-fashioned lock pick," Macdara said. "We tried it on the alley door to the bookshop. It works."

"That's huge."

He sighed. "It would have been had their paws not been all over it, not to mention the rain. But now we know how someone got into the back door. We just can't prove who, or when, or why."

"What did they say about this lurker?"

"Just that they saw him going through rubbish bins, and having a smoke."

What was it about this man and rubbish bins? Michael O'Mara was wealthy. It just didn't seem to fit the bill, unless it had something to do with drink. "Has Darren Kilroy heard back from Michael O'Mara?"

"As a matter of fact, Darren just called to tell me that Mr. O'Mara states he hasn't been off Bere Island for the past month."

"What about the gardaí responsible for Bere Island?"

"They said they don't keep that close of a watch on their citizens."

"Meaning they're not talking out of school."

"Correct."

"Are we just going to take Darren Kilroy's word for it?"

"Are you out of your mind?"

Siobhán knew that look in Macdara's eyes. "Are we going to Bere Island?"

"Does a bear—"

Siobhán held up her hand. "Enough said. When?"

"Can you clear your schedule tomorrow?"

Siobhán sighed. "I was hoping you'd say today."

"And have you miss book club?" His grin was back in full force. "Not a chance."

Chapter 25

As Siobhán stepped into the twins' sitting room, the wolfhounds greeted her first, then parted as if giving the floor to Emma and Eileen, seated behind them. Because the skies were spitting on them, the members of the book group were all huddled inside. The room consisted of a large yellow sofa, two turquoise armchairs, and four wooden chairs brought in from the kitchen table. Pastries covered the coffee table, and most of the members clutched steaming cups of tea. Siobhán hadn't thought to bring anything; she could have ingratiated herself with an offering of brown bread, but it was too late now. She hoped they wouldn't be thinking ill of her. *She works at a bistro this one and she can't even bring a dish to pass.* Aretta hadn't mentioned the food. Then again, Aretta probably wasn't eating the food.

Emma and Eileen each sat in one of the armchairs, legs curled in, a wolfhound by their side. Leigh Coakley and Nessa Lamb seemed the most startled to see Siobhán.

"Hang around after the discussion is finished," Aretta leaned in and whispered to Siobhán. "But don't let anyone see you."

"What?"

"The discussion will finish in an hour. Pretend to leave before it's finished."

Was she messing with her? Siobhán glanced around the sitting room. "Where would you have me go?"

"There's a covered trellis in the back garden. The ones who remain will be meeting underneath it. Perhaps you can find a tree to hide behind."

"Couldn't I have just skipped to that part?" Siobhán said, feeling a bit like she'd lost control.

"And miss the discussion?" Aretta said. "I assumed you were looking forward to it."

"Of course." Inwardly, Siobhán groaned. She hadn't brought the book either. She hoped she didn't get called on.

It was too warm in the sitting room. Between a mug of tea, a fire, and bodies gathered to read and discuss a book Siobhán had barely read, she didn't realize she had drifted off to sleep until she felt a poke in her side.

"Loved that part," she said reflexively, eyes popping open.

Mouths dropped open. "You did?" Leigh Coakley asked.

"Loved it," she repeated. "I think it was my favorite."

There, she sounded convincing. Why was everyone looking at her like that?

"I think what Garda O'Sullivan means is she loved the way Nessa Lamb spoke about the horrific abuse with such raw honesty."

Horrific abuse? She'd just said she loved the horrific abuse? Siobhán went to reach for a pastry to shove in her gob but they were all gone. *Savages*. Perhaps because they'd expected the woman from the bistro to bring more. At least then, maybe they'd have forgiven her for loving passages filled with horrific abuse. Apparently, the novel wasn't about a hill at all. "Indeed," Siobhán said. "Thank you, Garda Dabiri. It was the raw honesty that really got to me." She wanted to manufacture some tears to make up for her faux pas, but her eyes remained dry.

Never. Ever. Again. She would read books. Alone. Like a normal person. Like books were meant to be read. Otherwise they would be on telly.

"It's understandable if you fell asleep," Nessa said. "You've expended quite a bit of energy lately trying to get me to confess to murder."

"Murder?" Leigh said. "Our little Lamb?"

"Nessa is neither meek nor mild," Siobhán said. "As that outburst just proved."

"I'm also innocent," Nessa said. "And the more time you spend questioning me, the more danger we're all in." Tension filled the room. Even the wolfhounds were staring at Siobhán. Were they the ones who had snatched the last of the pastries? She wouldn't put it past the hounds.

"The sooner we eliminate suspects, the quicker we'll solve the case," Siobhán said.

"We were all there that night," Leigh Coakley said. Heads nodded en masse. "Are we all equally suspects?"

"Yes," Siobhán said. "And since you've brought up the subject, I'd like to ask you about the argument you had with Margaret O'Shea the night before she died."

Leigh gasped and her teacup rattled. "I wasn't arguing," she said. "Margaret was."

"What was it about?"

The twins leaned forward at the same time. "What does that poor old woman's death have to do with anything?" Nessa asked.

Leigh set her teacup down with a clink. "She was upset over something I said about *The Dragon Files*."

"What did you say?"

"I just said he was in top form with his latest book. That was it. She went mental." Leigh sighed. "I think it's a clear indication she wasn't feeling well."

"Was she arguing with Deirdre as well?" Siobhán asked, scanning the group to see who would answer.

Emma and Eileen nodded, then leaned back in their chairs. "She was behaving rather peculiar now that I think of it," Emma said.

Eileen held up her hand as if she was a schoolgirl. Siobhán gave her a nod. "She was under the impression that Michael O'Mara would be making a surprise visit. I think the agent had to inform her that he would not be making an appearance. After that, she argued with Deirdre, then Leigh, then poor Lorcan, who I really do believe accidentally opened her door." A clock on the wall chimed, and several in the group, including Siobhán, jumped.

Aretta leaned in. "It's time. Perhaps this is your cue to exit."

Siobhán stood. "I apologize. For falling asleep. Not for doing my job." She stood. "I have an early day tomorrow and must bid you all a good night."

"Do you need us to see you out?" Emma said, looking as if she did not want to move from her chair.

"Not at all," Siobhán said. She felt everyone's eyes on her as she exited out the front door. No one expressed any dismay that she was leaving. No one wanted her back. She knew she shouldn't let it bother her, but they'd warmed more to Aretta in a few days than they had to Siobhán in a lifetime. Up until now, she'd told herself it was because she was a garda. Enough. She was here to solve a case, not to make friends. And if they didn't want her as a friend, then they weren't the ones for her. She could have put more effort into it. Read the book. Brought pastries. Stayed awake. Perhaps next time she'd tell them about her reading-sleep gene.

The cool air and drops of rain helped revive her. She clomped down the steps, hoping they could hear her from inside. Then ducked down and scooted around to the fence leading to the back garden. She was thankful the hounds were inside. Not that she was afraid of the beautiful dogs, but she didn't need them drawing attention to her or sniffing her out. She headed for the trellis, hoping she could find a good place to hide, and hoping that whatever this was Aretta wanted her to see would be worth her time.

Her mobile buzzed with a text. It was from Aretta.

DON'T REACT. JUST WATCH.

She certainly had her interest piqued. She found a tree behind the trellis fat enough to hide behind and waited.

Soon, several members of the book club filtered out, including Leigh Coakley and Aretta. They gathered in the trellis. Several looked at their watches. Minutes later, a figure, dressed in all black, streaked across the garden coming straight toward them. He or she was carrying a large sack. Siobhán nearly bolted from her hiding place, and had to silently repeat Aretta's text. *Don't react. Just watch.* What on earth was going on? This looked like the figure on Chris Gordon's CCTV. The women didn't seem afraid of the figure; in fact, their excitement grew as he or she approached. It wasn't until the person was standing in the trellis underneath the twinkling lights that he whipped off his hood.

It was none other than Padraig McCarthy. He reached into his sack. "Be quick, ladies, there isn't much time. I've got Stephen King here."

"Me," a female voice said as a hand reached out and snatched the book.

"Three Michael O'Maras." More hands reached out to grab their requests.

"Three Jackie Collinses, and one *Fifty Shades of Grey*."

"I told you to whisper it," an older lady said as she grabbed her books and stuffed them in what looked like a pillowcase. "And I asked for the trilogy."

"*Fifty Shades Darker* and *Fifty Shades Freed* should be here by next week," Padraig said.

"Whisper!" the woman said, gripping her pillowcase and squeezing it.

"We're among friends here," he said. "No one is judging."

Siobhán, who was totally judging, leaned against the tree as he continued to hand out the goodies. Padraig Mc-

Carthy was peddling books like they were illicit drugs. Behind his husband's back. All marriages had their secrets, and the mystery of the figure in black with the large sack was solved. Was that the only secret he was hiding? Luckily, the meet and greet didn't take long, and soon everyone but Aretta scurried away. Siobhán emerged from behind the tree and they began their trek back home.

"Does that help?" Aretta asked as they strolled.

"It answers one question at least, so, yes, that helps."

"That he is lying to his husband?" Aretta guessed.

"It appears."

"Only appears?"

"There's always the possibility that the entire 'I only sell literary fiction' business was all about stoking demand, and that they are both in on it."

"This sounds like reverse psychology."

"Exactly." Then again, if Oran McCarthy was faking his aversion for genre fiction, he deserved an award.

"Where do you go from here?" Aretta asked.

"Bere Island," Siobhán said. She filled Aretta in on the reasons for the trip.

"But what if O'Mara is here in Kilbane?" she asked.

"That's a very good question," Siobhán said. "Do you think he is?"

"Me?" Aretta sounded startled.

"You have good instincts," Siobhán said. "I'd like to know what you think."

"I do not trust my instincts at work," Aretta said.

"You don't have a choice, do you?"

Aretta frowned. "What do you mean?"

"Instincts are like breathing. You can't just not breathe."

"I am not sure I agree that instincts should be brought to work," Aretta insisted.

"You're officially off the clock," Siobhán said. "I'm simply asking you, Aretta, for your opinion."

"I think he is here," she said. "If I were to listen to my gut, I would say he is here."

"I agree," Siobhán said. Michael O'Mara was here in Kilbane. She could feel it. Which was why she had to tell Macdara they wouldn't be going to Bere Island after all.

Chapter 26

Macdara was at the bistro bright and early. "I think we should change our plans," Siobhán said.

"What's the story?" Macdara asked.

"We think he's here," Siobhán said. "Aretta and I think Michael O'Mara is here."

Macdara gave a nod. "Then we stay." She let out her breath. It wasn't that he believed her as much as he believed *in* her. That was the kind of man every woman deserved. That was the kind of man you marry. "Does that mean he's lying to Darren, or is Darren lying to us?" Macdara mused.

"If the two of us go running off, we may be leaving everyone vulnerable to a killer." She was talking past the sale, but now that she'd changed their weekend plans, she wanted to prove it was for good reason.

"Where do we look?" Macdara said. "If he's here, where is he sleeping?"

"We might need to canvass town," Siobhán said. "Take Michael O'Mara's photo around."

"I could still go to Bere Island, and leave you in charge here," Macdara said. "But I wanted to go with you."

"I still want to go to Bere Island someday," Siobhán said. "But not to look for a murder suspect."

"How about we go when we solve the case?" Macdara said. "We'll have a nice romantic getaway. In fact, wouldn't it be a lovely place from which to set our wedding date?"

"It would," Siobhán said. She hoped it would still seem lovely when she told him it was going to be at least another year.

"It's a date then," Macdara said. He leaned in and kissed her cheek. "See you at the station."

"Do you want brekkie?"

"I do," he said. "But more than that I want to solve this case. Throw me an apple." Siobhán turned, picked up an apple from the basket on the counter, and threw it at Macdara. He caught it with a grin. "See you later."

"Not if I see you first." She could hear his chuckle as the door to the bistro closed behind him. Siobhán slumped against the counter. Even though it was the right move, Siobhán felt sorry that they weren't getting out of town.

"Who poured sour milk in your porridge?"

It came from Gráinne, who had snuck up behind Siobhán. When Siobhán didn't answer right away, Gráinne tugged on a strand of Siobhán's hair until she let out a yelp. Gráinne howled with laughter. "You should come into the salon, you're due for a snip."

"Bere Island is canceled," Siobhán said, giving her sister a gentle shove. "And I don't have time for a snip, we have more work to do here."

James walked through the dining room. His mobile rang. He stopped, looked at the screen, then shoved it back into his pocket before continuing into the kitchen.

"At least you're not Elise," Gráinne said, flopping into a chair and whipping out a nail file. "He's totally ghosting her."

Ghosting her. The same usage of the word had been mentioned by Aretta. Had Michael O'Mara and Deirdre been lovers? As Jeanie Brady said, there was a sad connection between love and death. Fame aside, he wouldn't be the first man to kill over a broken heart.

"I spoke with Michael O'Mara at length," Darren Kilroy said. "He insisted he hadn't left the island in a month." They were sitting in the front dining room of Naomi's Bistro. Macdara had arrived on with Darren in tow. Siobhán did not bother to tease Macdara for ordering a full Irish breakfast along with his guest. Darren Kilroy was the type of man who gave more answers when he felt respected. The station interview room was not the place for him. Fair or not, he sat at a table in the dining room with a mug of tea. They had finished eating and their breakfast plates had just been cleared. Darren Kilroy was their best chance of finding out if Michael O'Mara was in town, but first they had to try and ascertain whether or not Darren knew his client's whereabouts. It was possible he'd been left in the dark. It was equally possible he was covering for him. He would probably never have another megastar author such as O'Mara.

"Did Michael O'Mara mention Deirdre Walsh during any of your calls or e-mail exchanges?" Siobhán asked.

"Why would he?" Darren said, lifting his eyebrow and stopping midair with his teacup raised.

"Because you are here, where a woman has been murdered, and he's a writer. Would it not come up at all?" Macdara chimed in.

"I suppose," Darren said. "Perhaps it is strange that he didn't mention it."

"Especially if the two of them were lovers," Macdara said.

"In that case not mentioning her would be very suspicious," Siobhán added.

Darren's teacup clinked onto his plate.

Macdara glanced at the teacup, then stared at Darren. "Imagine if they were romantically involved and Deirdre tried to end things." Macdara leaned in. "I don't know about Deirdre, but if I ever tried to break it off with herself, you'd probably find me in the river wearing cement shoes."

Darren's eyes widened but his gaze did not dare move in Siobhán's direction. As for "herself," she nearly choked on her tea, and Macdara Flannery would pay for that cheeky little comment later, but for now she focused on the task at hand and dropped the final revelation. "And we believe that's what Deirdre meant when she said she had an explosive tell-all. She was going to tell all about Michael O'Mara."

Darren's head swiveled between the pair who were

purposefully trying to keep the information coming fast. Keep him on his toes. "You're not serious?" Darren said. "You think Deirdre's tell-all was about Michael O'Mara?"

"We were hoping you could tell us," Siobhán said.

"How? You know I tried to get my hands on that manuscript."

"By breaking into her room after she was dead," Macdara said. "Not a good look."

"Did she seem to you like the kind of writer who was into anyone's life or work but her own?" Darren said. "And I don't know what she could have said about Michael that hasn't already been said. Drunken bum who can still write. That's the gist of his reviews lately. Forget reviews, that's the gist of *him* lately. I don't think he'd be able to read her tell-all let alone muster up enough gusto to care about it. And well-played the pair of ye, almost had me going, you did, but let me be clear. Michael O'Mara is not any more a killer than Stephen King. He's a writer. It's fictional. Now. If you have any fire-breathing dragons gone missing, then he's your man. Otherwise you're on the wrong track entirely!"

"I guess it's lucky then," Siobhán said.

"How's that?" Darren's voice wobbled slightly. Good. They were getting to him.

"That you never intended on signing Deirdre Walsh in the first place."

He swallowed. Looked at Siobhán, then Macdara. "Who told you that?"

"We can ask a judge for a warrant to search all your client records, or you can tell us what we need to know," Macdara said.

Siobhán wasn't sure a judge would grant such wide

permission but she was proud of Macdara for threatening it.

He straightened his colorful tie. Today it was yellow with white polka dots. It went nicely with a white shirt and gray blazer. "As a matter of fact, I have signed Nessa Lamb."

"When did you sign her?"

He concentrated on his empty teacup. No doubt trying to figure out what they had already been told. "I signed Nessa Lamb the morning I arrived in Kilbane," he said. "I knew all along I wanted to represent her."

Siobhán and Macdara nodded, jotting things down in their notebooks, letting the space fill with silence. "Who else knew about this?" Siobhán asked when drops of sweat appeared on Darren's forehead.

"Besides myself and Ms. Lamb? No one."

"Not even Padraig or Oran?"

"Especially not Padraig or Oran."

"Why didn't you just wait the week as you had agreed to do?" Siobhán asked.

"Nessa informed me that she had other offers. I didn't want to lose her." He opened his arms. "I was leaving myself open to the possibility that I might sign Lorcan or Deirdre as well. If they had something that impressed me. There's no law saying I could only sign one of them."

"We're not in the business of telling you whom to sign," Macdara said. "We're trying to figure out if learning of this news was a motive for murder."

"But they murdered Deirdre, not Nessa," Darren said. "Do you think it was a mistake? Was Nessa Lamb onto something? Was she the intended target all along?"

"That's not the only way to look at it," Siobhán said.

Darren leaned back and crossed his arms. "Oh?"

"Maybe Deirdre found out you signed her and threatened to expose what you had done," Siobhán said lightly.

It took Darren a moment. When he realized what Siobhán was saying he pointed to himself. "But what had I done? Nothing illegal, I assure you." He waited. They continued to stare at him. "You think I'd kill an author for something so inconsequential?" A red hue flared along the side of his neck. Anger or fear?

"Was Deirdre Walsh blackmailing you?" Macdara asked.

"Over whom I chose to sign?" Darren sputtered. "We've already covered this. It's not against the law. I have no indications whatsoever that Deirdre or anyone else found out that I had already signed Nessa Lamb. But since you seem to enjoy playing devil's advocate, let's go there. Let's say Deirdre found out. What then? Would I be a little embarrassed that I didn't play by the rules? Of course. I don't know what books the pair of ye have been reading, but mild embarrassment has never been a motive for murder."

"We had to ask," Macdara said.

"Of course," Darren replied. "I'm sorry I can't be of more help. And I think it best to inform you that I'll be leaving right after Deirdre's memorial tomorrow."

Macdara nodded. "As long as we can get a hold of you if we need to speak again."

"Not a bother." He stood to go.

"One more thing," Siobhán said. "Have you ever published any books on interior design?"

He shook his head. "No. Why do you ask?"

Siobhán shrugged and looked around the walls. "I was

thinking some wallpaper might liven the bistro up. But I wouldn't even know where to begin."

"I'm afraid I'm of no help to you there," Darren said. He nodded and was out the door.

They watched him go. "What are you thinking?" Macdara asked.

"Once he leaves town the rest will follow," Siobhán said. "We'll be chasing a case with all of our suspects on the run."

Macdara nodded. "Unless we get some hard facts and soon, we can't force anyone to stay." He rubbed his face. "I'd say Michael O'Mara is looking like a good bet. It explains the note about not believing in ghosts. It explains Deirdre's claim that she had an explosive tell-all. It explains the pack of cigarettes found in her room, and it explains the sightings of a lurker in the trash."

"And now we know the figure in black was just Padraig running to the ladies' book club to sell popular fiction."

Macdara suddenly chuckled.

"What?"

"Nice segue with the wallpaper," he said. "That wasn't suspicious at all."

Siobhán laughed too. "He did look perplexed."

"Indeed."

"Speaking of wallpaper, any progress on where the sample came from?" Siobhán asked.

Macdara shook his head. "Aretta checked with the hardware shop and has been popping into businesses up and down Sarsfield Street. No one has wallpapered recently."

Ann entered the dining room at that moment carrying a large bouquet of flowers. "Leigh Coakley," she said, lifting them. "I helped with the arrangements for Ms. Walsh's memorial. She gave me these as a thank-you."

"Lovely," Siobhán said. Ann moved to take them into the kitchen. "Wait." Ann stopped at the table. Siobhán stared up at the flowers wrapped in decorative paper.

"Why are you staring at them like that?" Ann said. "If there's a bug on me just say so."

Siobhán tapped the paper. "Bring me this when you're done, will ya?"

Ann frowned. She whipped the paper off and handed it to her. "Just take it now." She shook her head and continued into the kitchen.

"What are you thinking?" Macdara said.

Siobhán held up the decorative paper. "I want Jeanie Brady to see this," Siobhán said. "Leigh brought flowers into the bookshop the day of the murder. What if it isn't wallpaper that was found in Deirdre's mouth?"

Chapter 27

Jeanie Brady and Siobhán sat at the picnic table in the courtyard of the Twins' Inn. The wolfhounds sat eagerly in front of Jeanie, who had been tossing them treats non-stop. Jeanie took the paper that had come from Blooms.

"I'll do some tests," she said. "But it's not consistent with the wallpaper found in Deirdre's mouth. However, you might still be onto something."

"I don't understand," Siobhán said.

"What if one day the florist ran out of this kind of paper to wrap her flowers in? What if she grabbed something else?"

"Like wallpaper," Siobhán said.

"Like wallpaper," Jeanie echoed.

"Does that make her the killer, or just the supplier?" Siobhán mused out loud.

"Good boys," Jeanie purred to the dogs. "Good, good boys."

"I didn't know you were such a dog lover," Siobhán said.

"My husband's allergic or I would have a house full of them," Jeanie said. She looked up. "Ready for my next piece of news?"

"Probably not, but go ahead."

"I found the same sample of wallpaper underneath Margaret O'Shea's tongue."

Even though Siobhán was expecting that would be the case, the news still delivered a shock. She felt tears filling her eyes before she could stop them. Jeanie reached over and patted her hand.

"I'm sorry, pet."

"We have to catch this killer," Siobhán said. "He or she will not get away with this." This killer thought he/she was so clever. Wallpaper. Arsenic. What did it mean? Why Margaret O'Shea? A squeal rang out, like someone in pain. Siobhán first looked to the dogs, but other than drool pouring out of their mouths, the noise hadn't come from them. A second squeal followed, then escalated into screams. It was coming from the cottage. Siobhán shot off her chair and ran toward the house. But just as she reached the door, Emma came barreling out with a Michael O'Mara book in her hand, followed by Eileen.

"What's the story?" Siobhán asked.

Emma held the book out. "This is brand new," she said. "I acquired it the other night."

Padraig's contraband. "Okay," Siobhán said. "I still don't understand."

Emma turned to the first page with trembling fingers.

There, in large sprawling ink, was an autograph: Michael O'Mara.

"That's nice," said Siobhán slowly.

"You don't understand," Emma said. "This autograph was not here a few days ago."

"Have you had it in your possession the entire time?" Siobhán asked.

Emma shook her head. "I left it in the trellis overnight."

"He's here," Siobhán said, pacing the hallway of the garda station. "And he's managed to keep out of sight for the most part."

"You need to speak with Padraig," Macdara said. "To confirm the book he sold Eileen was not already signed."

"Emma," Siobhán corrected. "Why would she lie about it?"

"Not lie per se," Macdara said. "But perhaps she didn't notice."

Or perhaps Michael O'Mara has been watching the inn. Listening in on the book club. Sneaking in to sign his books. Perhaps he wasn't so out of it after all. "I'm on it," Siobhán said.

A lorry was parked in front of the bookshop. *AL'S PLUMBING* was painted across it in blue. Curious, she entered the shop to find several nonfunctioning toilets sitting in the middle of the bookstore. Oran stood a few feet away tossing books into them.

"What are you doing?"

"Expanding our inventory as promised," Oran said.

"This toilet is for romance. That one for mysteries and thriller—"

"You're putting books in *toilets*?"

"They're dry as bone," he said, continuing to toss them in.

Padraig popped up from behind the counter. "Please listen to her. We can't do this. Think of the optics."

"I'm trying to think outside the box."

Inside the commode was outside the box, alright. "What about some nice claw-foot bathtubs instead?" Siobhán said. "People aren't going to want to stick their hands in there."

"It might make them give Joyce a second go," Oran said.

Padraig rolled his eyes. "We'll switch to the tubs."

"What are we going to do with these?" Oran asked.

"You'd better recycle them," Siobhán said. "Or you'll be paying very dear fines."

"What else can we do for you?" Oran asked. "I assume you're not here to admire our toilets."

"Definitely not." She shuddered. "Do you have any photos of this space before you started renovating?"

"You already took my design folder," Padraig said.

"It will be returned soon. And it did not contain before photos of the space. Do you have any?"

"Loads," Padraig said. "Why?"

"They were questioning the landlord about this very same issue," Oran said.

Siobhán cringed. Gossip was always detrimental to an investigation.

"I can't imagine what photos of the bookshop have to do with Deirdre Walsh's death," Padraig said. "Did she inhale toxic paint?" He clutched his throat and looked around. "Are we safe?"

Siobhán put her hand up. "I assure you, you're safe." At least as far as the walls were concerned. But none of them were safe from the killer. "I'd like you to send the photos you have to this e-mail." Siobhán handed him a business card with the e-mail. "Any photos of the space before you remodeled."

"You're not going to tell us what this wallpaper business is about, are you?" Padraig asked.

"I'm not," Siobhán said. Should she call him on his secretive visits to the ladies' book club? She discarded the idea. No use causing marital strife if it wasn't pertinent to her investigation. "Please just send the photos."

"He'll send them right away," Oran said.

"Of course," Padraig said.

Siobhán smiled. "Thanks a million." She glanced at the exit, hoping to keep her hands off the books in the toilets.

Padraig McCarthy wasn't ready to give up, she could see it in his eyes. "This doesn't have to do with my list, does it?"

Siobhán stepped forward. "List?"

Oran and Padraig exchanged a look.

"My dream list of rare books," Padraig said. "I gave it to all our visiting authors."

"They are in frequent contact with booksellers, and bookshops," Oran pitched in. "It was a long shot, but we want to be in the loop if they hear of any of these books circulating."

"Why do you think your list has anything to do with this case?" Siobhán was genuinely curious.

"Because of the wallpaper book," Padraig said. "Isn't that what you've been driving at?"

"Are you telling me there's a rare book about wallpaper?"

"There is," Padraig said. "Although we wouldn't have a chance of getting our hands on it. I think there are only, what? Five copies remaining? And they're all in the States."

"I wouldn't want it even if that weren't the case," Oran said. "Because we'd have to take very special care with it."

"Very special," Padraig repeated.

Siobhán stepped forward. "And why is that?"

"Because the wallpaper samples are from 1874," Padraig said.

"And they contain arsenic," Oran added.

Siobhán felt a chill go up her spine. "Do you have a copy of this list?"

Padraig nodded, reached under the counter, and handed her a sheet. There it was, the fifth on the list. *Shadows from the Walls of Death*.

"I need to know everyone who had a copy of this."

"That's easy. Deirdre Walsh. Nessa Lamb. Lorcan Murphy."

"Leigh Coakley?"

"The florist? No."

"Darren Kilroy?"

"We tried to give him one, but he wouldn't take it," Padraig said. From his tone, she could tell he was still sulking over it.

"Why not?"

"He said he didn't have time to be on the lookout. Instead, he gave us a few names of book dealers and shops that could help us."

"Did you call any of them?"

"Not yet," Padraig said.

"We had our hands full, even before our wee shop became a crime scene," Oran added.

"Tell me more about the book."

"It contains a hundred wallpaper samples. Each saturated with various levels of arsenic."

"Why?"

"Excellent question. It was conceived by Dr. Robert M. Kedzie."

"He was a Union surgeon during the American Civil War," Oran added.

"And a professor of chemistry," Padraig said.

Oran nodded. "He wanted to educate the public about the dangers of arsenic-pigmented wallpaper."

"Arsenic-pigmented wallpaper," Siobhán repeated.

"Arsenic can be mixed with copper and made into paints and pigments," Oran said.

"The Victorians," Padraig sighed. "They knew arsenic could be poison when ingesting it, but they thought nothing of plastering their walls with it. Can ye imagine?" He shuddered.

"That quote from the book," Padraig said, placing his hand on his heart. He leaned in. "He spoke of women falling ill and retreating into their wallpapered bedrooms to convalesce."

"All the while taking in . . ." Oran said.

". . . *an air loaded with the breath of death,"* they finished in unison.

The words echoed in her poor head. *'An air loaded with the breath of death.'*

"But as I stated, we never actually expected to get our hands on the book," Padraig said. "Only a hundred copies were ever printed, and they were all originally distributed in the United States, and out of those one hundred only four have survived."

"You said five earlier," Oran corrected.

Padraig frowned. "Four, five. What does it matter, we'll never see it." He turned to a stack of books and began sorting through them. "If it's poison you want to know about, you should read Agatha Christie."

"And yes," Oran said. "We carry a few."

"They're all sold," Padraig said. "To Leigh Coakley." He gave Siobhán a look. "She's writing her own mystery."

"Lovely," Siobhán said. "What happened to the remaining copies of the wallpaper book?"

"Most libraries destroyed them out of fear," Oran said. "The remaining copies have been sealed and you need gloves to turn the pages."

"Lest you lick your fingers and die," Padraig added in case it wasn't clear. "There's now a digital version online." He sighed. "I hear the real version is exquisite."

"But deadly," Oran said. "Exquisite but deadly."

Chapter 28

Siobhán had just arrived at the door to her bistro and was about to enter when a figure came up from behind, startling her. Leigh Coakley jiggled her handbag looking as if she hadn't slept in days. "Leigh," Siobhán said. "What's the story?"

"I know you have to be thinking I did it," Leigh said.

"Did what?"

Leigh scoffed. "Why, killed Deirdre Walsh of course."

"Have I said or done anything to give you that impression?" Siobhán asked. "Aside from doing my job, which is to question everyone who was at the bookshop the evening Deirdre Walsh was murdered?"

Leigh Coakley was still a neighbor and she didn't need to get all wound up. Some grudges were hard for folks to get over. Being accused of murder was one of them.

Leigh frowned. This wasn't the answer she had been

expecting. "Pages stuffed in Deirdre's mouth, and here I'm the one who said she should eat her words."

Siobhán nodded. "Come in." The bell tinkled as they entered the bistro. "I'll make us some tea."

They set up in the dining room. "It's an expression. It should clear me," Leigh began. "Nessa Lamb's prose is gorgeous. Uplifting. Did you hear the terrible things Deirdre Walsh was saying? I shouldn't have let her get under my skin, but of course I did. The green-eyed monster rises from the murky depths of humanity's underbelly."

"Can you stop speaking in prose?"

Leigh brushed lint off her sleeve. "It comes naturally."

"Did you murder Deirdre Walsh?"

Leigh collapsed at the closest table. "If I was planning on killing her I wouldn't have given myself away like that."

"Padraig McCarthy mentioned you purchased all of their Agatha Christie mysteries."

Leigh blinked. "He told you that?"

"Yes." She kept her voice casual, as if to assure Leigh that the gossip was trivial.

"I see," Leigh said. "Does that make me a murderer?"

"I think I've made my position quite clear. You're a neighbor. You run bake sales, and put together gorgeous bouquets, cheering up this village. We're questioning everyone, but no, neither Detective Sergeant Flannery nor I are doing anything but singing your praises."

Leigh finally smiled. "I'm so relieved."

Eoin ambled out of the kitchen. The lunch hour was over, and technically they were closed. "Can I get you anything?" he asked Leigh.

"If you could put the kettle on, pet, that would be grand."
She turned to Leigh. "Are you hungry?"

"Heavens, I've had no appetite since Deirdre Walsh
died."

"I have some fresh baked scones," Eoin said, turning
to return to the kitchen. Siobhán made herself a cappuccino and soon they were seated with their drinks and
scones.

"Do you read a lot of mysteries?" Siobhán asked after
giving them a minute.

Leigh nodded. "I'm writing a murder mystery if you
must know."

"Oh? Doing any research?"

"Of course. I'm a big believer in research. . . . Sneaky!
I see what you're doing. How did she die? Was it nuts or
poison?"

"How would you have done it?"

"Me?"

"As a writer. Agatha Christie was the Queen of Poi-
sons, wasn't she?"

"Fine. You want the truth?"

"I can't handle the truth," Siobhán deadpanned. She
may not have been up on her books, but she could quote
an impressive number of American movies. Leigh
frowned. "I'm only messing. Yes, of course I want the
truth."

"The truth is, I haven't read a single Agatha Christie
mystery. Yet. I intend to."

"You haven't read one?"

Leigh shook her head. "I thought they would moti-
vate me."

"I'd like to see your murder mystery."

"Really? Are you a fan?"

"No."

"I haven't gotten very far." Leigh stirred another spoonful of sugar into her tea.

"Show me what you've got."

"Are you going to make me? Is that legal?"

"I'm only asking. But cooperation during a murder inquiry is appreciated."

Leigh ran the tip of her index finger along the table. "If you must know, I'm still in the research phase."

Siobhán didn't think Leigh's manuscript, if it existed, would shed any light on the case, so she let it drop. It was Deirdre Walsh's manuscript that she wanted to get her paws on. The supposed tell-all.

"I've been meaning to ask about the decorative paper you use to wrap your flowers," Siobhán said.

"It's lovely, isn't it?"

"Tis."

"I get it from Charlesville." Charlesville was the next town over, a tad larger than Kilbane, with lovely shops.

"What do you use when you run out?"

Leigh didn't hesitate. "I never run out."

"I wonder if wallpaper would work?"

"Wallpaper?" Leigh frowned. "I never thought of it. But like I said, I never run out."

Siobhán believed her. Leigh was a world class organizer. Leigh's teacup was empty and only crumbs remained of her scone. "Would you like another cup?"

"Heavens, no. I have to get back to the shop."

"I'm sure you're very busy," Siobhán said as she pushed back from the table and stood.

Leigh followed suit. "There is a matter of the flower arrangements for Deirdre's memorial. It's going to keep me busy the rest of the day." Siobhán walked her to the door.

"I can imagine," she said.

"At least I don't have the unpleasant task of remodeling Margaret's room at the inn."

"Margaret's room?" Siobhán said. "Right, so." She felt a tingle at the back of her neck. Guards, accompanied by the twins, had already checked out Margaret's room. Nothing had seemed suspicious.

"And don't even get me started on how long it's going to take them to get that hideous wallpaper taken down." Leigh had just stepped onto the footpath. Siobhán followed.

"Wallpaper?" she said, trying to keep her voice light despite every nerve in her body firing on overtime.

Leigh nodded. "We were forced to have book club in her room that first night so Margaret could meet the authors." Leigh shuddered. "It smelled dusty. And the wallpaper might have been lovely once but it was peeling off. The twins are going to have an awful time freshening up that room."

Why hadn't any of them mentioned this detail at the book club meeting? She supposed they didn't think it relevant. No one knew they were looking at Margaret's death as foul play. Even now, Leigh wasn't picking up on Siobhán's alarm.

"Remember you asked me the other day about my argument with Margaret, and then I told you she argued with Deirdre next?" Leigh asked.

"Yes."

"I remembered something. I don't know if it will be of any help."

"You never know." Siobhán's mind was still on the wallpaper. They had to get there straightaway.

"I remember what Margaret said to Deirdre. 'That's trickery.'"

"That's trickery," Siobhán repeated. "What was she on about?"

"I haven't the slightest idea," Leigh said. "One minute they were talking about Michael O'Mara—at least Margaret was, and then I missed what Deirdre said because she was speaking in a normal voice, and then Margaret shouted: 'That's trickery.'"

The skies were blue and the air fresh. Siobhán could take her scooter to the inn. She loved her pink scooter nearly as much as her cappuccino machine, but she hadn't ridden it in ages. It would feel good to have the wind in her face, and it might help her process what she'd just learned. One of the frustrating aspects of investigations was that they involved other humans and often these other humans were holding on to valuable scraps of information that they didn't even realize were helpful to the case. She donned her matching pink helmet and called the station before hopping on. Macdara was not in the station, so at her request they transferred the call to Aretta. Siobhán asked her to bring the note about the ghost and the scrap of wallpaper from the evidence room and meet her at the Twins' Inn. It was actually a copy of the wallpaper as Jeanie Brady had the piece found in Deirdre's mouth, but it was an exact replica of the color and shape and would do the trick. She was missing a lot of pieces to the puzzle, but one thing was becoming clear. Her theory that Margaret had witnessed something was close but not exact. Margaret, it seemed, had instead stirred something up.

That's trickery.

I don't believe in ghosts.

Margaret O'Shea had written that note. The wallpaper had come from her room. Siobhán bounced along on her Vespa, enjoying the feel of the engine beneath her, the wind rejuvenating her, the smell in the air fresh, as if days of rain had breathed new life into everything. She hadn't planned on stopping at the park near the Travelers' caravans until she spotted the lad out with his donkey. She'd passed him the same morning she'd gone for her run. Had he seen anything?

The Travelers kept to themselves, and so did the villagers for that matter, but Siobhán had made it a point to nod or say hello and she received the same in kind. Siobhán parked her scooter far enough away that it wouldn't startle the donkey, and she approached slowly with a smile. The lad gave her a wave and a nod, then seemed surprised when she stopped in front of him.

"I was wondering if you saw a fella with a wheelbarrow around here?"

"You need a wheelbarrow?" He spoke fast, as if that might limit the extent of their interaction.

"No, sorry. I was asking after yer man. I saw him days ago, in the distance, pushing a wheelbarrow. That same morning I saw you as well." She pointed in the direction she'd seen him that morning. The lad followed her gaze, then gave a nod. "You saw him too?"

He nodded. "Do you know who it was?" He shook his head. She hadn't gotten a close look at him either. At the time, she thought it was a farmer. But what if it was the killer? This spot was the middle point between the Twins'

Inn and the footpath in front of the bookshop. She shivered, realizing that what she had witnessed was the killer transporting Margaret O'Shea's body. A man. Then again, from this distance the person could have dressed to look like a man. One always had to be careful about absolutes. "Have you seen him since?"

The lad looked quickly to his left. Siobhán followed his gaze to a lone caravan set a good distance apart from the others. He then turned back to his donkey. His message was clear. Someone was in that caravan. And now that she'd thought about it, that particular caravan was located outside the formal caravan park where the Travelers lived. Somehow, he'd charmed the Travelers, or offered money they couldn't refuse, to stay a few days. They'd probably agreed on the condition that the caravan be moved away from their homes.

The lad murmured something else, indicating he didn't want to get in trouble.

"It's grand," Siobhán said to the lad, in case he was thinking of tipping off Michael O'Mara. "Not a bother."

She walked a few feet into the park, closer to the caravan. She didn't want to strain relations any further, and the guards were not in the habit of entering the caravan park unless they were aiding a Traveler at their request. Which had not happened since she'd been with the gardaí. It could stir up trouble otherwise. But if Michael O'Mara was in that caravan, she couldn't give the lad the chance to warn him. Aretta was on her way to the inn, and Macdara hadn't been at the station. Aretta would surely spot Siobhán's pink scooter on her way to the inn, but she didn't know it belonged to Siobhán. She could call or text, but she didn't want the lad to overhear.

"I need to talk to him," Siobhán said finally. "Will you escort me?"

The lad hadn't been expecting this either. He had been leading his donkey away in the opposite direction and it took him a moment before he stopped and turned. He nodded to the caravan. "Go on."

It was permission. She'd have to settle for it. And although it would have been better to have backup when approaching the caravan, she would not step inside until backup arrived. But she would stand near it in case anyone came out. "Thank you," she said. "I'll try not to be long."

But he was already gone. Most likely he would tell the group that she was here, and if she stayed too long, it wasn't going to be appreciated. She called Macdara directly this time and headed for the caravan.

Chapter 29

Macdara responded that he was on his way with another guard and requested that she wait. Siobhán was standing a few feet away from the caravan when the door flew open and a man barreled out, head down, tearing forward. The suit gave him away. Darren Kilroy. He let out a yelp when he saw Siobhán and slapped his hand over his heart. She stood motionless, swallowing the urge to apologize for scaring him. How long had he known that Michael O'Mara was in Kilbane? When she didn't speak, Darren Kilroy nibbled on his lip and threw a glance back to the caravan.

"I was going to tell you," he said. She folded her arms and waited. He held up his mobile phone. "He only called me this morning. I've been taking care of him all day."

"Does he need medical attention?"

Darren shook his head. "He definitely needs rehab,

and yes, he needs to go to hospital. He's been refusing, but I think it's time we called an ambulance." He held out his phone, but she didn't make a move to take it. The nearby river gurgled, birds chirped, and the tall green grass swayed. "At least I won't be leaving town now until he's sorted, if that makes you feel any better."

"Did you ever meet Margaret O'Shea?"

He frowned. "The elderly woman who lived at the inn? And passed away near the bookshop?"

"That's the one."

"We weren't officially introduced mind you, but yes, we met."

"Did you ever go into her room?"

He swallowed and nodded. "They held the first book club meeting in her room. When she found out I represented Michael O'Mara she was quite pleasant. I gave her a signed copy of his latest book."

"You did?"

He nodded. That must have been the copy the twins discovered in the trellis. Unless she was being played. "Did he sign it while he was in Kilbane?"

He bowed his head. "It's a shame she'll never get to read it." He crossed himself, then looked up. "Why do you ask?"

"You need to stop lying. How long have you known he was in Kilbane?"

"Just today. I swear it on me life."

"How long has he actually been here?"

He bowed his head again. "He's in no state to tell me. But from the looks of the food containers, I'd say he's been here for days."

"Perhaps even before you arrived in town."

"Perhaps." He took off his glasses, and squeezed the

bridge of his nose before placing them back on. "It's not what you think. He was not romantically involved with Deirdre Walsh and he is not a killer."

"Did you ever see Margaret O'Shea arguing with Deirdre Walsh?"

He wiped his brow with a handkerchief. "Arguing? Do you mean during the book discussion?"

"At any time."

He licked his lips. "No. However . . ." He sighed. "I do have more to add to this story. But I only want to say it once. Perhaps we should conduct this in a more formal setting." His attention was distracted by something in the distance. Siobhán knew without turning around that Macdara had arrived. He and two other guards approached.

"Wait here," Siobhán said to Darren as they headed for the caravan.

"He's having delirium tremens," Darren said. "And he's a big man. Be cautious."

The door to the caravan gave a loud squeak of protest when they pushed it open. Macdara took the lead. Siobhán, standing on the ground, saw Macdara duck as a lamp whizzed over his head and smashed into the wall behind him. Then Michael O'Mara began screaming and cursing.

"I warned you," Darren said in the background.

Siobhán gave him a withering glare and he was smart enough to shut his gob.

Macdara began speaking to O'Mara, letting him know they were calling an ambulance and he could go peacefully or they would bring in more guards to assist. Michael O'Mara stopped screaming. He began to whimper. He sat in a corner and scrunched himself in as he began rocking back and forth, muttering to himself, stroking his red beard. Sweat poured off him in buckets. Siobhán could smell the alcohol off him. There would be no talking to him in this state. Macdara nodded his head to a nearby counter. On it sat a hammer, next to it a box of nails, and next to that—crime scene tape. Michael O'Mara had been the one to nail Deirdre's window shut. Return to her room. Replace the crime scene tape on the front door. Wheel Margaret's body to the bookshop, and break into the back door of the bookshop the night Deirdre was murdered. One of their own must have been careless with the crime scene tape and left a roll behind at the inn. Macdara signaled to Siobhán and they slowly backed out of the caravan.

"Got lucky there, boss," Macdara said in a low tone once they were outside. "He's definitely not well."

"I've never seen someone in that bad a state."

Macdara nodded. "From the rage he worked himself into, could be drugs involved as well." He held up his finger, then placed a call to the ambulance services.

"May I go back to my room?" Darren called. "I need to sleep."

"I'm afraid that's going to have to wait," Siobhán said. "We're taking you into the station." She took a deep breath. "But not until we get Mr. O'Mara to hospital."

Darren nodded. "Before we go to the station you should assist me to my room first," he said. "I have something you need to see."

Michael O'Mara had been transported to hospital. He wouldn't be in shape to answer questions for days, maybe

even a week. Siobhán, Macdara, and Aretta were headed
for the Twins' Inn in a guard car. Siobhán had messaged
her brood and James had agreed to walk over and ride her
scooter home. Darren Kilroy was on foot; he would meet
them there. Siobhán didn't know what he wanted to pick
up from his room, but she was going to give him some
leeway. "If Michael O'Mara is our killer, we're safe,"
Aretta said from the back seat. Macdara was driving—
Siobhán needed to concentrate on her thoughts.

"And if he's not, we're in even more danger," Siobhán
said. She brought up the crime scene tape. "How on earth
did he get his hands on it?"

Macdara sighed. "I'll have to check with everyone
who was assigned to the inn, see if any of them will admit
they may have left it behind."

"It's me," Aretta piped up from the back seat. "But I
didn't leave it at the inn." She placed her hand on her
forehead as if she was taking her own temperature.

"Where did you leave it?" Siobhán asked.

"At Blooms," Aretta said. "I had popped in there after
returning from the inn. I must have set it on the counter
while I was speaking with Leigh. I am so sorry. I've
failed."

Siobhán shook her head. "You've done no such thing.
We all make mistakes."

"Why don't you give Leigh Coakley a bell. Don't
alarm her, just see if she knows what happened to it,"
Macdara said.

Aretta took out her mobile phone and placed the call.
It only took a minute. "Leigh didn't remember but she
checked with her daughter, and given the counter was
piled with nonsense, Leigh told her to straighten up, and
she's worried the daughter might have thrown it away."

"And Michael O'Mara has been going through rubbish bins," Siobhán said. They were pulling into the inn. Macdara parked in front of Margaret's room.

"Should we search Margaret's room now?" Aretta asked. "Or am I off the case?"

"You're still on the case," Macdara said. "Growing pains are part of the job. You should have seen how often this one messed up." He jerked his thumb at Siobhán.

"I still do," she said. Siobhán glanced at Margaret's room, which was now cordoned off with crime scene tape. Searching it had been the plan, but she equally wanted to know what Darren Kilroy had to show them. Macdara must have been feeling the same.

"Let's take Darren Kilroy back to the station to hear him out. Then we'll return to Margaret's room."

"I can stay here and stand watch," Aretta said. "If you think that would be helpful."

"I don't know how long we'll be," Macdara said. "It might get a bit boring."

Aretta grinned. "Not a bother." She patted a lump in her pocket. "I found a good book in a toilet."

"As I previously stated," Darren said, "Michael O'Mara and Deirdre Walsh were not romantically involved." They sat at a table in Interview Room #1 across from Darren Kilroy. The briefcase Darren had fetched was on the table in front of him.

"What is Michael O'Mara doing here then?" Macdara asked.

"He came to warn me."

"Warn you?"

Darren nodded. "About a year ago Michael began receiving letters from an obsessed fan." He tapped the briefcase. "May I?" Macdara nodded. Darren pulled a stack of papers out and set them on the table. "These are all the letters Michael received from the very first to the last. They begin mild enough. She calls herself a fan. An admirer. By the third letter she confesses she's a writer too. By the fourth she's criticizing his portrayal of female characters. By the fifth she's suggesting a partnership. It escalates to stalking and threats." He lifted the stack of letters. "It's all here." Macdara gestured for him to slide the letters over and he obliged. "I don't know what you can do about it now, but I assure you Michael is no killer."

"These letters are signed *Your Biggest Fan*," Macdara said.

"That's correct."

"How do you know they're from Deirdre Walsh?"

Darren reached into his briefcase again and brought out *Melodies*."He received this. If you read her note to him in the opening, and compare it to the handwriting in the letters, I think it's quite clear she's the writer of these letters." He gestured to the book and then the letters. "You should have your handwriting expert compare the documents."

"Did Deirdre Walsh ever approach you about Michael O'Mara?" Siobhán asked.

"She said she had a proposal for me that she wanted to discuss. I assumed it was about her own book project. We never got the opportunity to speak, but after reading these letters I am convinced she wanted to propose writing for Michael O'Mara."

"Writing for him?" Siobhán asked.

Darren nodded. "Ghostwriting."

I don't believe in ghosts. Had Michael O'Mara written that note?

Darren was still talking. "When an author reaches the megastar level that Michael O'Mara has achieved, it can get tiring to keep up with the demand. Many authors hire a team of writers to keep their works going. With strict guidelines. The American author James Patterson is an example. He has loads of authors who write for him."

"Was Michael O'Mara looking to do the same?"

"No," Darren said. "He was not." Darren shifted uncomfortably. "But it wasn't a terrible idea. Given his drinking as of late."

"Did you suggest it to him?" Siobhán asked. Had it enraged him? Had it motivated him to murder?

"I hadn't worked up to it yet," Darren said. "To be honest, I often walk on eggshells around him. I couldn't afford to lose him."

Siobhán knew the truth when she heard it. And what agent wouldn't walk on eggshells around such an author? Michael O'Mara was Darren Kilroy's golden goose. "Why are you just telling us about this now?"

"I found out Michael was living in the caravan this morning. I went to him first. Perhaps I should have called you straightaway."

"You should have," Macdara said.

"I found these letters in the caravan. That's when I put it together—that Deirdre Walsh was his 'biggest fan.'"

"What exactly is he doing in Kilbane?" Macdara asked.

Darren pulled on his bow tie. "Apparently, he saw the flyer for my appearance at Turn the Page. I found that in the caravan as well. On it was the name of the authors in attendance. Deirdre's name, as well as the name of her book, was on the list, as you know. I can imagine his shock when he found out his stalker was attending an event with me. When he couldn't reach me on the phone—I silenced it during the book events—he came to warn me. Perhaps he was worried I'd be swayed by Deirdre's appeal and he wanted to stop me."

"Stop you or stop her?"

Darren looked away. "He wasn't even in the bookshop when Deirdre was murdered." He made eye contact. "I don't think he killed her."

"I don't understand how he connected Deirdre to the fan letters," Siobhán said.

"I can't say for sure," Darren said. "You'll have to ask him when he's able to answer."

"What if I told you we have evidence that he was in the bookshop the night Deirdre was murdered?" Macdara said.

Darren blinked. "I don't know what to say. What evidence?"

Macdara shook his head. "I cannot share that at this time."

"He's not himself when he drinks. I don't want to believe he's capable of murder. He has no history of violence." Darren removed his handkerchief and wiped his brow. "But if, as you say, he was at the bookshop . . . I'd better get him a good solicitor."

"You'd better," Macdara said, standing up. "We have work to do." Darren's chair screeched back. He snapped his briefcase shut and looked at the letters in Macdara's hands. "We'll be holding on to these."

"Of course," Darren said. "Will you be so kind as to give me directions to hospital? I'd like to be by my author's side."

* * *

Michael O'Mara wouldn't be in shape to answer questions for days. Over the phone the doctor insisted that he was in delirium tremens and he needed intensive care before he'd be well enough to be questioned.

"Do you think he's our killer?" Siobhán asked.

"He fits into several pieces of the puzzle," Macdara said. "Don't you think?"

"Yes," she answered honestly. "If we can confirm that those letters are indeed from Deirdre Walsh." Did he see Deirdre's handwriting somewhere else and make the connection between his "biggest fan" and Deirdre Walsh? Darren Kilroy had hindered this investigation by holding on to evidence. It brought the rest of his story into question. What else was he withholding?

"In the meantime, back to the inn," Macdara said. "Let's hope Margaret left us some kind of clue."

Chapter 30

This time the twins didn't argue with Siobhán and Macdara when they said they wanted to get into Margaret's room.

"Shall I call the judge?" Macdara asked.

"No need," Emma said. "It's technically our room."

"You won't last long in there," Eileen said. "It's sparse, and outdated."

They weren't there for a happy tour but Siobhán kept her gob shut on that matter. Eileen handed Siobhán a key to Margaret's room and the twins headed back for the cottage. Siobhán and Macdara removed the crime scene tape, unlocked the door, and stepped into her room.

Apart from the peeling wallpaper, which was an exact match to the wallpaper found in their victims' mouths, Margaret's room was a throwback to when she owned the inn. The decorations were stark, a cross hanging above the bed, and no other thrills or splashes of color. She did have a bookshelf but nothing adorned the top of it, not even a scrap of lace. The wallpaper, swirls of blue and white that may have been pretty in its day, was yellow with brown at the edges and peeling in multiple locations. Aretta set about trying to locate the pattern of the torn piece of wallpaper in Deirdre's mouth. They would run chemical tests on it to confirm it was the same wallpaper, but tests took time, and if they wanted to catch this killer time was running out.

"Here," Aretta called out, excitement in her voice. Siobhán and Macdara edged in. Near the window by the front door, Aretta had been able to match a missing piece. It fit exactly. "Our killer was in this room," Siobhán said. "Part of the book club meeting."

"That's most of them, as usual," Macdara said.

"What's this?" Aretta pointed to a notebook beside Margaret's bed. Next to it was a roll of tape. Siobhán and Macdara edged in. It was similar to the notebook they'd found in Deirdre's room where she had written passages from Lorcan, Nessa, and O'Mara. The ones where it seemed Deirdre had been practicing different writing styles. This matched Darren Kilroy's claim that she was interested in ghostwriting. Had she been trying to prove her skills? In all their interviews with Lorcan and Nessa, they had forgotten to ask them about these passages. Were they written by Lorcan and Nessa or were they imitations created by Deirdre Walsh?

With gloved hands, Siobhán opened the notebook in front of her. On the first page, someone had jotted down multiple lines from Deirdre's book, *Melodies*. The handwriting looked like Margaret's. Siobhán had seen it several times over the years in Margaret's annual Christmas cards. Next, in the notebook Margaret had jotted down multiple lines from a Michael O'Mara book. Similar words were underlined. Was this more evidence of Deirdre trying to plagiarize? There was no doubt Margaret was trying to make the connection. And Margaret had been a big Michael O'Mara fan. There was something else that drew Siobhán's attention to the notebook. The sheet behind it was torn and Siobhán could see raised bumps where a message had been. "We need tracing paper and a pencil."

"We have some at the station," Macdara said. He placed a call. They took a short break while they waited for the tracing paper and pencil to arrive, and headed outside to the twins' flower garden. They hadn't seen rain in hours but it was looming in the distance. The flowers blew in the soft wind. When another guard car arrived in short order, the three of them ran eagerly back to the notebook. Siobhán placed the tracing paper on top and began shading it with the pencil. She lifted it up to see the message. They all leaned in eagerly to read it:

I DON'T BELIEVE IN GHOSTS

"At least we know for sure who wrote the note," Macdara said. "But why would she care if Deirdre wanted to be a ghostwriter?"

It was a question Siobhán would ponder the rest of the day.

Siobhán stood in the dining room of the bistro, pacing back and forth. The memorial for Deirdre was at the bookshop this evening, and once it was over, all their suspects were going home. *I don't believe in ghosts.* Margaret O'Shea wrote that note. To Deirdre Walsh? Or to someone else? Michael O'Mara? Both? The handwriting in the notebook comparing Deirdre's work to Michael O'Mara's was the same as the handwriting in the note. It would be easy enough to check past records to confirm it was Margaret's signature.

What about the other notes?

The Hills Have Eyes

What are you doing here?

What are you doing here . . . ? That had to be either *to* Michael O'Mara or *from* Michael O'Mara to Deirdre. If Deirdre was simply a mad fan, a stalker, would Michael write that kind of a note to her? Didn't it suggest more of an intimate, or at the very least, familiar, relationship?

Something else was nibbling at her. Perhaps it was nothing, but sometimes the smallest inconsistencies were key. They'd found the notebook Margaret had used to write the note and the tape she'd used to presumably tape it to Deirdre's door, but they hadn't found a single biro in Margaret's room. She was a Michael O'Mara fan. Had Darren Kilroy given her a biro? And if so—was it the same one found at the murder scene? Siobhán needed to go back to the beginning. First, everyone had assumed that Margaret had died of natural causes. Once Siobhán suspected otherwise, she had assumed the killer had been practicing, testing out the poison, creating his or her rough draft before he or she hit the real target—Deirdre Walsh. Now she knew it was something else. Margaret O'Shea, may she rest in peace, was killed for the same reason Deirdre was killed. She was in possession of deadly information, and she planned on spilling the beans. Siobhán needed to speak with the remaining authors, not to mention Leigh Coakley and Oran and Padraig McCarthy, before someone stamped *THE END* on a story that was far from over.

The wood floors in Turn the Page were gleaming, and the smell of wood polish hung in the air. In the center of the shop a stunning wreath made of white and yellow roses was positioned in front of chairs arranged for the memorial. A large poster showed off Deirdre's book, *Melodies,* accompanied by quotes from it propped up on large easels next to it. A photograph of Deirdre Walsh was framed by flowers, as if it were a book. Leigh Coakley had outdone herself. Oran and Padraig, dressed in dark suits, stood in a dimly lit corner of the bookshop, arguing. Siobhán pretended to have a keen interest in the shelves nearby.

"After the memorial," Oran said. "Or we'll have the guards trampling all up in here before the poor woman finally gets her event."

"It's hardly an event she'd have wished for," Padraig said. "And we could get arrested for hiding evidence."

"We're not hiding it, we're simply waiting."

"Heya," Siobhán said, sneaking up on them. Oran yelped and slapped a hand over his heart. Padraig dropped the book he was holding. "What is it you two were waiting to show me?" she said.

"I swear to you, we haven't been hiding it," Oran said. "We've only just uncovered it." That was the same excuse Darren Kilroy had used about the letters.

Siobhán felt herself straightening her spine reflexively. "We didn't have any reason to open it," Padraig said. "It didn't seem disturbed."

People were starting to file in for the memorial. Siobhán agreed with them on one thing at least. She did not want this memorial postponed. This might be her last chance to speak with the suspects. "Whatever this is you are going to show me as soon as this is over, are we clear?" They nodded their heads in stereo. "In addition— whatever it is—I don't want you two going near it, is that clear?"

"Everything you say is very clear," Padraig said.

"Almost too clear," Oran added before they slipped away.

Leigh Coakley stood in front of the seated guests read- ing passages from Deirdre's book. Sniffles could be heard during the reading, and Siobhán turned to find they were coming from Darren Kilroy, who upon noticing her noticing him, reddened slightly and blew his nose into his handkerchief.

Siobhán was no expert on writing, but as Leigh read from Deirdre's book, she found her mind wandering again and again, or her brow furrowing in confusion. Were those passages that Deirdre wrote in her notebook from Nessa and Lorcan her way of trying to improve her own writing or was she trying to prove she was capable of being a ghostwriter? Siobhán had no proof that Deirdre had wanted to be a ghostwriter, apart from the supposed fan letters supplied by Darren, which would take time to analyze. Did everyone else think this was magnificent poetry and Siobhán was too thick to understand it? She'd snuck a look at a Michael O'Mara book the night before and had read three chapters before she fell asleep. She took a deep breath and forced herself to pay attention, alerted to a par- ticular passage as Leigh read it out loud.

"The woman, stripped of her wifely duties, wandered aimlessly about the meadow, and as a farmer passed her without a single glance, she wondered if she was invisible, if somehow in the night she had left this earthly vessel and had become a ghost."

"Ghost." Siobhán didn't realize she'd said it out loud until heads whipped around to look at her. "I don't believe in ghosts," she said, now that she had everyone's attention. Had Margaret simply been disparaging Deirdre's work? Had Deirdre murdered Margaret? Over an insult?

Hadn't people killed for less?

It still didn't ring true. If authors couldn't take critics, they shouldn't be writing. With the Internet, Siobhán assumed authors had to get used to negative comments about them, and probably considered themselves lucky to be read widely enough for people to pick at them.

"I believe it's a metaphor," Leigh said, frowning and looking at the passage again. "The character isn't actually a ghost."

"You asked us if we were writing about ghosts," Nessa said. "Does this have something to do with Deirdre's murder?"

"It's because of the note someone taped to Deirdre's door," Lorcan reminded her. Now that the guards knew about their affair they were seated close together.

"Note?" Leigh asked.

Nessa frowned. "Why didn't you ask her about the note?" she said, pointing an accusing finger at Leigh. "Are Lorcan and I the only suspects?"

"I'm sorry if this is an inconvenient time but I need to show you something." Siobhán had been waiting for this. She held up the two photocopies containing Deirdre's passages resembling Lorcan's and Nessa's work. She handed them to the authors. They each moved the paper closer to their eyes, read, and then frowned.

"What is this?" Nessa asked. "She . . . was practicing our styles?"

"Just the style?" Siobhán asked.

"What do you mean?" Nessa sounded defensive.

"Is this your passage?"

"No," Nessa said. "But it's an obvious attempt to write like me."

"And yours?" Siobhán nodded to Lorcan.

He glanced at his page again. "I didn't write that. But I must admit, it's a grand imitation."

"Did Deirdre Walsh ever accuse either of you of plagiarism?"

Nessa's eyebrow shot up, and Lorcan laughed. "Oh," he said off her look. "You're serious."

"I am."

"No," Nessa said. "She never accused me of something so vile."

Lorcan shrugged. "If she did, she didn't do it to me face."

Chapter 31

"Plot holes," Siobhán said to Macdara. They stood in the back of the bookshop as the memorial proceeded. "Everything has to fit to find the true killer. Not just bits and pieces."

Macdara murmured his agreement, letting her do her thing. It was swirling around her now, a ghostly narrative. But it all had to fit. Every single piece. Anyone who had ever spent hours or even weeks working on a puzzle knew the frustration of getting close to finished only to discover there was a missing piece. Maddening! It would never feel right.

Nessa found her one-star review taped to her door along with a note: *The Hills Have Eyes*. Deirdre presumably found a note taped to her door. *I don't believe in ghosts*.

And in Deirdre's room they found the third note: *What are you doing here?*

They had evidence that Margaret had written: *I don't believe in ghosts.* Presumably she had penned it just after she was seen arguing with Leigh Coakley, Lorcan Murphy, and Deirdre Walsh. Just because they found the note in Deirdre's room, did it mean it was originally meant for her? Or had the killer slipped the note into Deirdre's room to throw them off? And did this mean Margaret wrote the other notes? They did not find evidence of that in Margaret's room. That left: *What are you doing here?* And: *The Hills Have Eyes.*

What if *What are you doing here?* was the question and *The Hills Have Eyes* was the answer? Did that put Nessa Lamb in the crosshairs?

The notes were key. Not only who sent which note to whom, but in what order. She needed to speak with Michael O'Mara. She passed this on to Macdara. "I'll call the doc again," Macdara said. "Hopefully he's in a better state, and I'll tell him it's an emergency." He headed off to make the call.

Aretta met her over by a small table where pastries made by Bridie had been set. "It's been confirmed," she said. "Lorcan Murphy is divorcing his wife."

"You spoke to the soon-to-be ex-wife?"

Aretta shook her head. "I spoke to her attorney. He said the divorce has been mostly agreeable. Lorcan made a good sum. If he killed Deirdre Walsh it wasn't over grant money or getting an agent."

"And they are indeed getting a divorce meaning he didn't kill to protect that secret," Siobhán said.

"He did not," Aretta agreed.

"And Nessa's work?"

"I read through it all. I did not find the passage Deirdre wrote in her notebook."

Siobhán nodded. "That matches what Nessa and Lorcan just told me."

"Are they eliminated as suspects?"

"No," Siobhán said. "Not quite yet." But she was getting close to the killer. She just needed to find the missing piece.

"That was lovely," someone said once the memorial was over. Each participant had been given a copy of Deirdre's book and many were holding it as if they didn't know what to do with it.

"The books are on us," Oran said. "We've officially purchased them all."

"We think it's what Deirdre would have wanted," Padraig said. "Happy reading."

"And when you've finished with it, please come back to discover another great Irish writer, right here in Turn the Page." Applause rang out, Oran McCarthy beamed. They had indeed replaced the toilets with claw-foot bathtubs, filled to the brim with a variety of paperbacks, and people seemed to love pawing through them for their genre picks.

"Everyone is invited back to Naomi's Bistro where your meal is on us," Bridie announced. "We can continue our memories of Deirdre."

Folks didn't need to be told twice, they seemed eager for the feed, and nodded enthusiastically, although Siobhán knew that hardly any of them had memories of Deirdre Walsh to share. But the killer did. He or she had been alarmed by Deirdre's tell-all. Could *ghosts* have re-ferred to skeletons in the closet? *I don't believe in ghosts.* Had Margaret learned what this tell-all was about and threatened to spill the beans?

Margaret had been strong minded. She'd give you her opinion as easily as the weather forecast, and usually it was just as glum. *Tis a miserable day, isn't it? Spitting out of the heavens. Me bones have been aching for days. . . .*

If something was bothering her, Margaret O'Shea would let anyone know. And this time, it had cost her her life.

Macdara returned to Siobhán's side, breaking her out of her thoughts. "The doctor said we can visit him briefly," he said. "But he can't guarantee how forthcoming he will be."

"Better than nothing," Siobhán said.

"We're set for first thing in the morning," Macdara said. "It's the soonest the doc will allow it."

"That takes care of that," Siobhán said. "On to the next. Oran and Padraig have something they want to show us."

When everyone else had filed out of the bookshop, Oran removed the red book on the shelf and pushed open the secret door. Aretta gave a squeal of surprise. They en-tered one by one and Oran pointed to the safe in the cor-ner of the office. Inside they could clearly see a handbag.

"Deirdre's handbag," Siobhán said out loud. *Finally.* The one they'd found in Deirdre's room had been missing crucial items. Perhaps they were in this one. They would have to examine it.

Padraig put up his hands. "I swear to you, I only opened it this morning. I don't know how it got in there."

"Someone knew about this room, they knew you didn't

have keys to the back door, and they were able to figure out the combination to your safe," Siobhán said. "Besides the pair of ye, any clue who had access to that kind of information?"

"We've been thinking about this," Oran said. "There's only one man."

"The landlord," Padraig said. "It was his old safe, and we hadn't had a chance to get the combination changed— it's an old safe and the lock is built into it. And we used his recommendations to hire the lads to build the bookshelf, and it was he who said he didn't have keys to that back door."

Siobhán now wished she'd gone with Macdara when he interviewed the landlord. She had a feeling he'd been a chatterbox and had opened his mouth to the wrong person. One with deadly intentions. And she could only think of one person influential enough to weasel that kind of information out of an old Irishman. And even without speaking to him, Siobhán had a feeling she knew what type of book he liked to read. Michael O'Mara was not randomly in town. He had been here on a mission.

Macdara placed a call to the forensic investigation team to come and gather the evidence from the safe. Evidence that would take time to sift through. Another delay. And no doubt, if anything was incriminating it had probably already been scrubbed.

Unless it was someone other than the killer who had hidden the handbag in the safe. Siobhán had gotten word that none of the participants were leaving town until Michael O'Mara was released from hospital. That would buy her some precious time. She could only hope that it would be enough.

* * *

When Siobhán arrived home, weary and ready to drop into bed, she found her brood wide awake, reading a book. Together.

"It's poetry," Ciarán said excitedly.

"Grand," Siobhán said, plopping down next to him. Eoin brought her a cup of tea and James shoved the tin of biscuits toward her.

"Thank you." She wouldn't want to imagine life without a single one of them. Human beings got so little time on this planet to begin with. Nobody deserved it cut short at the hands of someone else. She wanted to be oblivious in this moment, to just enjoy her siblings, and a night of poetry reading—now that was inspiring. She tried to focus, tried not to imagine all their suspects taking off at first morning's light.

"I can't imagine writing a whole book," Ann said. "From start to finish, like."

"We can start with reading one," James said with a wink.

Gráinne was painting her nails. She didn't even look up. "I would just hire someone else to write it for me," she said, holding her nails out and blowing on them. "I'd give them the ideas, like, but let them do the work."

"A ghostwriter," Siobhán said, remembering Darren Kilroy's comment.

Gráinne frowned, then shrugged. "Now there's a fun job title."

"I'd feel let down if I discovered my favorite author was a fraud," Eoin said. "But maybe that's just because I couldn't imagine my own name not being on my graphic novels."

"It's like telling a lie," Ciarán said. "Isn't it?"

"I guess once you write so many it might get tiring to keep going, but you also wouldn't want to stop the product from going out."

"Product?" Ann said. "Are books a product?"

"Anything can become a big product when money is involved," James said.

"It's a win-win," Ciarán said. "Money and no work! How do I get that?"

But was it? A win-win? For everyone? Was it fun for a writer *not* to be recognized? What if what one had written went out to be a raving success? And this person was still not receiving their due. All the attention was going to the name on the book. And what if that name was a stumbling drunk, and yet he was still getting the credit? *And what happened if a ghostwriter no longer wanted to be a ghost?*

The Hills Have Eyes. Forget the horror movie, it meant someone was watching. Watching what? Was that a warning from the killer?

I don't believe in ghosts. What if Margaret was saying: *I don't believe in ghostwriters?*

Accusations of Nessa Lamb plagiarizing had never been proven. Nessa Lamb herself insisted Deirdre had never accused her of such a thing. It had been a lie. A distraction. Besides, Margaret O'Shea wouldn't have cared if Nessa's book had been ghostwritten. She wouldn't have cared if Lorcan's book had been ghostwritten. She wouldn't have cared if Deirdre's book had been ghostwritten.

But what about Michael O'Mara's *The Dragon Files?* What if he wasn't the mastermind behind them? Everyone had commented that as of late he'd been a fall-down drunk. And yet . . . his latest installment to the series was better than ever. Hadn't Leigh Coakley said that? What if those had been ghostwritten? Then, Margaret O'Shea would have cared. And she would have made that clear.

Deirdre Walsh had an explosive secret. A tell-all.

Deirdre Walsh's passages in her notebook were proof that she could write in other styles. She'd tried to make it on her own with *Melodies*. Only no one was interested. She had been overlooked. Passed over for grants, and awards, and accolades. And she'd been tired of it. Tired of keeping an explosive secret. Michael O'Mara was no longer writing his books. *She* was.

Siobhán's teacup rattled in her hand. She set it down, and moved to the back dining room where she could pace. She recalled that first event at the bookshop where Deirdre had announced her explosive new tell-all. But she wasn't the first to threaten to spill that secret. Margaret O'Shea was.

Who had the most to lose by that information coming out? One could argue it was Michael O'Mara. And yet, he was still behaving like a drunk. Rummaging through rubbish bins. Perhaps he did break into the back office during the murder, leaving the door open, creating the possibility that an outsider had snuck into the bookshop and murdered Deirdre by accessing the secret door. Maybe he broke into Deirdre's room and returned the notebooks and laptop after her tell-all had been deleted. And maybe he returned the handbag to the safe. But he wasn't the main character—the killer. He was an accessory. Someone else was the mastermind—someone sharp enough to pull it off, crafty enough to throw every misdirection that he could at the murder scene. And smart enough to throw suspicion onto all the others.

Darren Kilroy. He didn't just represent Michael O'Mara. He also represented O'Mara's ghostwriter. Deirdre Walsh. What a perfect arrangement. O'Mara was still selling out his popular series, thanks to Deirdre Walsh. Until she decided she no longer wanted to be a ghost. And in the bookshop that first evening, she dared to threaten it by mentioning her tell-all. Darren Kilroy could always get another ghostwriter, but he could not allow O'Mara's cover to be blown—his golden goose to go down. Not if he wanted those royalties to keep coming. Margaret O'Shea was proof that readers might revolt to the news. Margaret, what did you do? Did Deirdre Walsh let you in on her secret first? And did Darren Kilroy see you posting that note on her door?

I don't believe in ghosts.

Did Darren then demand that Michael O'Mara come to town and help him out?

Siobhán sensed eyes on her back. She turned to find her brood staring at her.

"What's the story?" Eoin asked.

"You look like you've seen a ghost," James said.

"No," Siobhán said. "I've seen a ghostwriter."

Morning didn't come soon enough. But the night had given Siobhán time to come up with a plan. At sunrise, she hopped on her Vespa and headed for the Twins' Inn. Macdara was on his way to hospital to get Michael O'Mara to verify what Siobhán already knew. That he was here to help out his agent. Deirdre's killer. That he had created a ruse by wandering through the village, going through rubbish. That he had befriended the landlord and picked the lock of the back door to the bookshop the night of the murder. A guard was bringing the land-lord into the station to confirm that he had indeed spilled too much info to Michael O'Mara. Perhaps in exchange for a signed book. Siobhán's plan would only work if the minor characters involved in this sordid tale told the truth. Meanwhile, she was on her way to the Twins' Inn to make sure none of them had checked out. It wouldn't be smart to confront Darren Kilroy on her own. But she loathed the thought of him getting away with it. She had to play it cool. He was probably confident that everything he'd thrown at the crime scene had done the trick of con-fusing them.

An umbrella, a rose, a biro. Red herrings, not to men-tion literary tropes. His accusation that Deirdre had ac-cused Nessa of plagiarizing. He had scribbled *The Hills Have Eyes* on Nessa's one-star review. He had printed it out, scribbled the note, and dropped it off to Nessa, knowing she'd either tell the gardaí about it or it would be discovered. He'd planted Lorcan's umbrella. Easy enough to grab in the dark. And while everyone was run-ning around in panic, he knew Michael O'Mara was breaking into the back door to leave it open. Simple. Make it appear as if someone had come in from the back and used the secret passage.

Another piece of news had come down this morning. An interview with Deirdre Walsh's brother. He informed them that Deirdre was not allergic to nuts. It had all been fabricated by Darren Kilroy. Perhaps he hoped that they would just assume she had been killed by her allergy. Most likely he just liked adding more smoke to the fire. Cloud everything up and slip away so that when the air cleared he would be long gone. And now that Siobhán thought about it, she had never heard directly from

Deirdre that she had a nut allergy. The warning notice did not mention *who* was allergic to nuts. Darren had managed to whisper that it was Deirdre without the rumor reaching her in time for her to straighten it out.

When the lights went out, Darren Kilroy was ready. Ready with his syringe to sedate Deirdre, and his arsenic. He'd already used it on Margaret O'Shea, no doubt pushing into her room, and deciding at the last minute to use the wallpaper for his next kill. He'd seen it peeling on the walls of her room, curled with age. He'd seen the wallpaper book on Oran and Padraig's list of rare books. *Shadows from the Walls of Death*. How perfect. He was adaptable, she'd give him that. This murder had been mostly planned, while taking advantage of the power outage, and Margaret's wallpaper. Siobhán had a gut feeling that Deirdre Walsh had been urging Darren to let her out herself as O'Mara's ghostwriter for some time. He'd been putting her off. Until she threatened to out herself in a tell-all. She hadn't written any fan letters to Michael O'Mara. Darren had written them himself. That was the real reason he hadn't mentioned them early on—he was improvising as he went, changing the story, throwing in plot twists, anything he could to obscure the truth. He figured as long as there were enough threads leading to other suspects, he would get away with premeditated murder.

Michael O'Mara hadn't been so careful. That was the problem when you asked a drunk to be your accomplice. The one person he could trust not to say anything. But O'Mara left his cigarettes on the back of the toilet in Deirdre's room, most likely going through it to get rid of any reference to his books, or her part in writing them. He'd also left his cigarette butts underneath Deirdre's window and in the back alley of the bookshop. They would have to wait for the tests to prove it, but they could still use it as leverage. Poor Margaret O'Shea. Darren had killed her, cleaned up, and wheeled her body to the footpath in front of the bookshop. What he didn't realize was that Margaret O'Shea had not ventured from the inn in years. That was his first mistake.

The air was cool, and due to more storms in the forecast, the morning skies were dark. The scooter's engine hummed beneath her. Siobhán pulled up to the inn and set her gaze upon the rooms. They were all lit up. Her suspects had not yet left town. Especially the one she really wanted. Darren Kilroy. Siobhán stopped to send a message to Macdara and Aretta. She could only hope that they would get through to Mr. O'Mara and that he would be able enough to participate in the ending Siobhán had planned. A twist that even Darren Kilroy would not see coming.

Chapter 32

"Michael?" Darren Kilroy hissed into the dark. "Where are you?"

"Confess," a deep voice called out from the far corner. It was Michael O'Mara.

They had left one dim light in the bookshop on, and Siobhán could see Darren freeze in the middle of the bookshop. He threw a look over his shoulder as if trying to assess his chances of making an escape. "You're not well," Darren said. "You have no idea what you're saying." Darren scanned the room again. "You're not alone, are you?"

"Deirdre Walsh is one of your authors," Aretta said from another dark corner.

"I never said otherwise," Darren said. "But I have a duty to protect the confidentiality of my authors."

"Even if she was intent on cracking your golden egg?" Siobhán said, happy that she'd come up with a book pun.

"You killed her," O'Mara said. "I didn't ask you to kill her."

Darren let out a moan. "I don't know what he's told you, but he's not well. He's hallucinating." Siobhán only wished she could see the look on his face. Did he have his hands up in surrender, or was he looking around for the closest exit? Was he holding wallpaper coated with deadly arsenic?

"We have Deirdre's tell-all," Macdara said. "And she did tell all."

"That's a lie," Darren said. "I destroyed it." He gasped, realizing what he'd said. They didn't have Deirdre's tell-all, but soon a computer technician would find it.

"Thank you for verifying that," Siobhán said. She flicked the lights on. At first Darren flinched, then he flew into action. He reached out and grabbed the nearest book off the shelf. He hurled the book at Siobhán's head.

"Over here," Macdara said. Darren whipped around and tossed a book in Macdara's direction.

"It's not nice to throw books," Aretta said.

"It's not my fault. I have a duty to protect the readers!" Darren began tossing weighty tomes in every direction as fast as he could, backing up as he continued to throw books like projectiles. If any of them were damaged, Oran and Padraig would be inconsolable and they would all have to pitch in to replace any destroyed books, but that paled in comparison to the lives that Darren had destroyed. He had an excellent arm and Siobhán had to duck nonstop. One *War and Peace* to the noggin and she could be out of commission forever.

"Stop," she yelled. "It's over. You're caught."

He stopped, his eyes wild, sweat running down his full face. "I can reinvent myself. Go into hiding. Mold the next James Joyce." He sounded delirious and hopeful. He continued backward, not seeing the claw-foot bathtub in his way. A look of confusion came over his face as the back of his legs slammed into the tub and he lost his balance, falling into it.

"Don't move," Macdara said as he and Siobhán and Aretta flanked the tub.

Darren flailed his arms and legs. "I did this for you, Michael," he shouted. "I did this to keep your legacy going."

"My books will keep going," Michael O'Mara said. "But you won't be a part of it." Sober now, shaved, and dressed, he looked like a new man. Siobhán hoped he'd keep it up, continue to fight to stay sober the way her brother James was doing. O'Mara wasn't completely out of the legal woods, but his help in nailing Darren Kilroy would go a long way with a judge. Lucky for him not Judge Judy or he'd be eating his shoes.

"You traitor." Darren tried to sit up but continued to slide on the books in the tub. "I made you. I propped you up. I found Deirdre Walsh when you were nothing but a drunken husk of a man." He finally righted himself, and hands up, slid out of the tub and onto the floor. "And what happened? Your sales skyrocketed. Because she was better than you. Much better." He turned away from Michael and focused his gaze on Aretta. He reached his arm out as if he expected her to help him up. "If only she wasn't so naive. Nobody wanted her books. They wanted dragons." He dropped his arm. "Fire-breathing writers are a much more dangerous creature than anyone realizes. The egos! The fragile, fragile, stupid egos." He reached into the tub, grabbed more books, and flung them one by one at Michael O'Mara, who simply ducked. When he tired of that, he hung his head and grasped the back of his head with his hands, rocking back and forth. Had he not murdered two women in cold blood Siobhán would have almost taken pity on the state of him.

"You seem to be the one with the fragile ego," she said. "But I'm sure Margaret O'Shea confirmed your fears. That readers would not want to know the legend of Michael O'Mara was a sham." She threw a glance at O'Mara and mouthed *Sorry.* He shrugged. He knew this was part of the plan. "It drove you to the breaking point," Siobhán said. "Didn't it?"

Darren looked up for a moment, as if she was on his side. Then he glared. "What do you know?"

"I know that when Padraig McCarthy mentioned the rare book of arsenic-laced wallpaper, you started writing a story of your own, didn't you?"

Darren reached for a book in the tub to toss at Siobhán. She was fine with it. She could duck all day. But there were no more pages left for Darren Kilroy to turn.

"If you throw one more book at the woman I love, you won't like what happens next," Detective Sergeant Mac-dara Flannery said. "I promise you that." Darren Kilroy dropped the book, curled up into a ball on the floor, and wept.

* * *

Siobhán entered the bistro after a much-needed afternoon walk about town. The bell dinged, and she crossed the hall to the French doors leading to the bistro.

"Surprise!" a chorus of voices shouted. She stood in shock at her friends and family, who had gathered around a birthday cake glowing with candles.

"Look at her face," Gráinne said. "We got her."

Siobhán laughed. "You certainly did." She caught Macdara's eye and he winked. Everyone began to sing "Happy Birthday." She edged closer to the cake, to see what was written on it this time:

HAPPY BIRTHDAY SOS

She laughed again. "It's perfect."

"Do you need help blowing them out?" Ciarán asked. "There are a ton of candles." This time everyone laughed.

"Everyone can help," Siobhán said, holding her hair back and leaning in. Her brood didn't waste time, as multiple folks leaned in to help her blow them out.

"Look at all your prezzies," Ann said, pointing to a table in the back dining room filled with colorfully wrapped gifts.

"I am definitely spoiled," Siobhán said.

"Recognizing it is the first step," Gráinne quipped.

"Shall I play 'Happy Birthday'?" Ciarán said, lifting his violin.

"Let's cut the cake," Eoin said. Siobhán couldn't help but notice he'd been standing apart from most everyone except for one person: Aretta. She tried not to grin in their direction.

"What's your hurry?" James said as Eoin stepped up

with the knife. Siobhán was surprised, but happy to see that Elise Elliot was in attendance. It appeared as though the mercurial lovebirds had patched things up yet again.

"Aretta and I are going to exchange recipes," Eoin said.

"I've never made a proper Irish stew," she said.

"In exchange for her pepper stew," Eoin said.

"Wonderful," Siobhán said. "We all look forward to sampling both." The next hour was filled with what a birthday party should entail: chatter and laughter, and cake, and gift opening. It was a wonderful surprise, but also somewhat draining, so Siobhán was relieved when the attention was off her and folks went back to their regular routine. She felt a tap on her shoulder. She turned around to find Elise staring at her.

"Heya," Siobhán said. "Thanks a million for coming."

"Can we talk?"

That was never a good starter. "Of course."

Elise looked around. "In private?"

"Let's speak in the garden." They headed out. Elise was wringing her hands. "You can tell me anything."

"I don't know exactly when James and I are getting married. I think he's avoiding it."

Siobhán was not going to share her brother's confidence with anyone, not even Elise. "I'm sorry, luv," she said. "Sometimes these things take time."

Elise gave a half nod. "I have a birthday gift for you," she said. "Only it's not something that could be wrapped."

"You don't need to give me a thing."

"The abbey," Elise said. "I'm giving you the abbey."

"Pardon?"

"You and Macdara. That's where you should get married. I was wrong to covet it."

Siobhán knew her mouth had dropped open and tears formed in her eyes. She tried to think of anything to push them away. "Thank you." She ambushed Elise in a hug.

"I hope you aren't going to put that man off much longer," Elise said. "He may not tell you how much it hurts, when you want nothing more but to marry the person you love—but take it from me. It hurts."

A pulse in Siobhán's neck started to throb. "Thank you," she said. "For everything."

Elise let out a sigh of relief. "Now that that's sorted, I'm going to have a proper drink." She headed back inside, leaving Siobhán in the garden. Macdara came out soon thereafter.

"Hey, birthday girl." She ambushed him in a hug. "Are you ready for your present?"

"You already gave me presents." A gift certificate to the bookshop, which she was over the moon about, and a gorgeous bouquet from Blooms. He held up a luggage bag.

"What's this?"

"We're going to Bere Island for the weekend," he said. "I've arranged backup at work for us." She didn't realize how much she needed that until it was right there in front of her. This time she didn't hide her grin. "Ready, boss?"

"Race you to the car."

* * *

The water surrounding Bere Island glistened. Siobhán had prepared her speech. Her let's-wait-for-a-year-to-get-married, logical, planned-out speech. Macdara came up behind her and wrapped his arms around her.

"It's okay," he said. "I can wait."

She hadn't expected this. "Is that what you think I'm going to ask you to do? Wait?" He nodded. "And how do you feel about that?"

"I don't want to. I want to marry you right here, right now. But I wouldn't do that either."

"You wouldn't?"

"I'm a garda," he said. "I intend to have as many witnesses at our wedding as possible. Especially since half of them will be loaded before the night is through."

Siobhán laughed. "You're not wrong about that." She took a deep breath. "Elise gave me an interesting birthday gift."

"What was that?"

"She's agreed to change their wedding venue."

"We can have the abbey?"

She felt tears well behind her eyes. "We can have the abbey."

Macdara took a step forward. "What are you saying?"

Siobhán took a deep breath. But this time the butterflies were happy ones. She wanted to marry the blue-eyed, messy-haired man in front of her. "I planned on asking you to wait a year. And maybe that's a prudent thing. Because there is a lot we have to figure out." She took his hands. "But I don't want to wait. It's spring. We need time to plan. But not too much time. Let's marry in June."

He squeezed her hands. "As the sun is going down over the abbey," he said.

"That's perfect." She could see it now, strips of orange and red filtering in through the gorgeous five-light window. Her abbey. Her village. Her love. Surrounded by friends and family. She nodded, trying not to pay attention to the tears in his beautiful blue eyes.

"I didn't expect this," he said, his voice husky. He put his hands on her waist and pulled her into him. "I intend to make it the best chapter of your life."

"Don't do that," she said, taking his hand and squeezing it as they began to walk along the water's edge.

"Why not?" he asked.

"Because the good stuff always happens at the end."

"Not for us," he said. "We're going to fill every single day with the good stuff."

"I want baskets of curried chips at the reception," Siobhán said. "And loads of chocolate."

"That goes without saying."

"And Ciarán is not playing the violin."

"Ciarán is definitely not playing the violin."

"Where are we going to live?"

"I don't know," he said. "But we can take it one step at a time. And if we keep bouncing from my place to yours until we figure it out, then that's the way it will be."

"Maybe one day we'll buy an old farmhouse and James will fix it up for us."

"I like the sound of that. I like the sound of anything that has to do with you and me."

She rested her head on his shoulder as they looked out at the water. She thought of her mam and da, wishing she could share the good news. Just then, as they gazed out at the ocean, a dolphin shot out in a perfect arc, then dove back underneath a wave. She grinned, knowing she had her answer. Macdara held her tight. "There's one more thing."

"Hit me."

"I've given this a lot of thought. I'm not taking your surname," she said. "But if you want to change yours to O'Sullivan the matter is open for discussion."

Eoin's Irish Stew

Ingredients

1½ pounds stewing beef—cut into chunks
¼ cup oil (extra virgin or vegetable oil)
2 beef stock cubes dissolved in 1 pint of water
1½ ounces flour*
3 minced garlic cloves
3 carrots and/or parsnips
1 onion
Salt and pepper
1 cup Guinness Extra Stout
1 cup heavy red wine
2 bay leaves
2 tablespoons tomato paste
2 tablespoons fresh cut parsley
1 tablespoon sugar
1 tablespoon dried thyme
1 tablespoon brown sauce
2 tablespoons Irish butter
2 to 3 pounds russet potatoes, peeled and cut into ½-inch pieces

Brown the beef:

Sprinkle salt on the pieces.
Heat the olive oil in thick-bottomed pot over medium-high heat.
Cook in batches, browning meat on both sides
Add garlic and sauté, then add beef stock, Guin-

ness, wine, tomato paste, thyme, sugar, brown sauce, bay leaves. Stir to combine.

Lower heat and simmer for 1 hour, stirring a few times.

In another pan, melt butter. Sauté onions and carrots/ parsnips until golden (approximately 15 minutes).

After stew has simmered for 1 hour, add the onion/carrot/parsnip/butter mix. Add potatoes, black pepper, and salt. Simmer 40 minutes. Discard bay leaves. Spoon off excess fat. Add salt and pepper to taste. Garnish with parsley.

*If you prefer your stew on the thicker side, coat beef in flour before cooking.

Pepper Stew

I have not tried pepper stew yet, but you can find a Nigerian pepper stew recipe at: Mydiasporakitchen.com.

The wedding of Siobhán O'Sullivan and Macdara Flannery in the village of Kilbane in County Cork, Ireland, comes to an abrupt halt when the skeleton of a groom is unearthed...

If only her mother could be here! The entire O'Sullivan brood—not to mention the regulars from Naomi's Bistro—have gathered at St. Mary's Church for the wedding of Siobhán and Macdara. It's not every day you see two gardaí marrying each other. Only Siobhán's brother James is missing. They can't start without him.

But when James finally comes racing in, he's covered in dirt and babbling he's found a human skeleton in the old slurry pit at the farmhouse. What farmhouse? Macdara sheepishly admits he was saving it as a wedding surprise: he purchased an abandoned dairy farm. Duty calls, so the engaged gardaí decide to put the wedding on hold to investigate.

James leads them to a skeleton clothed in rags that resemble a tattered tuxedo. As an elderly neighbor approaches, she cries out that these must be the remains of her one true love who never showed up on their wedding day, fifty years ago. The gardaí have a cold case on their hands, which heats up the following day when a fresh corpse appears on top of the bridegroom's bones. With a killer at large, they need to watch their backs—or the nearly wedded couple may be parted by death before they've even taken their vows. . .

Please turn the page for an exciting sneak peek of Carlene O'Connnor's next Irish Village mystery MURDER ON AN IRISH FARM coming soon wherever print and e-books are sold!

Chapter 1

The big day was here, June 16th at half-nine in the morning, in the village of Kilbane, County Cork, Ireland, where it seemed the entire town had flocked to Saint Mary's, the gorgeous collegiate church with the five-light windows, to witness and celebrate the marriage of Detective Sergeant Macdara Flannery and Garda Siobhán O'Sullivan. And what a grand day it was, the sun was shining down on them, and the forecast was more of the same. Given their reception was going to be held outdoors in the remains of the Dominican Priory, Siobhán couldn't have asked for a better day. A day that took ages planning and loads of money would pass in the blink of an eye, but be remembered and celebrated for the rest of their lives. *I do.* He would say it, she would say it, Siobhán O'Sullivan and Macdara Flannery would be wed in less than an hour. The Mister and Missus, Herself and

Himself, the wedded bliss, the old ball and chain. Then why did it not feel real?

"Hold still," Gráinne said, jerking Siobhán's head back and tightening her grip on Siobhán's auburn locks. Siobhán would have regretted allowing Gráinne to fix her up but even the regret was futile; saying no would have meant years of resentment from her younger stylish sister. The dressing room in Saint Mary's was suffocating, and Gráinne had every inch crammed with sprays, brushes, gels, tweezers, perfumes, patches, and pins. It was a full-on beauty assault. The emerald tiara given to Siobhán by her siblings was on top of her head and secured with so many pins Siobhán was half-expecting to receive incoming messages from alien spacecraft. She was probably going to have a mad headache before the day was done, but it was a stunning addition to her attire, and although the emeralds in the tiara were not real, the one in her engagement ring was, and so were the studs shining from her ears. They had belonged to her mam, Naomi O'Sullivan. *Something borrowed.* And tucked into her bodice was a blue pin her father Liam had worn as a member of his hobby club collecting and trading model trains. *Something blue.* This way her parents were with her in spirit, and she knew they were looking down from heaven, and were thrilled with the union. Siobhán O'Sullivan had made a lot of mistakes in her young life, and would continue to do so, but Macdara Flannery would never be one of them. "It doesn't feel real."

She felt a sharp pinch on the back of her arm, and yelped. Gráinne laughed. "How's it feel now, pet?"

Siobhán shook her head and stared at herself in the mirror, feeling beautiful but wondering if it was a little *too much.* She was terrified to ask her sister to ease up a little on the make-up. She couldn't afford to get into a row. "Make sure he still recognizes me when you're done with me." She smiled to soften the message in case Gráinne took the comment as a first strike.

"You'll look so good he'll marry you anyway," Gráinne replied. "Now sit still."

Siobhán sighed, looked at her eyes illuminated by dark lashes and eyeliner and shadow. They did look stunning, even if they belonged to someone else, someone with an affinity for glamour. Gráinne was trying to turn Siobhán into a version of herself. Siobhán's hair was in curls and piled on top her head with tendrils hanging down. She wasn't even wearing her wedding dress yet and already the corset and tights alone were cutting into her skin. Perhaps they should have eloped after all. A short ceremony in a comfortable dress with a stop at the chipper and she would have been happy-out.

"Woah," Ann, the youngest O'Sullivan girl said, as she careened into the tiny room, her emerald dress swirling around her heels as she came to an abrupt stop. "Would you look at dat." Siobhán was thinking the same thing about Ann as they studied each other in the mirror through their heavily-made-up eyes. Three beautiful women. Ann was blonde, Gráinne with her dark shiny locks, and Siobhán the redhead— although technically, her hair was auburn. But it was Ann that Siobhán couldn't look away from. She looked way too beautiful and womanly for a girl just shy of sixteen. Siobhán had an irrational urge to take a wet cloth and wipe away all the make-up on Ann's young face. But if she did, there would be war.

"You look lovely," Siobhán said to Ann instead.

"You look. . . . woah," Ann replied.

"You're both gorgeous," Gráinne said. "You're welcome."

Siobhán turned to Ann. "Was that a good 'woah' or a bad 'woah'?"

Ann shrugged. "I dunno." She crossed her eyes and stuck out her tongue. "Just messin'. You look gorgeous. I don't even recognize ya!"

Siobhán closed her eyes and imagined what life would be like without siblings. *Bliss.* Gráinne pinched Siobhán again until she opened her eyes, then tilted her head back as she loomed over her. "Do you think you need a touch more eye shadow?"

"No," Siobhán and Ann said in unison. Noise filtered in from the church, the murmurs of friends and family. Maria and Aisling, her Maid of Honor and bridesmaid, (along with Gráinne and Ann), were dressed and in the church, helping to usher people in. The bridesmaid dresses were a lovely shade of emerald green, and the groomsmen would all have matching bowties.

Siobhán's stomach tingled and a smile broke out on her face. It spread to Gráinne and Ann. Siobhán held out a hand to each sister, and soon all hands were all clasped, squeezing, and bonding. It was a mental snapshot Siobhán knew she'd remember the rest of her life, the three O'Sullivan lasses grinning like eejits in the mirror. Ann stuck out her tongue again and tears welled in Siobhán's eyes.

"Don't you dare start the waterworks," Gráinne said. "You'll ruin my artistry."

"Right, so." Siobhán took a deep breath and thought about non-sentimental things. Who was at the Garda Station right now? Their newest member, Garda Aretta Dabiri would look after things. It was astounding how quickly she was turning out to be a valuable member of the garda family. Aretta planned on popping in at some point during the ceremony to share in the good wishes, and enjoy some food and drink from the reception. Why did it feel like there was someone they'd forgotten to invite? This time when Siobhán's stomach tightened it was from worry.

"Let's get you into that dress," Gráinne said. "It's nearly show time."

It did feel a bit like a show, one where Siobhán was worried she was going to flub her lines. Siobhán stood as Gráinne and Ann reached for the dress. It had been a special order, a creamy satin dress that came close to Siobhán's liking, then was transformed by their dear friend Bridie into something out of a fairy tale. She had removed the sleeves so it wrapped around Siobhán's shoulders, more cleavage than Siobhán usually flashed, but nothing that would incite chins to wag. The bodice was framed in tiny white pearls and the bottom of the dress flared out in a tulle skirt. A lovely emerald satin ribbon would cinch her at the waist. As she prepared to step into it, Siobhán felt the moment in her bones, the absolute joy of the here and now. She could hear her Da's voice, feel his hug: *I love the bones of ya.*

I love you too, Da. I know you're with me . . .

"I swear on me grave I'll box you in the ears if you start the waterworks," Gráinne said. Siobhán bit her lip and nodded. "You can cry all you like after the photos are taken."

Photos. The photographer. She'd nearly forgotten all about him. "Has he arrived?" she asked.

"I'll check," Ann said.

"Help me squeeze her into the dress first," Gráinne said.

"Squeeze me?" Siobhán said. "There's no need to be squeezing me." She'd stayed away from curried chips and sugar for an entire month. Her sisters each held a side and Siobhán stepped into the dress. They gracefully pulled it up and zipped it up and as she'd attested, there was no squeezing to be done. They twirled her around and for a moment even Gráinne was speechless. Gráinne reached for the long veil that would attach to the back of the tiara. Siobhán was nearly giddy with adrenaline as it was securely attached. Gráinne and Ann spread the veil behind her then stepped away to have a look.

"Gorgeous," they all three said in unison. Ann whirled around and zipped out of the room. Siobhán turned and picked up the bouquet of wildflowers sourced by the local shop and dressed up with white roses and baby's breath with an emerald ribbon. They were sublime. Everything was absolutely picture-perfect. "I'm ready," Siobhán said with a nod to Ann and more confidence than she felt. "Tell everyone I'm ready."

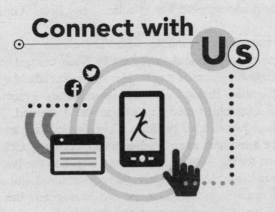